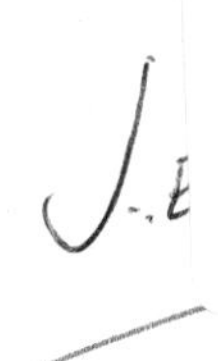

The Headmaster's Daughter

Jane Allison

Cahill Davis Publishing

First published in Great Britain in 2024 by Cahill Davis Publishing Limited.

First published in paperback in Great Britain in 2024 by Cahill Davis Publishing Limited.

ISBN 978-1-915307-10-1 (eBook)

ISBN 978-1-915307-09-5 (Paperback)

Cahill Davis Publishing Limited

www.cahilldavispublishing.co.uk

To my dear children and their spouses, Philip and Catherine, Caroline and Roshan, for their unstinting love and support.

Chapter 1

1921

Philip Manners, newly reinstated headmaster at Shadworth Quaker School after a long term of convalescence, sat peacefully in his wheelchair in the garden at his home at Holt House, enjoying the winter sunshine. Spring term was still some way off and the holidays stretched into January, giving him the time he needed to prepare himself for his return to his old study at last.

There were already signs of snowdrops peeping out from the soil in what had once been Jack's garden. Emma's hens were clucking happily amongst the seeds she had thrown for them only minutes earlier, and Philip felt an immense relief that she belonged to him now after the long, long months, nay years of anguish.

My wife. What did I do to deserve this gift?

His thoughts were interrupted by noises from indoors, where Emma had been busy baking. A stifled cry, a groan and what could only be retching. He had become adept at managing the heavy wheelchair alone, and he wheeled himself hurriedly into the kitchen.

He stopped next to Emma, who was leaning over the sink vomiting, and reached out to touch her back.

"*My darling, what is it? You are ill, sweetheart. See if I can reach to support your head. Steady.*"

Emma, the sickness all spent and her face as pale as a ghost, wordlessly put her head on his shoulder, and he looked at her with all the love he felt for her on his anxious face. Eventually, she managed a reply.

"*My dearest, I'm alright, truly. It's passed over, and I feel much better already. Can we go into the garden and just sit quietly for a minute or two? Maybe I've caught the bug they had at Tempests' Farm. Florence said she has been feeling sickly.*"

Together, they wheeled and walked to the sunny terrace, and she sat at the foot of his chair, her head on his lap.

Philip stroked her hair, which cascaded over his knee. He loved the way her chestnut curls refused to be contained by her ruthless tying back.

"*Darling, have you had any other symptoms? I'm puzzled that it came on so suddenly. You would tell me if there was anything else?*"

She looked up at him with a strange smile playing on her lips, a kind of glow about her head. And he looked back at her, astonished.

Of course, she's caught something. It can't possibly be anything else? But the look on her face...

"*Is it something that I can hardly dare believe, my love?*" Philip's words shook with emotion. "*Emma, you surely can't be? We're too old, aren't we? Emma, tell me.*"

Tears were welling up in her hazel eyes as he searched her face for the answer.

"*I thought I was in the change. At my age, that's what happens. But, Philip*"—she shook her head and laughed—"*this sickness is so like the sickness I had with Will and with Harry too, that I do believe it's no sickness bug, though I've been pretending it is to myself for days now."*

Emma herself could hardly believe what seemed to be true. The evidence had been quietly creeping up on her as the signs became more and more apparent. The nausea was familiar, her breasts were fuller, but there was no more blood, which, of course, must be normal for a woman of over fifty in the change.

And yet, this miracle, begotten of such love, might actually be more than a pipe dream. Just maybe she was carrying his child. And she wanted to get down on her knees and thank God for this special honour that would be her gift to him after all the sufferings he had had to endure.

"*My beloved man, I think I'm going to be a mother again and you will be a first-time father. I hardly dare believe it."*

Philip's voice shook as he allowed himself to believe her words, his own taking on a serious tone. "*We need Leonard straight away. He's our friend as well as our doctor. He must check that you are safe to have another child, my Emma. We cannot put you at any risk."*

Emma laughed. "*Philip, oh, Philip. I've borne three big sons and a healthy daughter, and my hips are as ready as ever they were to carry your baby. He, or maybe she, will slip-slide out of me easily. I can hardly wait."*

And with that, she returned to the kitchen, where she could smell her cakes burning.

Philip simply sat in silence now, and there were tears in his eyes as he offered his gratitude to God. They had shared their passion for each other, at first gently after the terrible amputation of his leg, then more confidently as they expressed their tender love for each other after the long wait they had endured. All the pent-up longing and the discipline they had exerted over the years had been expurgated at last. That time in York was still seared into their minds when she had begged him to consummate their love and he had held back. They rejoiced as they made love now that they could belong together freely and damage no one. But this... he could never have imagined this.

His anxiety for Emma got the better of him. He wheeled back into the kitchen, already redolent with the scent of newly baked bread. Emma was busy getting her cakes out of the huge old oven, and he regarded her with something approaching exasperation for he knew she would not rest, however much he pleaded with her to take it easy. This baby, if there were one, would have to cope with its industrious, unstoppable mother.

"I'm sending for Leonard to come over at once, love. Let's at least get the idea confirmed before we go any further. And, Emma, you will, for once, do as I tell you. Remember how you promised to obey me, my darling."

She looked at him then with her face flushed from the heat of the oven and came to sit on his knee. He pushed back the chestnut curls from her forehead and took her face in both his hands. And then he kissed her passionately.

The good doctor was more than astonished when he heard what his friend had to say, and he arrived at Holt House almost before either Emma or Philip had drawn breath. They made their way to Emma and Philip's bedroom.

"Will you lie down on your bed, Emma? I'm going to feel your pelvis and just very gently feel your tummy. Forgive my cold hands." He looked across at Philip, who was watching guardedly as Emma made herself comfortable in an uncomfortable situation. *"All will be well, my friend."*

Leonard's hands expertly examined Emma's body as she stared silently at the stippled white ceiling and Philip held her hand. He nodded at what he could feel.

"I need to check your blood pressure, my dear, but I think there is no question that you are both to become parents." Leonard shared their joy, knowing how much this would mean to them.

Philip shook his head and whispered, *"Oh thank God."*

Leonard shook his friend's hand and then bent and kissed Emma's forehead as tears of wonder and relief fell.

"My God, Philip. What wonders are now in store for you two? Get out that whiskey I bought you for Christmas and let's have a drink. But, of course, Emma, you are getting old to bear a child and it's still early days, I believe. We must get proper confirmation and you will have to be careful. I can rely on Philip to make sure of that." He smiled at his friend, who was looking on anxiously.

"Courage, you two. We will monitor you, Emma, very carefully and make sure everything is in order. But I believe this birth will be no more difficult than when you brought Will into this world."

"I know it, Leonard. I'm on top of the world."

Philip leaned down to his wife very tenderly, and the two embraced while Leonard looked on somewhat embarrassedly. He knew they had forgotten him in their new-found delight, and he crept away to give them the space they deserved.

Chapter 2

January, 1922

For Philip, the return to his position as head of his beloved Quaker school was not an easy one. He had gradually returned to work under Alan Lorimer, his best friend and ally throughout all the traumas of his convalescence in Scarborough, Jack's death and his own marriage to Jack's widow.

He had picked up the pieces of his teaching, part-time, especially with his sixth formers studying English. But with Emma's support and encouragement, he had relaxed back into life at school. James Thompson, Leonard's son, was now fully installed as gardener and groundsman at the school and it was he who chauffeured Philip up to school every day in his rather large automobile, into which the wheelchair fitted comfortably. James had indeed become something of a right-hand man, which delighted his mother and father.

Beatrice, Alan's wife, now well-established as head of Ayton House, sat beside Alan around the large dining table at Holt House, eating one of Emma's delicious dinners. She had excelled herself as usual with a huge piece of pork surrounded by the crispiest crackling and roast potatoes to die for.

Alan crunched on a luscious chunk of crackling and then sat back. "*I really do think you should reconsider returning full-time as headteacher. Think how glad all your staff will be to welcome you back, not least Kath Hanson, who has found me an old grump in comparison with my predecessor.*"

"*Nonsense.*" Philip clapped Alan on his back, though he couldn't deny missing his old secretary. "*The whole school respects and admires you, not to mention their respect for Beatrice. You belong in that study and particularly in the house on the grounds where I spent long, difficult years with Harriet during my first marriage. I could never return there nor take Emma away from Holt House, as you well know.*" He sighed at the memory of those days.

"*Philip, nobody is expecting that of you. Your travel arrangement with James works well and there is no reason why you can't continue it. You will simply live off-site but can do all you ever did just the same, even down to your much-loved visits to the houses at evening time. Emma, am I right?*"

Beatrice and Emma looked at each other and smiled.

"*Of course you can, my dear. I might even do it with you.*"

As the boys began returning in mid-January, they found the head's study once more occupied by the man who had made it his own for many long years before his tragic confinement. Those who knew him, whom he had taught before the illness that had finally taken his leg, were jubilant that he had taken up the reins again. The young first and second years looked on at the older boys who seemed to visit the study often, as if to check that he was really there.

And he, more often than not, would be sitting behind the desk in his wheelchair, while the chair that had spent many years behind the desk was now in the corner of the small room.

"There will be no staring at his wheelchair, no signs of shock or surprise when you first see him and no fear of being called to his study. There never was a better, kinder head, but beware if you break the rules or treat anyone unkindly. He doesn't suffer meanness or malice in any boy."

This comment by a prefect in Fox House was overheard by James one morning after he had delivered Philip into the loving hands of Kath Hanson. James had to smile, not least at the pleasure in Kath's face at Philip's return to his old place.

As the weeks of term wore on, Philip and Emma rejoiced secretly at their pregnancy news every moment they were alone together. As half-term came and went, Emma's bouts of morning sickness disappeared, much to Philip's relief, but she knew that her body was beginning to show the secret, erstwhile hidden by her loose-fitting blouses.

Emma stretched her legs out in front of herself, a blanket under her creating a barrier from the grass. The early afternoon sun framed her in an almost holy glow in the garden of Holt House. "*Philip, dear, I think it might be time.*"

Philip turned to look at Emma and ask what she meant, but as he watched her look down at her stomach, one hand stroking it affectionately, the answer came to him. "*Of course. If you are ready, my love.*"

"I..."

They heard the click of the gate before Florence came into view, hitching the side of her floral dress up as she ran across the garden. Emma stood up and held out her arms to Florence, Florence's long dark hair flying out behind her as she almost ran into her mother's embrace.

"*Mother, Philip, I have to tell someone, or I'll burst.*" She pulled away from her mother, though she still gripped her hands with affection and excitement. "*Mother, I'm pregnant. I've seen Dr. Thompson and he's confirmed it. Can you believe it? Isn't that wonderful? Ned is over the moon and . . .*"

Florence stopped short as she looked at her mother and her stepfather smiling back at her.

"*That's truly the best news ever, my dear Florence,*" said Philip, "*but Mother must tell you our news herself. She's been anxious that you might mind her keeping it from you till now.*"

Florence's face lit up as she registered Philip's words with great joy. Though a shock, it was only a very slight one, as she'd had suspicions.

"*My darling Florence, you've guessed what it is, I can see from your face. Philip and I are like Ned—completely astonished that this miracle is happening. And now you and I can share it together.*"

Florence could not quite hide the emotion that followed the joy—fear for her mother who was so much older than she showed in the frown that puckered her forehead.

"*Oh, darling, don't look like that,*" pleaded Emma. "*We'll both be fine. I'm just as tough as you, you know.*"

"*But what about your age, Mother? It's incredible, scary and wonderful all at the same time.*"

Florence hugged her mother tightly while Philip watched them. An anxious smile played on his lips as he watched Florence reflecting his fears for Emma.

Come on, Philip Manners. Don't let your worries spoil this special time for Florence and for Emma. Rejoice.

He sat back in his chair and allowed himself to relax as they put their heads together and shared their due dates and the special coincidence that they would be giving birth on almost the same day in September. Florence's tears began to flow as she took in this astonishing correlation of dates. Philip quickly wheeled himself from his vantage point to take her hands.

"*My dear Florence, you have been our best companion throughout all our painful days. Now I am delighted that you and Mother share this joy. Do you think Ned would mind if we all go down to the farm now so that he doesn't get left out? Anyway, I feel I should see the Tempests myself and break our news to them.*"

Emma and Florence looked at this man they loved and, together, they pushed his chair out onto Long Lane and headed for the farm.

Easter was approaching, and the rooks in the tall trees were cawing their pleasures. Primroses were peeping out from the hedgerows and even a few cowslips raised their long necks in salute. They smiled with sheer pleasure as they strode along, Philip begging Emma to be careful, then feeling ashamed that he was not protecting Florence too. In the end, he wheeled himself into the farmyard to be greeted by Ned's two collies and by Ned himself, busy shovelling coal into buckets ready to take into the house. Ned, all clad in his workaday farm gear and his large wellingtons caked in mud, looked up and smiled as he wiped the sweat off his brow.

"*Congratulations, Ned. Florence has broken the news to us, and you must be thrilled,*" said Emma as Philip shook Ned's hand.

"*We've got a bit of news ourselves,*" added Philip while Ned looked questioningly at him.

"*Ned, you won't believe it,*" Florence interrupted, clapping her hands excitedly. "*Mother is going to have a baby at nearly the same time as me. They are expecting too.*"

Ned, a man of few words, stood there with his mouth open in surprise, then suddenly began to laugh before yelling at the top of his voice, "*Mum, Dad, come out here and listen to this.*"

Ron and Mary appeared at the farm door, years of hard work in all weathers showing on their ageing faces. Emma ran to Mary, whispering the news before anyone else could tell her.

Philip held out his hand to Ron. "*Ron, I am so happy to share the news that I am going to be a father. Rather late, I know, but nonetheless true.*"

"*I'm so pleased for you. Congratulations.*" Ron took the extended hand and shook it firmly and with delight before Mary hustled them all into the kitchen. The old farm kitchen was redolent with the scent of Mary's baking bread and warm with the heat coming off the Aga.

"*Oh my, oh my. I'm lost for words. As if it's not enough that we're going to be grandparents, but you, Philip and Emma, are starting all over again. Philip, you never thought you'd be a father, I know. Oh my,*" cried out Mary, hastily wiping her eyes on her apron.

"*There's one particular thing on my mind with regards to becoming a father,*" said Philip. "*I don't want this little one to know its father always sitting in a wheelchair; I really think it's time I persevered with the crutches again. I'd rather given up on them, but I'd like to be upright on the day this child meets me. What do you think, Ron?"*

Emma and Florence looked aghast, but Mary Tempest took in, with one look, the huge emotion that was evident in Philip's words—a longing to be back as strong as he had always been, a longing for Emma to know she could lean on him as of old.

"*Now, don't you women even think of stopping him in this resolve,*" Mary spoke sternly but lovingly. "*He can do it gradually; after all, he has a good five months to practise. You agree, don't you, Ron?*"

Ron nodded with amusement at Emma and Florence's cries.

"*I believe my main concern now must be to tell Will and Harry this news,*" said Philip, "*and especially little George. I couldn't bear Harry's youngster to feel pushed out in any way. He practically lives with us and Emma takes him to Howard School every day, just like all the other mothers. And how will Harry react? He's become very comfortable handing George over to our care.*"

"Philip," remonstrated Emma, "*it won't make any difference to George's routine. And I think he'll love it that he has a baby to care for, not to mention a new cousin as well. He's seven now and prides himself on being the big boy. When the time comes, that will certainly be true.*"

Mary and Ron nodded their agreement, and Florence, rousing herself from her own private idyll, jumped up and announced, "*Come on, Ned. Let's go and hunt Harry and George down. I think they've gone to the playing fields up at High Shadworth to play cricket. Mother, we'll bring them back to Holt House for tea and then share all this with them. I'll knock on*

Will and Laura's door as we pass and invite them too. That is, my dear mother, if you feel up to feeding us all?"

Philip could not hide his frustration that Emma's role as "great provider" was still being taken for granted. He gently huffed.

"*Philip, stop looking so worried; she's still the same iron-willed lady she ever was.*"

"As *if I didn't know that, Florence, my love. But seriously, you know we really must look after her now.*"

Emma simply frowned at these words, and, after embracing Mary once more, she took hold of his wheelchair and began to push him home. He reached out his hand to where hers lay on one of the handles of his chair and squeezed it hard.

"*My beloved wife, forgive me. I'll try to restrain my overprotective instincts. But, darling, there are two of you to consider now.*"

And so the news was shared that spring afternoon, and there was an air of celebration as Will and Laura helped Emma lay out the tea, a tea with all the hallmarks of Emma's culinary delights. Laura whispered in Emma's ear how pleased she was for them both. Florence, blushing with the joy of her own news, hugged Will, while Ned, Will's old friend and companion from the trenches, shook his hand vigorously.

"*Grandma, how I love your meringues,*" yelled George as he wolfed a second one down, "*and, Uncle Philip, are you really going to be a daddy?* Won't that *be fun?*"

The Holt children looked on with something like a mixture of amazement and relief to see George so completely unruffled by the news. Harry Holt could not help but be pleased for the man who had made his mother so happy, but he reserved in his heart that special place where he kept the memory of his father intact. He walked to the window and looked out at the sky that was just beginning to change in colour, not wanting anyone to see the tears welling in his eyes. He wiped them away with the back of his hand. Emma approached and placed a gentle hand on his shoulder.

"*I hope my dad can see us now and that he is pleased for you and Philip. Oh, Mum, I still miss him, you know.*"

He turned to face her, and she hugged him, understanding the deep-felt loss of the man he had so looked up to all his life.

Will, standing nearby, understood the silent gesture. He kept to himself, not wanting his own emotions to spill out.

Philip, presiding at the big kitchen table, smiled to himself. *Jack, you are part of this too, my dear old friend.*

Chapter 3

1922

That summer in Shadworth excelled itself. The sky, piercingly blue, barely admitted even a few white clouds, which seemed merely to dance around the heavens and then skim away into the distance. The trees were in their full and brightest green, effulgent, full of the sounds of birds rearing their young and tweeting madly. In Emma's lavender, the bees were busy about their business untroubled by George peering closely at them, though Emma kept a careful eye on him.

Rosebuds gently swelled and burst out under the warming sun, roses planted by Jack long before and now disporting themselves in every shade of pink and peach, to Philip's particular delight. Their scent was extraordinary, and Philip, just like a young lover, wished he could bottle the perfume to give to his beloved Emma.

Up at the school, James' garden, once Jack Holt's domain, was flourishing. James had a special love of rhododendrons and had planted them to line the pathways up to the head's study and the main entrance. His vegetable garden was a match for what had once been Jack's particular pride. James had determined it should be capable of furnishing not only the school's requirements, but also those of the village. James Thomson, once destined for university but denied by the horrors of his wartime experiences, was putting all his intelligence to work for the community. He knew the dangers of these post-war years, when men and women might still find themselves in abject poverty. He often shared his thoughts with Philip as he drove him to and from school, and Philip respected his views and, like him, thought long and hard about what was happening in the world.

Emma and Florence, meanwhile, were blossoming in the heyday of their pregnancies. Florence rejoiced in the small and gentle movements from her womb and her cheeks took on a healthier bloom than they had ever shown before. Indeed, she bounded with energy.

Emma observed her sweet Florence with admiration and not a little envy. Emma's age was making the pregnancy tougher, though she would not admit that to Philip.

The sun seemed to broil her as she set out for the little junior school holding George's hand tightly. He skipped along beside her practising his times tables aloud ready for the exigencies of Miss Prior, who was something of a dragon in his innocent mind. Emma's baby seemed to skip along too and often now pummelled her insides like a young footballer. When Philip was in the vicinity, she would place his hand exactly where the kicks were strongest so he could share the sensation, and it usually conjured a huge smile. But for herself, on these particularly hot summer days, the sweat would roll onto her forehead and she would sigh inside with the effort of keeping up with George's bounces. She did not realise that the little boy was very aware of her tiredness.

"*Uncle Philip*," he announced one day after he had been tucked up in bed at Holt House, "*we must look after Grandma, you know. I think the little mouse inside her is making her a bit tired.*"

"*You're right, George. We must keep an eye on that grandma of yours. The little mouse, as you call it, is heavy inside her, and she won't admit to you or me that the mouse makes her tired.*"

"*Uncle Philip*," said the little boy, snug in his blankets, "*I love staying here best, you know. You have the best bedtime stories ever, and Daddy is always too busy. Mousie won't spoil our times together, will he?*"

Philip had to hide his sadness that George should have even thought such a thing and instead leaned over and kissed the little hand that was peeping out from the blankets.

"*My darling, Grandma and I will expect you to take care of Mousie and stay very, very close to us as we teach him to be a good boy like you. You will be his best friend, sweetheart. Have no fear. And, George, 'he' may be a 'she'. Would you mind that?*"

"*Oh no, Uncle, but I think a boy might be more fun.*"

"*Well, we shall have to wait and see, my love. Now, it's time for your prayers. Let's say them together.*"

"*Gentle Jesus, meek and mild, look upon a little child. Pity my simplicity. Suffer me to come to thee. Amen.*"

The little boy's eyes were already tightly shut as Philip finished the prayer, and he touched him gently, smiling quietly, before he wheeled himself out of the room. He found Emma leaning back on a kitchen chair, exhausted.

"*Thank you for putting George to bed tonight. The weeks are going by and our little one is very active now, and I just felt too tired to do it, darling. I do wish*

I could have more energy, like Florence, who is so full of vigour."

"*When the time comes, my dear, you will find all the resources you need. But George has noticed that we need to take care of you. He has christened the newcomer* 'Mousie', *and I rather like it.* And, *Emma, don't try to hide your weariness from us. I'm going to get Leonard over to check you and make sure you are not overdoing it.*"

She protested furiously but was secretly pleased that the good doctor would ensure her child was growing safely.

And indeed he did, reassuring them that "Mousie" was growing just as he or she should at the seven-month mark. Philip thanked God a hundred times a day that they had such support from his old friend; meanwhile, he had to entrust Emma to George and the family, as term was demanding much of his time.

One particular morning, Kath ushered Will's wife, Laura, into Philip's office. Philip, watching her slowly enter, could not help but notice the streak of a tear on her cheek and her sagging shoulders.

"*Come and sit beside me, sweetie. What is it?*" He knew that some of the boys in the lower school were a menace to the younger members of staff.

"*I have such a difficult time managing boys like Graham Biggins, Philip. And I worry about Will. He's not sleeping.*"

"*Is it still memories of the war, Laura?*"

"*I believe so. He cries out for Ralph. You know he was my husband and also Will's captain. It's such an anomaly. And all I want is for Will to settle down to be content with me.*" Laura shook her head tearfully, then she put her head in her hands and wept. "*Gordon Biggins is very insolent, but. . .*"

Philip touched her hair gently. He noticed how her blonde hair shone brightly and golden in the rays of sun from his window even though she was feeling so wretched. He felt sorrowful that she was suffering and angry still at these tragic consequences of war that tormented his family. "*Come, my dear Laura. Let's go and sit awhile in chapel and pray for that peace that only God can give us. I know I find that helpful. Let's hand Will over to Him for His help. And you must certainly send Biggins to me. I won't have him upsetting my staff.*"

Laura lifted her wet face to him and smiled. Kath overheard this small encounter from her office next to Philip's and nodded to herself. Her head had not lost his loving touch despite all the months away from his desk. To Kath's mind, there was no one better to help the lovely girl than Philip. And she rejoiced that, at home, he had Emma beside him now.

That night, he told his wife Laura's story and she at once forgot the weariness that was now a daily issue for her, one she quietly kept to herself.

"*Philip, my poor Will.*" Emma put her hand on her heart and gasped. "*We must get him to share these agonies and unburden himself of it all. And Laura needs us just as much. Did you manage to cheer her?*"

"*I hope so, darling. I took her down to the chapel and we sat awhile. I said a prayer for them both in the hope it might give her confidence. But, Emma, I sometimes feel the world has too many sorrows.*"

"*She must have loved Ralph, and life has hurried her on. It's almost as if she needs more time with Will to grieve for him,*" Emma said, hoping to comfort

Philip with her words. She needed him to be his old reassuring self. "*I know Will loved him and could hardly bear to leave him on the field. Only his friends dragged him away from staying there beside him and dying himself. Oh, my love, the war has not finished its ugly business still.*" She shuddered at the thought.

"*One thing I will do is sort those little urchins in her third-year class. They need a rocket. But, my darling, you're done in.*" Philip wheeled himself closer and clasped her hands in his. "*Let's retire to our bed and rest now. Tomorrow, I'll get James to drop me off at their cottage and bring them both home with me.*"

He barely slept that night, however, for he could not forget that Will and Laura were struggling. It brought back all the agonies he had endured in Scarborough and how it had at times overwhelmed him. He desperately felt that they had to find a way to pull Will out of the depths of his memories, had to help him be able to look up at the light again. But he also knew that there were no easy answers to these hurdles.

Chapter 4

July 1922

The last days of term were smoulderingly hot, and tempers were frayed in the classrooms. Boys were constantly being brought in to see Philip for one misdeed or another, but there were great successes amongst the older boys who had achieved high honours in their exams.

At their final staff meeting of the year, Edna, Beatrice, Alan and Philip, the senior management in the school, discussed with pride the boys' achievements and congratulated their staff for their hard work, which was seen to reap its rewards. Laura, too, seemed better and more refreshed at last, though Philip noted the lines under her blue eyes.

"*Thank you, Philip, for your understanding. I think Will is feeling a little better. He doesn't cry out in the night so much now and Mother has spent ages with him getting him to talk it all out. This summer holiday, we're going to do some exploring of the countryside around Shadworth, but we'll never be so far away that we're not on hand when the babies arrive.*"

"*Thank you for that. I need all the reassurance I can get. Emma is so tired now and Leonard says her blood pressure is high. We're going to have to make her rest.*"

Laura bent down to him and hugged him, and Alan and Beatrice grinned at each other.

"*Come on, Alan,*" Philip said, laughing. "*She's my daughter-in-law.*"

They all joined in the laughter, and so term came to its close. Florence and Emma had just six weeks more of waiting and Philip had just that time to master the crutches.

How he toiled with them. Managing the heavy sticks at the same time as keeping his balance, then hauling himself forward with them before putting his good foot down was completely wearisome. Many times, he fell to the floor, gasping with the effort and furious with himself for failing again and again. It made him almost despair.

Maybe this child of mine will, after all, have to be content with having a father in a wheelchair. Oh God, thank goodness Emma hasn't caught me on the floor.

Kath knew his efforts in the quiet sanctum of his study and sent up many a prayer for his safety every time she heard him fall, but she kept her counsel and held her peace.

If only he would give up and be grateful for being alive.

At long last, Philip's special moment came.

He allowed James to drop him at the gate of Holt House, with his wheelchair left on the doorstep. He groaned as he picked up each crutch and fitted it onto his arm, but he was determined to show his wife his progress, knowing how thrilled he could make her with such a performance. He meticulously arranged the crutches, struggled slowly to the front door and knocked. He could hear George inside playing with his toy train and Emma laughing at something Florence had said. *Oh dear, I forgot they're all coming to tea.* Nevertheless, he remained steady, head held high.

George answered the door and gave a cry of delight. "*Uncle Philip, you're standing up.*"

Emma turned from the oven, where she was unloading her cakes, and screamed. Seeing him standing upright with the help of his crutches reminded her of the many times her heart had missed a beat on the station platform as he'd stepped out of the train, tall, smartly dressed and as handsome then as she found him now. She'd loved him though she hadn't been able to claim him. Now he was her husband, standing erect after so long incapacitated, and her passion for him could be expressed. She ran to him just as his balance was about to give way and caught him in her arms.

"*My darling, what am I seeing? How long have you been practising this and not telling me? I will have to give Kath a piece of my mind, for I'm sure she knew all about it. Come in, my love, and sit down,*" she demanded lovingly.

He looked around at them all gaping with wonder and felt huge pride swell inside him. Then he laughed and laughed as he staggered with Emma's help to the big old armchair and collapsed into it.

"*I did it, Emma Manners, and our baby will have a father who can stand up. It may not be for long, I admit, but at least I've made it.*"

George leaped up onto his lap and everyone broke into applause. Ned and Will grinned at each other and Florence hugged her mother.

"*I shall make the tea,*" announced Laura, smiling.

***

The clock at their bedside registered 10 p.m. when Emma woke, the sheet soaking wet underneath her. She stifled a moan, and Philip woke instantly with a protective start, reaching out to tenderly stroke her arm.

"*What is it, my love?*"

"*Philip, my waters have broken. I felt a huge gush, a sort of cascade. Oh, Philip, we need Doctor Thomson. Oh God, I'd forgotten the worst of it.*" She grasped his hand tightly as a sudden sickly pain shot across her back.

Philip wasted not a second fulfilling her request and thanked God a thousand times that he had insisted on bringing their phone upstairs to be close to their bed. But it was not Doctor Thomson who answered the phone.

"*Mrs Thomson, I do so hope you are well, but I desperately need to speak to Leonard. Would you be able to put him on the phone at all?*"

"*Oh, Philip, my dear, is it the baby?*"

"*It is,*" he confirmed.

"*He's already gone out to Tempests' farm, for Ned rang to say Florence is in labour. I'm so sorry, Philip. But have no fear. I will ring Mrs Townsend, who will be sure to attend, and then I'll ring the farm and warn Leonard. Mrs Townsend is the most competent midwife, just as much an expert as Leonard at birthing.*"

Even so, Philip's heart sank, for he could see Emma was really struggling with the contractions as she lay. He moved from the bed to his wheelchair and sat beside her, tapping the arms of his wheelchair as fearful thoughts raced through his mind. As Emma's cries intensified, he stroked her forehead and prayed fervently for God's help as he had never prayed before. Emma held his hand tightly, trying to keep her courage up.

The time ticked by as they waited for the midwife to appear. It seemed like an eternity till, at last, Molly Townsend arrived and pushed the front door open. She hurried up to the bedroom, smiling reassuringly.

"*Mr Manners, you must trust me to bring this baby into the world. I'll boil a kettle, and can you tell me where Emma keeps her clean laundry? We need towels too.*"

Through her stifled cries, Emma managed to direct her to the cistern cupboard where she stored all her laundry. When Molly came back, she carried a kettle and had towels draped over her arm.

"*Mr Manners, it is time for you to leave the room.*" She held the bedroom door open for him. "*Fathers should not be present at a birth.*"

"No," Emma screamed in protest. "*He must stay with me. I refuse to do this without him, Mrs Townsend.*"

The old midwife opened her mouth to remonstrate when they heard the front door opening and quick footsteps up their stairs. James strode into the bedroom, much to Philip's intense relief.

"*Mother said to come while Father is still at the farm. Philip, let me move you to the corner closest to Emma. Then you won't get in Mrs Townsend's way but still be able to watch over your wife. Mrs Townsend, is there anything more I can get you? I'm here to help.*"

Philip felt keenly at that moment his weakness and incapacity to do more, but he allowed James to take over and sat silently in the room, praying hard for his beloved wife.

Molly Townsend, if she would have admitted it, was very grateful for the presence of the doctor's son. She knew James and his enormously practical usefulness and that he would fetch for her and carry whatever she needed. She was concerned, for she could see from her examination of Emma that her cervix was not dilating as it should despite the intense contractions and Emma's obvious agony. She knew very well that Emma's age militated against an easy labour, and she felt sure this baby would need a forceps delivery.

Emma's forehead was wet with sweat, and Philip was at least able to wipe it with a cold cloth to relieve her a little. But he felt so inadequate and indeed frightened.

If I should lose her because she's bearing my child, I cannot go on.

As he uttered the thought, the door was again opened, and here at last was Leonard.

"*My God, Leonard, help her. She's having such pains.*"

"*Leonard, how is my Florence?*" a very weak voice came from the bed. "Is *she alright?*"

"*Emma, Philip, no more of this dreadful angst.* Let's *see where this baby has got to. It needs to join its new baby cousin in this world.*" The doctor began his examination as Molly stepped aside. "*And yes, Florence and Ned have a daughter, who slipped out with the least amount of fuss and is even now sucking milk from her mummy's breast.*"

A murmur of delight came from Emma.

Philip sighed. "*God, Leonard, I'm pleased, but please bring our baby now.*"

"We'll need forceps to help this one out, Dr. Thomson," said the midwife. *"Mrs Manners is getting very weary and the baby's heartbeat is slowing."*

"What I've got to do, you do not need to see, Philip. All will be well. Take him away, James. Go, *Philip. You aren't doing any good here now."*

Philip groaned but allowed James to help him into the next room, though Emma cried in protest. She was by now crying with exhaustion, and at last, Leonard could see the cervix had dilated enough for him to extract the very tired baby. What agonies Emma now endured, she would never forget. Unlike her other children, who had emerged relatively easily, this little one was entering the world painfully for her mother, herself and the good doctor. James was glad he was there and able to help, whatever was needed. Leonard kept a close eye on Emma's pulse as she pushed and pushed, scarlet with the effort. But at last, he pulled the child out, the head clamped hard inside the forceps, the slippery shoulders following. Molly Townsend sat with a thud on the chair by the bed, having wrapped the little one tightly in the blanket James had found for her. They all waited with bated breath. Would this baby give out the cry that would say all was well?

"James, get Philip as quickly as you can."

As James helped Philip back into the bedroom, his child let out a valiant and full-throated cry.

"She's greeting you, Philip. You have a daughter, perfect in every way. But my God, she took her time over it. And here she is."

Philip could not speak as he was handed the tiny, wrapped-up parcel and held her close to his breast for a second, kissing her blooded forehead as he tenderly placed her on her mother's breast. Emma was too exhausted to speak, but her eyes spoke of all her love for the small creature and for the man whom she adored. And the tears came for them both. Indeed, even Leonard and James Thomson wiped away a tear or two. But dear Molly Townsend cleared up the afterbirth and checked and double-checked that everything was as it should be as Leonard applied the stitches needed to mend the tear caused by Emma's exertions.

"*I'm away home to my bed, Doctor. A good night's work and thank God all is well,*" said the good midwife as she bustled out of the room.

"*Mrs Townsend, we are for ever in your debt,*" Philip cried after her. "*Thank you, thank you.*"

And, with a backward wave, she was gone.

Chapter 5
Elizabeth May – Early Years

And so I arrived safely despite my beloved daddy's fears, only a short while after my niece, Daisy. Daisy beat me to the date, for she was born before midnight on the seventh of September 1922 and I had to wait till the early morning of the eighth. My father enjoyed this particular fact and shared stories with Daisy's father about it.

The best story is of how my beloved George—my nephew—took one look at me and announced that I looked just like a monkey. My father had to prevent Mother from ticking him off for it, or so I was told.

George liked Daisy best, I think, for she was always ready for adventures in the fields and round the farm, while I followed them around, trying to keep up. Maybe I was a little jealous of her, for her daddy used to carry her around up high on his shoulders to help look after the animals. How I longed for my daddy to be able to stand up and throw me in the air like Ned used to. But I never told him this; instead, I would snuggle on his lap as Mother pushed the both of us, with George giving her a helping hand on the way.

Mother was so strong, so determined and so full of gaiety and vitality, just as if she were twenty years younger. Indeed, I was told that she had even acted as the railway's station master during the war. She was older and greyer than Daisy's mother, but I knew my sister, Florence, still relied on her and talked to her as if she were still growing up at home. I also knew how much the whole village looked up to her for help and guidance, especially in the years of hardship when everyone was struggling to make ends meet. As for my father, he had a special look in his eye whenever he looked at my mother. He had been forced to wait so long to be able to claim her.

They both loved and respected Mr Firbank, the old station master who had given Mother the job at the station when the war was at its worst. One of my earliest memories is of the day they heard he had died. I think I was about three years old, and Mother, Father and I went down to the station cottage to see his wife. She was a dear old lady who always gave me sweets from a big pot she kept on the sideboard, but on this occasion, she was swept up in Mother's embrace. The two of them stood with their arms interlocked and cried loud sobs. I expect I remember it still because it was so harrowing to watch. Daddy took my hand and nodded at me to follow him outside while they comforted each other, then he put his hand on my head and closed his eyes. I knew he was praying for the old lady, so I kept very still.

We walked home very slowly as Mother pushed the wheelchair. As she dried her tears, they smiled. I know now they were remembering those long desert days when the only times they had a few moments together were snatched in the Shadworth Station waiting room between Mother's duties. Father would have been on his way to London to see Frank Jacques or the bereaved parents of his boys who had died in the war. He was always so sad on those trips, he told me, yet he found enormous comfort in those clandestine minutes in the shady waiting room, when they could hold each other and assure each other of their love, though at the time it was forbidden and seemed impossible.

There were two people at that time who made it difficult for them to pursue their relationship. George used to talk about Grandad Jack, and I knew he was Florence and Will and Harry's daddy. He was the school gardener before James.

"*Nobody loved this garden as much as Jack Holt,*" James told me, "*and it was thanks to him and your father that I came to be the gardener today. He taught me all I know about growing the best vegetables and the most beautiful roses, and that was when, my little Beth, I was still very poorly after the war. I couldn't even get my words out, but it never mattered to Jack. He just taught me without needing to speak, and as I looked at the glories of his garden and worked with him, I gradually got better. But you mustn't worry your head about all that. Just remember that Jack was a wonderful man who loved your mother then, just like your daddy does now.*"

I frowned and internally protested at that, for no one could even approach the love my father had for Mother. Or so I supposed. So, I asked Father one day.

"*Daddy, tell me about Grandad Jack. James said he loved Mother very much and he was the daddy to my big brothers and sister, wasn't he?*"

Father went very quiet then, thinking back, I guess, over the many years he had shared the life of the school with Jack Holt and watched him with what must have been envy and pain and, indeed, guilt as he fell in love with my mother.

"Darling, Grandad Jack was a wonderful man and a dear friend to me. Your mother and I are still so grateful for that. He looked after Mother and stood by her right through the war years, when your brothers were out in the killing fields of France. And we all shared all the awful suffering the war brought to us.

"Then when your daddy's leg became very, very poisoned and the doctors had to amputate it, Grandad Jack let your mummy help me through that dreadful time. Oh, Elizabeth. That was very, very hard. I had to go to a hospital far away and Jack looked after Mother back here in Shadworth. And then, one terrible day, James found him in the school garden lying dead. And Mother was left alone." As he spoke, his eyes welled up with tears.

Back then, despite Daddy's tears and all the amazing things he had to say about Grandad Jack, I still couldn't comprehend how Grandad Jack could have loved Mother just as much. Now... I can't help but think what a wonderful man he must have been.

"But, Daddy, she had you."

"No, darling, I was many miles away, still getting used to having just one leg. Sweetheart, you have never known me to be able to stand up just like Ned and Will and Harry. But it meant that I could not go to Mother at first. She had to stand all alone. My poor Emma."

He had lost all thought of the little girl listening to him.

But there was another who had left a scar on him, and I vividly remember *her* appearance one summer's day at home. It would have been when I was around seven years old, a schoolgirl by this time, just home from school and playing with Daisy in our garden. Daisy would have been staying for tea, for my sister, Florence, was always so tired with all the farm work and my own mother was busy taking all the work from her as best she could. James had brought Father home from school, and he was sitting watching us. It was a glorious day, late September, not long after Daisy and I had celebrated our birthdays together, as we always did. The sunflowers had reached a pinnacle of height in the garden and shone yellow and dazzlingly bright near the chickens, which were clucking away in their pen. Father had his book open on his knee, but he was really watching us vying with each other to see which of us could perform the best handstands, and smiling to himself. We heard the front gate and clapped our hands. It must be George home from the big school in Cranston.

But instead, my mother came out to us, rubbing her hands on her apron, accompanied by a very elegant lady dressed all in white, with a very large hat crowning her outfit.

"*Philip, my dear, we have a visitor.*"

I shall never forget Father's look as he saw who it was. A mixture of horror and sadness passed over his face as she came towards him, behaving as if my mother was not even there.

"*Well, Philip, so this is where you have ended up.*" She placed her hands on her hips and looked around. "*I never believed you would actually come down here and live in Low Shadworth, even if you are a cripple.*"

"*Forgive me for not standing up to greet you, dear Harriet. As you can see, it's not so easy. But how are you? And how is Godfrey? To what do we owe the pleasure of this visit?*" He forced a smile. "*Let me introduce you to my daughter. Elizabeth, come and say hello to this lady.*"

The lady was visibly astounded at the sight of me and looked from me to Daisy and back to Mother as I held out my hand to her. I knew Father would never forgive me if didn't do as he asked. And Daisy, giggling, held her hand out too.

"Children, perhaps you had better go inside with Mother and help her get a cup of tea for this lady."

Mother, very pink but smiling, ushered us indoors. There, she gave us both a huge hug and put her finger to her lips to stop us from shouting out questions.

I know now it was, of course, Father's first wife, Harriet, who had presided over his years living in the headmaster's house at the school and who had given him little sign of affection or warmth through all the years she was married to him. Finally, she had left him for another man and had come that afternoon, I think, to persuade herself that he was bound to be regretting a marriage to such a common woman as Emma Holt.

The truth was that she had committed her life to this man, Godfrey, who had trailed her around the casinos of Europe and kept her as his plaything. She had remained childless and now bitterly wanted to believe that her former husband, crippled as he was, was as miserable as she.

Oh God. If only I had been older, I would have liked to have taken a cricket bat to her, as George would have put it. Yet when she drove away in her grand chauffeur-driven automobile, Father wheeled himself into the kitchen, where we were devouring our sandwiches and some of Mother's most delicious cherry cake. He took Mother's hand and pulled her onto his lap. Then he shook his head oh so sadly.

"Emma, she is wretchedly unhappy I think, and I am so sorry for her."

"I know you are, my love, but I find it difficult to forgive her for coming here and upsetting you. How dare she? How dare she step across our threshold and speak to you as she did?"

"Sweetheart, do I look upset?"

Mother looked at him, at the genuine smile on his face, and she smiled too.

"Darling, I am the happiest man in my own kingdom. She can't touch us now. Let it go."

Fortunately, the gate slammed at that moment, and this time, it really was George back from school, satchel over his shoulder. That was enough to distract Daisy and me, and we left Mother and Father to share their feelings in the peace of the kitchen whilst we bombarded George with questions about his day.

Chapter 6
1929

Philip's school went from strength to strength during years of much hardship for many across the world, not least in Shadworth. Unemployment reached its height and, in school, Philip found himself subsidising many of his pupils whose parents could not otherwise have kept their sons there. The school's senior management spent many hours discussing the finances required to maintain this situation, and Philip had to argue hard for the boys he knew deserved to stay and thrive.

Alan and Edna fought him over the issue, for they were ever practical and could see the school would struggle to maintain such subsidies. Nevertheless, Beatrice defended him and Will's Laura supported him after several stressful encounters.

"The staff are really behind you, Philip. I know not one of them would choose to send boys away because their parents could not pay. They are meeting with Alan this afternoon to plead the cause."

"Laura, my dear, thank you. I think I know Alan well enough to believe he'll give in and accept that material funds are less important than the lives of children."

He sighed, and Laura felt a stab of pain for him and for herself, for she knew that she and Will were indeed struggling. Will's work at the cobbler's shop, where he was still treated as an apprentice, was depressingly low paid and her wages had to make up the difference. It also made it very difficult to consider starting a family.

How can I have a baby when my earnings are so important and Will is so inclined to surrender to the black dog that still haunts him?

"*One thing I am grateful for, Laura,*" continued Philip, "*thank God George won his scholarship to The King Edward School in Cranston. At least I'm not pleading for my own sake. And George is supremely happy, which means everything to Emma, not to mention his father. I know Harry is busy getting on with his own life, but that doesn't mean he does not feel deep concern for George.*"

"*I agree,*" ventured Laura. "*And just look at the girls. Both growing up so fast. How they worship him. They fight for his favours every day, and I've a feeling Daisy usually wins. Yet your little Beth seems to suffer gladly. At least she has the pleasure of having him in her home; Daisy has to go back to the farm every night.*"

"*Don't, Laura. I can't bear to think she's second choice. At least she has her adoring big James, whom she treats as her very own slave.*"

Laura had to laugh at that, and they parted company a little more relaxed and hopeful.

Alan Lorimer was, in the end, just as Philip had predicted, brought round to supporting the measures, and peace prevailed in the senior team once more. No one could resist Philip's urgent appeals for compassion and, as a Quaker foundation, everyone knew that the school was not run as a mere business. Indeed, Philip's letters to more wealthy parents, requesting temporary help, were not written in vain.

That night, after they had tucked first Elizabeth and then George into bed, he sat in his chair, beside the fire, with Emma on the floor, her head in his lap.

"*I have news from Florence, my love,*" Emma said. "*Special news, and I feel so happy for her.*"

"*Can I guess, sweetheart? A baby?*" Philip had been observing Florence's quiet manner of recent, not so unlike how she'd been before sharing the news of her first pregnancy.

"*You are far too clever, Philip Manners.*" Emma wagged her finger at him. "*I'm sure you have a second sense for these things. Yes. Another grandchild for us. Isn't that just wonderful? Ned and his parents are hoping for a boy this time. And do you know, Philip, I have a fancy for a boy, to balance up the girls a bit.*"

"*My wicked girl. And yet I do believe you're right. Laura and I were discussing George this very afternoon. I hope he's not overlooking our own little treasure. Laura thinks he favours Daisy, yet they both adore him equally. Emma, there are so many difficulties in this troubled world our little one is going to have to face. I wish I could wrap her up in cotton wool and keep her safe.*" A frown passed over his face.

"*Philip, stop. She can manage her own small world very well, and we must let her. And another baby in the family will be a blessing for us all. I only wish Laura and Will could have such a pleasure. Will is struggling with his bad dreams again and is often back in the trenches with Ralph.*" She sighed, as if her love was being stretched beyond its limits.

Philip pulled her up onto his lap and kissed her tenderly. "*Keep faith, my love. Let's pray for help and healing. And let's go to bed.*"

Chapter 7

Late 1929

1929 was waning now and autumn was in the fullness of russet and gold. A new term was well underway and the school buildings were wrapped in dewy mist each morning as term proceeded. Boys of all backgrounds, rich and poor, found themselves huddled into their warmer clothes, and Edna, in her classroom, was busy with Emma, sorting out warm jerseys for those boys who had little.

"Emma, I've never seen such poverty amongst our pupils before, but I'm very glad Philip has insisted on helping parents out in this way."

"He's very preoccupied at the moment with the news from Germany, Edna. Poverty and unemployment there seem much more extreme than ours, and he is, I know, really afraid that Hitler, that awful man, is growing in power and popularity as people look for a stronger leader. He's in touch with Frank Jacques—they have, of course, been friends for years—and I know he is hearing of dreadful events over there."

Edna fell silent as she smoothed out one of the jerseys. "*We can't afford another war like the last; we've both seen so many deaths of loved ones. I can still hardly bear to think of my poor brother, and I know that Laura is haunted by her memories of what happened to her first husband. But, Emma*"—she lowered her voice even though they were alone—"*I have a suspicion that something good may be about to happen in their little family. Laura often comes in for a cup of coffee at break with Kath and me, and she's been refusing it recently. It may sound silly, but I wonder if she could possibly be pregnant.*"

Emma looked back at Edna, stunned. She had begun to lose hope of Laura having a child, and now, here was Edna suspecting something she herself had not noticed. "*I'll go and see if Kath has the same idea. That would give us all something to cheer us up.*"

She hastened round to Philip's study. She knew he would be working hard on marking papers, but Kath would be ensconced in the next room, on her own. She found her there typing away on her desk.

Kath looked up as Emma appeared at the door. "*Hello, Emma, do you want a word with Philip? He's busy, but he won't mind.*"

Emma glanced across to check that the door adjoining Philip's office was closed. "No, *Kath, I just wanted a quiet word with you if I'm not interrupting.*"

"*That's alright. I have a pile of letters to type up asking for financial help for the school, but I can come back to it. How can I help?*"

"*I just wanted to ask you about Laura. I've been with Edna and she has a theory.*"

A voice from Philip's sanctum interrupted Kath's answer. "*Do I hear my wife in there, Kath? Why has she not come through to my study? Kath?*"

Kath scurried past Emma and into his study with a smile. "*Just occasionally, Mr Manners, your wife and I share a little time together.*"

Emma appeared behind Kath. "*Philip, you know quite well I'm here and can't wait to see you, but I want to hear what Kath thinks about an idea Edna has put into my head."*

The wheelchair rolled slowly towards them, and he folded his arms and looked at them both. "*If this is about Laura's pregnancy, you two gossips, I was going to tell you, Emma, tonight. She really is pregnant and overjoyed and bursting to tell you. But I must say she came to me first.*" Philip smiled knowingly, clearly proud that he had been told first.

Emma threw herself onto Philip and playfully pummelled his chest. "*Philip, how could you? I am so thrilled with this news. It almost beats Florence's—old news now—but at least I was first to know about Florence's baby.*"

"*My goodness, Emma Manners, that's two more grandchildren now. How shall we ever cope with them all? Beth will be in heaven.*"

Philip's words were said in mock horror, at which Kath had to smile, but then she left them to their moment of pleasure, thrilled that her beloved headmaster had found such happiness.

But Frank Jacques' letter, when it arrived, cast a dark shadow over all the celebrations.

Westminster
22nd October, 1929

Mr Philip Manners,
Headteacher
Shadworth Quaker School
High Shadworth
Yorkshire

My dear Philip,

I hesitate to trouble you with my anxieties, but I find myself very troubled over events in Europe. My wife's cousin

Franz lives in Frankfurt, where unemployment is now at an unbelievable high and the resulting depression is far worse than anything we are experiencing here.

You and I have discussed Hitler's activities before at length, but I sincerely believe he is now working towards taking power with his fascist supporters, who are gaining in strength every day. Franz is frightened by moves to close down Jewish businesses, subtle moves at present but increasingly emerging. His wife, Esther, is from a wealthy Jewish family—her father is a professor at the university in Frankfurt—but he feels constantly under scrutiny from various colleagues of his who support Hitler.

Their chancellor, Muller, is failing and Bruning, waiting in the wings, is no better. Hindenburg seems unable to manage the Reichstag and Franz believes he will enforce Article 48 of their constitution to pass laws by decree without reference to the Reichstag at all. Democracy seems no longer viable, so you can imagine who will pounce on the potential in the situation. Philip, I really need to talk to you about all this. Can you get down to London, or shall I come up?

Our government seems totally helpless to act despite protestations of growing emergency from various members of the house. No one wants to acknowledge the danger Hitler poses, empowered by that silver-tongued propagandist Goebbels.

Most of all, I'm afraid for those groups they are targeting. They are playing on the idea that Jews are a threat to the racial purity they preach, which is so esteemed by the Nazi party as the answer to the failure of the Weimar Republic. Franz believes Hitler will, most of all, make Jewish folk the scapegoats. And heaven help them if he ever gets into real power. The SA over there are behaving like thugs, according to Franz, because they use violence to intimidate anyone they don't like.

Philip, get back to me as soon as you can, please.

Yours urgently,
Frank

Philip put his head in his hands, appalled. He had known from the early days after the Great War that the Treaty of Versailles would cause untold dangers. Germany had to pay far too high a price in reparation. Now here it was, unfolding as he had dreaded.

He replied swiftly.

The Quaker School
Shadworth
Yorkshire
25th October, 1929

Mr Frank Jacques
Westminster
Dear Frank,

Come up and stay. This minority government appears to be asleep. I suspect Ramsay MacDonald is too preoccupied with managing our failing economy and trying to lead without real power.

The Wall Street Crash has rendered us all weak and impoverished. Some of my students' families are suffering terribly and we are doing our best to enable them to keep their sons at school with us.

You and your colleagues must arouse MacDonald to action if that is possible. I suggest you come for the weekend if you can get away. Emma will be delighted to welcome you. Let me know train times.

Yours as ever,
Philip

Frank Jacques duly arrived as a drab November followed half-term. After the joys of the potato picking down at Tempests' Farm, now an annual delight, the contrast was stark. Rain was pouring down in grey swathes, as though the clouds had unpacked their burdens over the whole landscape. Black rooks had gathered on the telegraph wires, feathers all drab and dank with wet. The station, where Philip and Emma had admitted their love so long before, struck Philip with a huge pang of nostalgia, but it was a deserted place. Only Frank stepped off the train that day. James had driven Philip to meet him and now drove them up to school, where Alan Lorimer and Beatrice with Edna were awaiting them. Emma had insisted they all come to Holt House for dinner afterwards, though Philip had protested that she was working too hard.

"*My darling, this man is very dear to you after all that's happened, and I am determined to do it. Anyway, it will be a delight to entertain Alan and Beatrice, and besides, Edna really deserves a treat. She doesn't get many.*"

He had given in gracefully, knowing how stubborn she could be, and so she was busily preparing a huge roast dinner whilst Elizabeth, now age eight and loving to cook with her mother, was mixing the Yorkshire puddings with great vigour, much to her mother's alarm. George, having arrived home from school wet through from his journey from Cranston, was much amused at the sight of Beth, who greeted him with a squeal of delight as he tickled the back of her neck affectionately.

"*Why all the food?*" he asked his grandma.

His face took on full seriousness as Emma told him of the visitors and their reason for coming.

"*Grandma, we have been discussing these issues in my history class. Thank goodness Uncle Philip is on the case. We have to wake people up to the dangers of all this unemployment, not just in our country. I'd like to stay up, to hear what they have decided.*"

"*My darling, have you any homework to get done first?*"

"*Only some maths problems from Mr Seely. I can get them done quickly.*"

"*Alright, sweetheart. Then you and Beth can lay the table. We need the leaf out to fit everyone in.*"

Alan Lorimer's car brought the party to Holt House whilst James ferried Philip and his wheelchair. They were all glad to sit round Emma's table, but there was very little merriment that evening. Frank's wife's cousin, Franz, had painted a tragic picture of Frankfurt and its Jewish population in his correspondence, and Philip's staff had listened in horror to the details of the violence and thuggery that was rising day by day in the streets of every German city.

They had concluded that one thing the school could do would be to take in children of such victims of racism and antisemitism if such a need arose. And, as one, they had all committed themselves to welcoming Franz's own son, Pieter, to become a pupil at the school. Frank had been overwhelmed at such an offer and, aware of the dangers of being Jewish in Frankfurt, agreed to put the wheels in motion.

Philip sat back in his chair and thanked God for his colleagues. He lived and breathed the Quaker ethos, recognising the dignity and worth of every individual of whatever race or creed, and he felt keenly that his precious school should be a beacon of hope in this dire world.

Later, after the staff had all been transported back to school, Frank Jacques to Edna's house, and Beth and George were tucked up in bed, Philip and Emma sat by the roaring fire in the kitchen, she on his lap with her head on his shoulder.

"Emma, darling, I can't walk and I am sickened by that. If only I could get out of this chair and feel a complete man again. I could use the crutches or maybe even try to acquire a prosthetic leg if such a thing could really help. I long, my darling, to be able to travel without the wheelchair. We could get to Germany and see how things are there, for ourselves."

"Philip, stop it. You are the most complete man I have ever known, but you are jumping ahead of yourself." She stopped for a moment to swallow down the huge emotion welling up inside her. *"Your soul is not crippled. You are the most shining thing in my life, my dear, but you really must content yourself as a first step to welcome Franz's son to Shadworth School. He's George's age, isn't he? Perfect. And then let's try the crutches again if you feel so determined. Heaven knows, my darling, we all love you just as you are, and your chair is simply part of the family."*

"God, Emma, words cannot describe how much I love you."

And with that, she helped him into bed and lay next to him, embracing him with all the old passion of the years.

Chapter 8

Elizabeth May – School Days, 1930 - 1933

I was very little the day Frank Jacques came to the school, but I can still vividly remember mixing the Yorkshire puddings for Mother and sitting at the table to eat the most wonderful roast chicken Mother had managed to cook for so many, surrounded by the grownups and my dear George, all very seriously discussing grave things. I was not so little that I didn't comprehend that my darling daddy was very troubled and kept trying to guide everyone into finding something positive we could do. They all looked to him for his wisdom and, strangely enough, I know he looked to my mother for hers.

As the year moved into 1930, the end result of the debate that day was the arrival of Pieter Staab, all the way from Frankfurt, escorted by Mr Jacques.

He was the same age as George but much smaller and much more fragile-looking. Daisy and I decided he wouldn't be any good at climbing the trees down at the farm, but I felt so sorry for him and had promised Daddy I would help to make him feel at home at Daddy's school. He was in Beatrice Lorimer's House—Ayton—and George used to hurry home from Cranston to visit him there. Sometimes he let me follow along in his wake, and sometimes he had permission to bring him home with us for tea.

The best thing about Pieter was his love of books, and I liked to show him my favourites. Daddy had brought them home for me and I helped Pieter to read them. Daddy said it helped him to learn English, of which he was a quick learner. But he wouldn't talk about his home or his parents, no matter how hard we tried to bring him out of his shell. Yet he listened, oh so carefully, when Father and James were sharing with George what was going on in Germany. Mother drew me away because she knew it was all very frightening. My father was planning, with other Quaker people, to bring more children over to England.

But there were two pieces of news that gave us all a break from the exigencies of those years. My big sister, Florence, gave birth to a little boy, to everyone's delight, and Daisy became very possessive of her little Edward, or Teddy as we all called him. It meant I got to keep George to myself a bit more, and Pieter and he studied together in our gloriously warm kitchen while Father sat in his chair watching them quietly and I sat on his lap.

Then it was Laura's turn to bring her baby boy into the world. Will, at last, became a father and somehow seemed to find this little one a salve for all his deep-felt pain.

"He shall be called Ralph, Laura. No other name will do. Ralph, after your husband and my beloved captain, and Holt for my part."

When he said it, Laura simply went to him and put her arms around him while Mother snuggled the little scrap in her arms. Father shut his eyes, and I knew he was praying that this little family would be able to thrive now in a fresher light.

How I loved sweetie Ralph. Daisy and I both now could taste "the great emprise of motherhood," as Daddy put it, quoting from a poem he loved by Evelyn Underhill.

Meanwhile, Father was very proud that at last he was using his crutches more and more and was comfortable with them. He hadn't abandoned his wheelchair at all but used it as an old and comfortable friend when he was tired. But Mother and he loved to be able to walk together at last as she held on to him with one arm. It gave him a freedom he had almost forgotten.

As 1930 passed through into 1933 and we all grew up apace, George, now close on eighteen, was studying very hard. He wanted to get the most prized award from Cranston Boys' School, the Freiston Scholarship. It would mean a place at Oxford if he could win it, but the competition in Cranston Boys was very tough, and Father and he sat together studying in preparation for the exam many an evening while I read books. How I loved *What Katy Did* because I knew in a very particular way what it was to live with the need for a wheelchair. I knew all the hard things that my daddy had to manage, so I felt very close to Cousin Helen and Katy. *Little Women* came next in my favourites list, and how I longed to be just like Jo. It was strange that Daisy hardly ever looked at a book, being far too busy helping her daddy and mummy on the farm. But she and I remained the best of friends, though we were very different.

The truth was that we were all growing up really quite fast and school was getting more and more important for me. I knew Daddy wanted me to get a place at Cranston Girls' School, and it meant I would have to pass a test in arithmetic and in English. Daisy cared nothing for this, and my sister, Florence, did not bother her with it at all, meaning she would just go to the senior school in High Shadworth. Daisy accused me of being a swot, which I hated.

I shall never forget the day I had to sit the tests in my classroom at Shadworth. I had been sick with the anxiety of it all, and Daddy had almost decided I shouldn't do them after all. But Mother reassured us both and took me over that morning. I could feel her hand squeezing mine as we walked together.

"My darling girl, don't be scared of this. Daddy just wants you to be happy, and your happiness is what matters to us both. So, just do your best and then let's enjoy all the lovely things we have around us—little Ralphie and Teddy and all our family and friends. Daddy and I will be thinking of you every minute and so will James, and we know you'll be fine."

I was dawdling behind her, feeling anxiously sick, and she was having to drag me along in her wake. *"Are you sure he won't mind if I don't pass, Mother?"*

"Of course not, sweetheart. Your father knows what the really important things in life are, and he's busy helping George and Pieter to do their exams too, you know."

We reached the school gate, and she hugged me very close before handing me over to the headmistress, who was waiting for me with a smile.

"Come on, little Beth. It'll all be over before it's time for lunch."

And, of course, it was. Imagine my pleasure as I stepped out of the school to find Daddy and James waiting for me. I flung myself into Daddy's arms and then James swung me round and round with a whoop at the relief of it all.

That spring of 1933, I had no idea of the grim news from Germany. I could not have conceived then how worried my father was as he joked with us all at the tea table that night.

But in Berlin and other cities across Germany, books were being burned as the symbol of the purification of German values. And Father knew that Hitler had passed the Enabling Act, which meant he could more or less do as he liked without the control of the Reichstag. Mr Jacques had talked to him on the phone that very morning while I was sitting my test in my eleven-year-old innocence. Worse still, he had told Father that one of his very good friends, the lawyer Hans Litten, had been sent to a place

called a concentration camp, having been already harassed frighteningly by Hitler's gang of storm troopers. I had no conception then of the meaning of such a camp.

Yet Mother and Father did not allow anything to taint the happiness I felt as I awaited the results and as George awaited the news of the Freiston. And at last, it came. I was the first to hear from my headmistress, dear Miss Forster, waving a piece of paper with the glorious news that I had got a place at the Girls' Grammar School in Cranston for September. How I wish I could have bottled the joy on my mother's face as I ran into Holt House and announced it.

"*My darling clever little thing. Let's call James and get him to give us a lift up to see Daddy at school.*"

It had been a long time since James had stammered, for he had it well under control now, but he beat both me and Mother up the path to Father's study and ran in before us, and that old stammer returned, though only for a moment.

"Ph-Ph-Philip, B-B-Beth has got a p-p-place at the school."

Kath let out a shriek of delight and Father just sat back in his chair and opened his arms to me.

"Why, Emma, we have got ourselves a very special little daughter. How did we manage it?"

And such an astonishing combination of circumstances now completed that glorious day. For, as I hugged my parents, never forgetting my dear James, the study door flew open, and in strode George with a huge grin on his face.

"Grandma, Philip, I've won the Freiston. The head called me in to tell me the news, and I believe he was as pleased as I was. The Freiston, Philip, and it's all thanks to you and your hard work with me."

My father shook his head vehemently at that, for he knew very well how hard George had worked for his prize. He held out his hands to George.

Such news for us both coming all on that one day was almost overwhelming. But I can truthfully say that it warmed all our hearts and cheered us. All that lay on my father's heart, all the anxieties about Frank Jacques and the people in such imminent danger in Europe, was laid aside that night as we gathered the whole family together to celebrate over one of my darling mummy's delicious meals. And we did not forget to include Pieter, who was as delighted as George at his good news. But as Daisy commandeered George as she always did, I contented myself by sitting beside Pieter, knowing he was very afraid in his heart for his own family, assuring him with all the love I could muster that he was very much part of our family too.

Chapter 9

1933

"May I come in, Mr Manners?"

Pieter Staab's voice outside Philip's door called him back from ruminating on Beth and George's achievements, both so thrilled by their successes. He was quickly recalled to the cares of his school and to the growing fear he had for the Jewish families in Germany. Frank Jacques, his friend and comrade through the years, had kept him in constant touch with the abhorrent activities of Hitler's storm troopers. And now, here was a very anxious Pieter.

"Of course you may come in," Philip said gently, already sensing the stress of the deeply troubled boy.

"Mr Manners, I am so worried about my grandfather and grandmother and for my mother. Now Hitler is chancellor of my country, what will become of them? He hates all Jews and his henchman, Goebbels, is calling them subhuman and blaming them as the main cause of Germany's financial problems. Mr Manners, I really think I should go back."

"No, no, Pieter, my very dear boy, that would be disastrous." Philip put a reassuring hand on his shoulder. *"Your mother and father are at least grateful that you are here in safe hands. It wouldn't help them to know you are back exactly where the danger is greatest."*

"But the news reports terrify me, sir. How can I go on here while they are suffering?" The boy sat down by Philip's desk and put his head in his hands to hide his tears.

Kath, hearing his sobs, came hurriedly into Philip's sanctum. She seemed to consider offering support but noticed Philip had the situation under control. She tenderly looked on at the boy, her own heart breaking.

"Pieter, we must put all our resources together to support them. And we will. You are part of our family now and we will do our best to help them. Wipe your tears, my dear boy, and let Kath make you a drink."

He looked at Kath, and she nodded back, then disappeared to make him a cup of tea.

"Give yourself a few quiet moments here with me and then, if you feel up to it, do you think you can face returning to your class? Remember, you are near the end of the school year now, and next year, it will be your turn to try for a scholarship like George's. And, Pieter, remember how I have taught all our boys to pray to God for His healing and help? You too must trust."

Philip drew himself up onto his crutches and took the boy's hands in his. He himself felt the lad's pain.

"I will, sir. I'll try."

"James will bring you home to Holt House tonight with me, and you can let Emma and Beth cheer you up. Now, go find Kath."

He sat wearily back down in his waiting chair and put his head on his desk as Pieter left the room.

***

As home time drew near, Philip thanked God for his wife waiting for him, but he also resolved that he must find some way to assist those in such need, Pieter's family in particular. The first thing would be to talk to Frank Jacques to see if they could bring Pieter's family over to Shadworth.

He looked up as there was a knock at his door. James was standing there, waiting to take him home.

"James, are Beatrice and Alan back in the School House yet? Can we go over there and have a word?"

"What's wrong, Philip? Is it young Pieter?" James had been keeping a quiet eye on the lad, desperately wanting him to feel more settled.

"Yes it is, and we need to hear some of Alan's wisdom on this issue. I am confounded by it all. On top of all this, news from Germany appals me. Did you hear, James, that they have set up a concentration camp in a place called Dachau? God alone knows what they intend to do there and who they will send there."

A few minutes later saw them approaching the front door of the School House. Philip had deliberately not returned since taking up the headmaster position again and only the urgency of the current situation moved him to do so. His memories of those years with Harriet were painful and, as Beatrice welcomed them in and ushered them into the sitting room, all those old emotions crept back. Once Alan appeared, Philip quickly adjusted to the very different appearance of the room and the character of its hosts. The room was just as large and comfortable as he remembered, but he could immediately see the love Beatrice had put into the furnishings. She had arranged a beautiful bunch of tulips to sit beside the fireplace and everything displayed a care for the room's décor, which Philip's first wife had not cared to give. Quietly, he thanked God that the School House now had hosts who cared to make it beautiful.

Alan listened carefully but shook his head as Philip began to outline his concerns.

"*Philip, we can't bring all the world and his wife over here for shelter. We must keep a perspective as to what would be the best part we can play in all this. Pieter's parents won't want to leave Frankfurt and his grandparents behind. Surely the world has not gone completely mad. This man Hitler must still answer to President Hindenburg. I do believe we have to wait and see how things develop over there.*"

Now it was Philip's turn to shake his head. "*Alan, Alan, the SA under Röhm is pursuing a policy of thuggery towards anyone opposing them. They won't be answerable to Hindenburg.*"

"*I hear you, Philip. Of course, this school can indeed be a sanctuary for those who flee here, and I know all the staff and governors will support you in this. But we must work to maintain it so we are ready when the time comes. In the meantime, I believe we must be patient.*"

James had been watching Philip carefully during this exchange and noted how pale he had become in his distress. His hand was shaking as he spoke and his many sighs suggested that he was now extremely tired after the long school day. It was time for James to step in.

"*Beatrice, Alan, I'm taking this overstretched man back home to his family. Thank you, both of you. I think you're right, but it's been a very long day and Pieter is to come home with us. He'll be waiting at* Ayton House, *I guess. Our Beth will do him good, and Emma will do Philip good.*" James stood up purposefully and took hold of the handles of the wheelchair.

By this time, Philip was smiling his old wry smile, knowing they all were patronising him as in the old days of his convalescence. "*Alright. I hear you all. I don't know how you dare treat the head of this school so overbearingly, but I give in. Let's pray for God's grace to guide us all.*" And he allowed James to push the wheelchair along the pathway leading to Ayton House, where they found a much happier-looking Pieter waiting for them.

As they took their places in James' car, Philip allowed himself the luxury of sitting back and letting James take the lead until they at last reached Holt House. James pushed him indoors, where Emma was standing anxiously watching for him. He held out his arms to her with a huge sigh of relief, and she kissed him tenderly.

Beth had already whisked Pieter off to find George, which was, of course, her way of cheering him up.

The long summer days stretched before them. The harvest was being brought in down at Tempests' Farm, and the Holts and the Manners drew close to the Tempests and worked together. Florence liked this time of year best of all. Emma and Mary concocted wonderful picnics for them all, spreading rugs out beside Philip and laying the food on the big cloth brought from Holt House. Little Ralphie and Teddy enjoyed nothing more than to scamper all over the feast till they were picked up and thrown in the air by Ned or Will. They were both three now and up to all sorts of mischief, but Laura and Florence gloried in them. And both boys liked to snuggle up on Uncle Philip's lap when they got tired—a fact that gave untold delight to him and to Emma watching.

Beth was making the most of every minute this summer with George, for she knew he would be leaving for Oxford in October. Daisy, too, confided in her mother that she was scared of losing George. Florence was astonished at the depths of Daisy's feelings and saw a new side to her tomboy daughter.

"*Mother, how is Beth at present?*" Florence asked Emma as they packed up one of their picnics. "*I am quite concerned for Daisy, who is already fretting at the idea of George going away. Both girls adore him, don't they?*"

"*Oh, my dearest Florence, I think we are going to have to help them when he goes. He is more than a brother to them. They will really feel the pangs of a new emotion when they have to say goodbye. Hopefully the little ones will occupy them, but even Teddy and Ralphie can't quite match up to their special companion.*" Emma shrugged in a resigned gesture. "*Daisy, I'm afraid, will also miss Beth when she has to get Turton's bus every morning to go into Cranston. Daisy will be walking up to big school at High Shadworth, I suppose.*"

"*Oh, Mum.*" Florence absentmindedly poured out a full cup of tea all over the grass. "*How hard it is being a mother sometimes. You know all about that, I know. When I think what you have had to go through, it humbles me.*"

"*Don't say that, my darling.*" Emma placed her hand on her daughter's shoulder and gave a gentle squeeze. "*We've been through it together. And we keep those we love in our hearts, though we can't see them anymore. I sometimes dream, my dear, that your brother, George, comes back to me and is still the young soldier who joined up in his innocence, keen and full of life. I still find the way of his death in the war almost unbearable but I have to concentrate on the moment we are now living in."*

Florence clung to Emma, and Emma hugged her closer.

"*But remember, now we have another George, dear Maggie's son, leaving us for Oxford, a far better place than the fields of France, thank goodness. How I wish Maggie could only see him now. It's our job to set him on his way with smiles and assurances and without a trace of our sadness showing. Can we do it, Florrie?*"

Emma felt Florence nod against her cheek.

"*We will, Mum. I promise.*"

"*And look, Florence. Look at Philip besieged by the youngsters and enjoying himself enormously. At least they take his mind off the troubles of Germany, about which he worries so.*"

Emma let go of Florence and smiled at her before running over to Philip and leaning down to kiss him. He looked up in wonder at her.

"*What have you and Florence been up to, my love?*"

"*Just vowing to ourselves that we'll keep Beth and Daisy from missing George so much if we can.*"

"*Darling, they'll both have their new schools to keep them busy. Don't be anxious, sweetheart. We must let God deal with them and with George. And we, Emma Manners, have Pieter to care for and others too if I have my way.*" He leaned back in his chair and stretched. "*I'm hoping Frank Jacques will bring some more children over on his next visit to Frankfurt.*"

"Philip Manners, be careful. One thing at a time, my love. Let's see what MacDonald can come up with in talks with Hitler."

At this moment, little Ralphie let out a howl, and Emma hastily gathered him up in her arms. Philip smiled to himself. He knew his wife would support him in all his efforts to save as many as he could from the evils of Nazi Germany. He pictured in his mind the upright figure in her station uniform, hat atop her head, flag in hand, waving trains often laden with troops through Shadworth Station, and he knew her indomitability. His heart missed a beat as he remembered her standing, waiting for him to descend from the carriage on his return from London, pretending he was just any other passenger but longing for the moment when the platform emptied so she could take him in her arms. It was always a moment of healing and peace after the agonies of painful meetings with grieving parents or wearing business meetings in Westminster. For those few minutes, she gave her heart to him, though fraught with the guilt of betraying those at home. It was an intense relief to him to know, at last, they belonged together and there was no more need for guilt.

As they walked home after the harvest supper—Beth and George ahead, arms entwined, in thoughtful conversation—Philip looked up at his wife pushing his chair along the rutted lane and suddenly spoke up.

"I do believe you're right about Beth and Daisy. They're going to miss George dreadfully and we've got to pull them through that. But, Emma, I am determined somehow to get these persecuted Jewish children out of Germany. I contacted Miss Hollingsworth at the

hall to see if she could possibly house any we can bring over when the time is right, and she was her old gracious self. She hasn't forgotten the dance she gave for us all those long years ago. God, Emma, do you remember how we danced that night and let the world go by? We were risking a lot, my dear, not least in front of the governors and Harriet. But, darling, it was very sweet." He looked up at her as she held the wheelchair handles and sighed at the memory with tears brimming in his eyes.

Emma bent down to kiss him and a tear dropped on his cheek. "*Philip, how could I ever forget it?*"

He smiled at that and allowed himself the luxury of the memory for a moment. But then he turned back to the issue at hand.

"*Darling, a Germany Emergency Committee has been set up by our Quakers, and I've been asked to be a part of it with Frank Jacques. They are in touch with the Friends Service Council who are reporting on all the conditions out there and trying to get help to those who have been thrown into prison for no more than their religious and racial profiles.*"

"*That's wonderful, Philip. It gives you a link with those who are out in Germany itself. When I look at Pieter, in all his earnestness, my heart breaks for him. But I guess we must be patient and allow these things to move forward at the pace of the folk on the front line. I know you of old and I know you will not give up until you feel you have shared in the agonies of this world. But one thing at a time, please. I am with you as always in everything you set out to do.*" Emma sighed, feeling the immense stress of keeping everyone calm and hopeful and, most of all, keeping her beloved husband from fretting over the boys and the ever-changing news from Germany.

***

Summer passed into autumn, and the trees began to shed their already golden and russet leaves. The swallows took to the air to return to their southern climes, and the parting with George at Shadworth station, en route to Doncaster and thence to Oxford, was all Emma and Florence had dreaded. Elizabeth and Daisy clung to him while their parents, dealing with their own grief, tried to comfort them. It was acute and, for Emma and Philip, deeply reminiscent of the anguish they had often felt on that very platform long before.

Then, as if to divert them from the awful gap they all felt at George's absence, the telephone rang the next evening. Elizabeth had already been tucked up in bed after a long day in Cranston and a lot of homework set for that night, which she had worked through with her daddy's help. Shattered, she was already fast asleep.

"*Philip*," said Frank Jacques, his voice cracking with emotion, "*I have been in touch with the new secretary of the emergency committee, a lady called Bertha Bracey, who is as concerned as we are to bring the Jewish children over to safety. Perhaps you could see your way to make space at the school if it comes to it.*

"*But, my dear friend, I've got something even more urgent on my mind and the real reason for ringing you.*"

"*Is this to do with your own people, Frank? You know we will do all in our power to help. One good thing to report is that Pieter is settling down well. Indeed, he is a blessing to us all."* As he reassured Frank, he wondered and worried about what was coming.

"*It is indeed. It's a great relief to know that Pieter is in a good place, but, Philip, it's come to a crisis point in Frankfurt. Esther's father has been stripped of his position as a professor at the university and they've taken him away to God-knows-where. Franz is trying his best to find out, but Esther's mother and Esther herself are distraught. Esther's brother, Otto, is in danger of losing his position in his school in Frankfurt and he's brought his son, Anatole, to stay with the Staabs. If I do nothing else, I must try to get Anatole to safety here. He and Pieter have always been close cousins and it would be an immense relief if he could join Pieter with you in Shadworth.*"

Emma watched Philip as he listened to Frank, his brow furrowed with the challenge Frank was setting him.

"*Philip, what is it?*" she asked urgently.

Philip moved the phone away from his ear and covered the mouthpiece with his hand. "*Emma, it's another boy for us to rescue—Pieter's cousin. His father may be taken away by the Brownshirts any day.*"

Emma's eyes grew wide. "*Well, how can we get him, darling? Can Frank fetch him alone, or does he need someone to accompany him?*"

Philip shrugged and put the phone back to his ear. "*Are you still there, Frank? Try not to panic. We will ask this Miss Bracey to get us the papers we will need and then, I suggest, we drive down to the coast with James and get a boat over to Belgium. Presumably, there will still be train services from Antwerp into Germany, and we can train it through to Frankfurt.*"

Emma gave a gasp of horror. How could she bear for Philip to undertake such a journey into, what seemed to her, the jaws of deathly danger?

"*Is this at all viable, Frank? Would the lad be prepared to make the long journey back with us? We would have to take potluck at getting a boat back to England and then I am sure either Alan Lorimer or James would pick us up and bring us home.*"

"*One thing is sure,*" said Frank, "*There is no time to lose and we will need to make sure he is given permission to enter Britain. Can we do it?*"

Philip nodded and reassured him, "*We can, Frank, and we will.*"

Frank exhaled with something akin to relief. "*We will try all we can, Philip, but we must act immediately. I trust you to put all that is necessary into action in Shadworth. Thank you, my friend.*" And with that, he hung up the phone.

Emma put her face in her hands in anguish at what she was hearing. "*Philip, you cannot be serious. I know you want to save the lad with all your heart, but I beg you to think of everything here, not least your own beloved Beth. You would be risking your life in the hands of evil. Philip, please consider. Please.*"

Philip heard a kind of terror in Emma's voice, but he knew this was something he had to do. It almost felt like the voice of God calling on him to help—irresistible and urgent. The young Anatole represented a child in need whom he could not simply wave away. He knew Emma would face up to it, as she had faced up to so many things before.

"*We'll sleep on it, my darling, and see how to manage it in the morning. Do not be afraid.*"

Chapter 10

Elizabeth May – New Horizons, September 1933

The new term began and with it, such a change of circumstances. At last, I was a grown-up schoolgirl, catching Turton's bus to Cranston each morning to my school, unaware of my parents' anxieties for me as I waved goodbye. Mother only told me later how Father would fret for my safety and then reprimand himself for having so little faith. Yet they were both so proud that I had got the place and now wanted me to try my wings in the world.

As for Daisy, she was the most wretched lost soul without George and lost all her sense of fun. She detested her school and could not wait to get home to the farm, where she had her chickens and her horse, Sacha. But I loved my school and even enjoyed doing the homework each night.

My studies saved me, the piles of homework keeping me busy, that and my beloved books. Daddy called me his little bookworm and Mother used to get frustrated with me for ignoring all her appeals for help in the kitchen. Knowing there was no George to confide in cast a heavy shadow over me sometimes and then I would write him long rambling letters to reassure me that he was not so far away.

Daisy would arrive at our house and run to Mother for a cuddle. She had turned into a proper grandmother's girl, and it was only Mummy who could cheer her up. She would set her to help with baking her cakes and scones, which she continued making to send up to school for the staff—old habits die hard, and Mother never forgot those days when she used to take her old bike with the basket on the front full of packages of goodies for everyone. She whispered to me once that she always hoped against hope that she would catch a glimpse of my father in the window of his study.

"*Mother*," I would say, "*he was the headmaster of the school. Did you not feel a little in awe of him?*"

"*Beth, you surely know your daddy by now. When he saw me pushing the bike with the heavy cakes or the laundry, he always made me feel welcome.*"

There was much between Mother and Father in those dreaded days of 1933 that they kept back from me. Daddy was fretting terribly about the situation in Germany and what evil Hitler was planning as he gained more and more power. Mother told me how he had many sleepless nights after conversations with Frank Jacques over the phone. He could see that the influence of all this was beginning to infect the school too.

There were some sixth formers in school who were persuaded by what they read about the Blackshirts led by Oswald Mosley. And Pieter, our own Pieter, had been bullied one day by a group of them who were leaning towards antisemitism. Mother told me how Father had brought them to his study and had raged at their attitudes. Kath had sat silently in her office as he dealt with each one in turn. She had never, in all her time as his secretary, heard him so angry. And then he had taken them down with him to the school chapel and sat in silence with them. They each begged his pardon and promised they would apologise to Pieter.

I knew that day how upset Pieter had been by them, for Father brought him home with him in James' car and handed him over to Mother. Pieter would not look at me but just stood by Mother as she prepared the vegetables for our dinner. How I wished George were home that day instead of in Oxford. I grabbed Pieter's hand and forced him out of the door.

"*We're going to the farm, Pieter. That's what George would have made you do.*"

Father shouted after me, "*Beth, be gentle.*"

It was a slow walk, for Pieter dragged his feet and pulled away from me.

"*I hate those boys, Beth. They call me Jew boy and talk about wanting to join the Blackshirts. Your father made them apologise, but I know they are still tempted by the idea of being a military force and wearing the black uniform. There's so much evil, and my mother and father are still in real danger from it in my country. I really long to see my mum, Beth.*" Pieter dropped his head against his chest, and one tear dripped from his face before he wiped the others away with the back of his hand. The sun and glassy effect from the tears made his eyes stand out, bluer than ever.

It was agony to hear all this from my close friend. I did my best to comfort him, but I felt scarred by his pain.

What was perhaps the most shocking to me at this time was the news that Daddy and Mr Jacques were going to travel to Europe to bring back Pieter's cousin, Anatole, from Frankfurt to safety with us in Shadworth. His father was Pieter's uncle, Otto

Czernik, who had lost his position as a teacher when Hitler began ruthlessly stripping the Jews of every right and privilege they should have had as human beings. Pieter's grandfather had already been taken away to a camp, somewhere no one knew where, and they knew Uncle Otto would probably be taken any day. It was truly horrific.

That was an excruciating time for Mother and me. We had to stand by while we tried not to think of all the perils Daddy and Mr Jacques would have to face to get there and back with the boy. I thank God for Will and Laura, who took over our big kitchen during those frightful days, days that seemed like an eternity to us. Having no contact with them to hear how they were managing the long sea crossing by boat, then the train, then all the way back again to the coast was almost unendurable. How would my beloved father manage with his crutches, always such an encumbrance, and without his wheelchair? I could hardly bear to think.

Many times during those days, Will walked with Mother into the garden and talked quietly to her. Laura cooked for us, as it was as though Mother had no energy left to do the practical things. She was using absolutely every ounce of her energy in her anxiety, and even our darling Ralphie did not distract her. That was left to me. I honestly felt I would find it hard to forgive Father for putting us through that. Could he not have let Frank Jacques do it alone? And James was just waiting for the telegram to tell him to drive back to the coast to pick them all up in the car. I raged at James, almost blaming him for allowing Father to go. He got it all from me and never once winced at my cruel words or answered me back.

All in all, they were away for ten days until, at last, we had a call from James to tell us they were docking in Newhaven Harbour and he would shortly be bringing them home. Mother sank to her knees and cried as I'd never seen before—I think it was with sheer relief.

I can never forget the moment James hooted the big horn on his car to announce their arrival. How can I forget my first sight of Anatole Czernik? I see again the slim, tall figure jumping from James' car as Daddy hauled himself from it on his crutches. I see again the look of joy on Pieter's face as he ran down the steps of Holt House to greet his long-lost cousin. The dream fades, but I try so hard to get it back, to see again that arrogant boy, that toss of the head clearing the dark hair from his forehead as he clasped his cousin to him and laughed at Pieter's white face. But the vision has gone, and I am back in my bed with only the memory of it.

Chapter 11

1933

As Philip emerged from James' car, Emma took one look at James' face and knew he was trying to hide his anxiety from her. She knew she must greet the fifteen-year-old who must have suffered so much from having to leave his home and parents. She rejoiced to see Pieter's reunion with his young cousin, which was being observed closely by her own Beth. Yet her real concern was for her husband.

"*Emma, we have managed the rescue, and Frank can see we have started a process of getting all his wife's family to safety here. James drove Frank home, and we parted with reassurances that we stand behind all his efforts. So, my darling Emma, we're not through with this project yet, but we've made a start at least.*"

He faltered, and Emma rushed to his side. His mouth was blue and his face had gone very pale. She looked desperately towards James.

"*My dearest, let's get you indoors; you're done in.*" She turned anxiously to Beth. "*Beth, please get Father's wheelchair for him. And now let's get you all inside. You have had an ordeal much worse than ours back at home.*" She ushered them towards the door.

"*Emma, don't fuss. I'm just a little exhausted from the long journey.*"

As he spoke, Beth managed to wheel his chair till it was right beside him.

"*Oh God, Beth, thank you. What a relief to sit down once more in my old friend.*" But even as he spoke, his words getting fainter and fainter, he went completely white and his head flopped to one side. Beth screamed, so afraid for her beloved daddy.

James flew into action and caught him just before he fell. He carried him up to his room and gently laid him on the bed.

"*Daddy!*" screamed Beth, appalled to see him quite unconscious, but James was already picking up the phone to ask his father to come and see the patient. Her mother lay a gentle finger on her lips to shush Beth as Philip slowly began to come round.

"*Courage, Beth. Dr. Thomson knows Daddy and will make sure he's alright. There's nothing to worry about.*"

Pieter peeped his head round the door, looking from one to the other of them and at the prone figure on the bed. His concern was palpable.

"*May we come in, Mrs Manners? I am so sorry we've been the cause of this.*"

Before Emma could respond, Anatole rushed into the room and hurried to kneel by Philip, burying his head in the bedcovers.

"*Mr Manners, will you ever be able to forgive me for causing you this hurt? I will always be in your debt, sir.*"

Emma touched his head very gently and helped him to his feet. "*Don't be afraid, Anatole. You are very welcome, and I know my husband will tell you so.*"

"Boys, Beth," James stepped in, "*leave Mother to sit with Philip and wait for my father.*"

It was not long before Leonard entered the bedroom and James led them all out. Leonard looked at his old friend and took his hand, feeling the inside of his wrist.

"*His pulse is thready, but it's already strengthening. And, Emma, have no fear, it's only a faint. See the colour coming back into his cheeks. James has told me all he's been doing and the terrible journey he and Jacques and the boy have undertaken.* No *wonder he's exhausted. He simply needs to rest. When will he learn to measure his activities to his disability? Emma, we've been through much worse with him.*"

"*Waiting for him to come home over these ten days has matched the horrors of those dreadful days and his sepsis. I really thought they might not make it.*" Her face hardly differed from the pale colour of Philip's, as if she too may faint from the days of anxiety she'd just lived.

Philip raised a feeble hand from the bed and opened his eyes in a squint. "*Emma, what happened? My darling girl, what am I doing on the bed, and what's Leonard doing here?*"

Emma turned to Philip, her hands on her hips, but she didn't get a chance to respond before Leonard broke in.

"*Philip, you really are a most infuriating man.* You *fainted because you've been overstretching yourself undertaking such a venture.* You *could have left the journey to Frank Jacques and not put your poor long-suffering wife to such torment as she has endured these last ten days,*" Leonard spoke very sternly, though his smiling face belied his words.

"*Emma, Leonard, am I really home?*" Philip looked around the room for familiarity, as if Emma's face wasn't enough for him to believe. "*I can see I have been thoughtless in going through with this. But, Emma, I thought you understood that it was somehow a calling I could not resist. I had to be beside Frank for Pieter's sake and for young Anatole. And, Emma, I'm so relieved to be home and to see your face. You must forgive me now."*

He looked so sadly earnest that Emma could bear it no longer. She stooped to him where he lay and kissed him with all the passion of her younger days. He pulled her into his arms and sighed.

Leonard coughed, and they jumped.

Emma abruptly stopped kissing Philip and moved to sit at the side of the bed, the brightly patched quilt now crumpled. "*Leonard, how could we embarrass you so? Sorry.*"

Leonard Thomson, smiling, left them. Downstairs, he reassured them all, gathered as they were, so anxious to hear if all was well. James shook his father's hand in relief and gently pushed Beth towards the stairs.

"*Go and see him, Bethy. As for you, Anatole, there will be no one happier that we have brought you to Shadworth than Philip and Emma. Now's your time, Anatole, to make yourself a new life here in school under Philip's wing.*"

Beth wasted no time in hurrying back to the bedroom, where she threw herself on her father and pummelled him with her fists.

"*Daddy, never leave us again like that. Take us with you on your next adventure.*"

He laughed and pulled her to him. "*My little lady, how dare you attack me when I know you are truly glad to see me. Your job now is to make this very smart young man, Anatole, feel welcome and at home with us and to show him how the world ticks here and at school. Can you do that for me?"*

"Mother and I will do it together, my wicked daddy."

Beth leaped off the bed and hurried down to the two boys, Emma closely following. A much-recovered Philip emerged a couple of minutes later on his crutches, and the newly extended little family settled down to one of Emma's glorious teas.

The Quaker School at Shadworth received a new pupil as October turned to November, Anatole Czernik taking his place under Edna's careful eye in Fox House.

Chapter 12

1934

Anatole was no gentle Pieter Staab even though they were cousins. He grew taller and taller, as if he would never stop growing, while the staff in school despaired of his wild antics around the grounds. As the year turned to 1934 and the new term moved on, Laura confided in Kath that he was almost unmanageable in class and that other members of staff found him very difficult to discipline. Laura sometimes took her morning coffee break with Kath in her office and found her a helpful confidante.

"*Shall I tell Philip, do you think, Kath? I don't want to worry him with it really, as I know he is very much Philip's protege and Philip so dearly wants him to settle here and put his energies into his work.*" Laura stood beside Kath's desk as she expressed her exasperation. "*His English is immaculate, you know. I believe he had English lessons as a young child because his very wise father knew it would stand him in good stead.*"

Kath nodded and put her finger to her lips. "*Careful, Laura. Philip is almost despairing of him and Emma tells me that it keeps him awake at night, what with all the horrible news from Germany. Mr Jacques is in constant touch with his mother, who lives in terror of being dragged off to one of the camps they have opened, where Jews are already being sent.* No *one has any idea where they have sent his father.*"

The door between Kath's study and the head's study opened, and Philip wheeled himself into the room determinedly.

"*I heard all that, Kath.*" Philip gave a frustrated huff, disappointed they had discussed Anatole without coming to him first. "*Laura, you come to me immediately if Anatole causes you stress. What would Will say to me if I allowed him to disturb you? Emma would never forgive me. I shall send for him straight away.*"

"*Oh, Philip,*" pleaded Laura, "*don't be angry with us. Edna is trying her best to manage him and I didn't want you to worry.*"

Philip shook his head, unwilling to listen to any excuses. "*Kath, you know me well enough to know that is ridiculous. The lad needs discipline and woe betide him if he doesn't stop his antics,*" he spoke firmly before wheeling himself back to his study whilst Laura and Kath looked at each other much dismayed.

"*Don't worry, Laura. Philip will deal with this because he is very aware of the boy's anxieties whilst he's trying to guide him to a more mature approach to his studies.*"

Laura nodded and knocked gently on Philip's door.

"*Come in, Laura, my dear.*"

As Laura nervously entered the office, Philip stretched out his arms in reassurance and gestured to the chair beside his desk. She sat down, relieved that Philip's tone, though still firm, was much calmer.

"*We will sort this young man out one way or another. I believe him to be exceptionally intelligent. Am I right?*"

"He *really is*." Laura smiled. "He's *due to take the School Certificate this summer, as you know. If only he would settle down to his work.* Mr *Lorimer takes him for maths and has the same issues with him as I have in English. And you know* Alan *won't stand for any nonsense from any boy*."

"*I hear you, my dear. I'll call him in and try to get to the bottom of this behaviour*."

Philip could see the stress in Laura's anxious face and the stoop of her shoulders, and he wished, for the hundredth time, he could wipe away all the huge concerns that haunted her.

"*Thank you, Philip. Bless you. And, by the way, our darling Ralphie is loving school and I'm so relieved that he does. He asks to see you and Grandma every day as* Will *meets him out of* school, *and* Emma *is so good to him. She stands at the gate of* Holt House, *and he practically jumps into her arms*."

"*He is very special,* Laura. *And I think it does* Will *good to be so involved in all this. Is* Will *sleeping any better?*"

She laced her fingers in front of her stomach and looked down. "*I think so, but he still has the nightmares where he's back in the trenches. If only his work at the cobbler's shop was more than half-time. He does enjoy it and is quite a master cobbler now*."

"*My dear Laura, let's pray that the job is extended for him. If that happens, Emma will ensure Ralphie gets looked after by us, as and when. Now for Anatole. Try to feel more relaxed now, but send him straight to me if he does not conform*." He looked at the door, as if he could see straight through to Kath, and raised his voice. "*Kath, will you send for the young rascal?* Let's *see what he has to say for himself*."

Laura quickly dismissed herself, not wanting to watch Anatole's ticking off after so many misdemeanours.

Anatole's knock came soon after, and he stepped into the study very slowly, with his head down.

"*No need to look so abjectly humble in front of me, Anatole,*" said Philip. "*You know quite well that all we want is your happiness. But, my boy, you have really deserved a sound reprimand. You have caused anxiety to my staff, even Mr Lorimer, so I'm told. Your behaviour is not at all what I would expect of you. What on earth makes you believe that you can do what you like in class?*" The vein in his forehead stood out, betraying his controlled voice. "*You are not far from the summer exams, which are so very important if you are to go forward into the sixth form and to university.*"

There was dead silence, and Anatole's whole demeanour remained downcast.

"*Anatole, are you hearing me?*"

Anatole finally lifted his head to meet Philip's glare, and he licked his lips. "*Mr Manners, I can't concentrate in class because I have this awful vision of what's happening in Germany. What good are exams if my mother is taken away and killed? I might as well give study up. I don't understand Pieter, who just works and works and will never share with me how he's feeling. I hate my work. I hate the dormitory in Fox House. I just want to run away and live wild. I know I could do it.*" His brown eyes hardened, his hands becoming fists at his sides as his whole body seemed to tense.

"*So what to university if my country is under the yoke of that man Hitler and I a Jew? Some of those boys in the sixth form have been mocking me and*

Pieter because we're Jewish. They fancy themselves as followers of that man Mosley," he scoffed.

Philip sat back in his chair and groaned in sorrow. "*Anatole, you are looking at this from the wrong way round, my dear boy. You make me very cross but at the same time extremely sad. You must listen to me now. Think back to our journey from Germany across the sea and up the country to Yorkshire and remember the thankfulness your mother demonstrated as you parted from her. She was sad, but she was also thankful because she knew that with us here in England, you would be safe and could grow and learn and move forward into a more secure future.*

"*Remember this to keep yourself from despairing. We must take one day at a time and trust that we shall come to better times. But, Anatole, you must now try very hard to conform to this school's rules. Indeed, I will not countenance bad behaviour in class.*"

Philip looked straight at the boy, and he returned the look as tears formed in his eyes. He put his head in his hands and allowed the tears to flow.

Kath knocked on the open door, holding a small tray with two glasses of lemonade on it. She came in and put them down next to Philip. "*Please forgive me, Mr Manners, but I have a young lady in my room who's got off Turton's bus by the fingerpost at the crossroads instead of going straight home. And she is desperate to be let in to see you.*"

Anatole's head lifted. "*Is it Elizabeth, sir? Can she come in?*"

Philip shook his head in disbelief that the arrival of his own dearest daughter should stop the boy from his tears. But before he could dwell too much on it, Beth rushed at him.

"Beth, what are you doing here, you little mischief? We must tell Mother so she doesn't get worried that you're late."

"Leave it to me, Philip. You deal with these two rascals." Kath hastened back to her office to ring Holt House.

"Daddy, stop being a cross patch. I just wanted to see you." She ended the embrace with her father and now really noticed the mood in the room. Even though Anatole's tears had stopped, his face was still red. *"And now, what are you doing to make Anatole cry?"*

Through all his many difficult days, Philip had never faced such a situation as now lay before him and he needed to resolve the issue for the sake of equilibrium and discipline. His beloved daughter was very clearly growing up, and he could not protect her from the world as he would like any longer. He wheeled his chair round his desk and took Beth's hands in his. Anatole watched in silence and stood up.

"Don't you be sad, Anatole," begged Beth, turning to him. *"Daddy will look after you, and you can come home with me to tea. Can he, Daddy?"*

"First, my darling," said Philip very seriously, *"first, we are all going to the chapel to say some prayers for God to help us to know what to do for the best."*

Kath watched the small procession as it wound its way to the chapel, Anatole pushing the wheelchair and Beth keeping up with them. She knew that, somehow, Philip could and would bring Anatole to a peace he needed to feel. But she shook her head at the thought that little Beth was taking on cares that should not have affected her yet.

That evening, Anatole sat with Emma, Philip and Beth as they all ate dinner together and listened as Philip outlined a timetable for extra studies in English and maths. Anatole promised Philip he would undertake them conscientiously as a way of helping him to pass the School Certificate.

As the months sped by and summer term dawned, Anatole studied with the extra tuition Philip set in place for him, though it was not without the odd outburst of fury at the demands it made on his freedom, nor the occasional wild excursions he embarked on.

In April, he climbed the school clock tower as a dare and he abseiled down it whilst half the school watched with delight. Only Elizabeth, in whom he confided later, knew it was to show the secret Mosley followers in his year group that nothing they could say or do would frighten him. But this was one confidence Beth could not keep, and she hastened to tell her father what he had said. Philip brought the three boys in question to his study and warned them with expulsion from the school unless they promised to keep away from such influences. He asked Beatrice to keep them under careful scrutiny, which she gladly did.

Then in June, not long before the Certificate Exams, Anatole disappeared completely, much to everyone's horror. Hours later, he strolled into Holt House kitchen talking and laughing with Beth.

Emma and Philip looked up from their places at the kitchen table, where they'd been sitting wearily, discussing what to do to find Anatole and where he could have gone. His appearance, though it provided relief, was also somewhat irritating after all the worry he'd caused.

Emma swallowed her anger, stood up and wandered over to the kitchen sink to wash up, knowing Philip could handle the matter.

Philip crossed his arms on the kitchen table and frowned at them each in turn, his disapproving silence somehow feeling harder to take than if he'd shouted.

Anatole stepped forward as Beth bit her lip silently, fading into the background. She had never seen her father so angry.

"*Mr Manners, I am very sorry, but my motives were good, sir. I know Beth likes my company for the bus instead of sitting all by herself, so I took the bus to Cranston and waited for her. And my afternoon timetable was only PE and Fitness, hardly academic, so I was not neglecting important work, sir.*"

"*Anatole, I like to think that I can decide when your studies are important. Or not. It is not up to you. You will spend tomorrow morning under Matron's eye in the Sanatorium.*"

"*Daddy, how could you when he was only thinking of me?*"

Philip folded his arms, and Beth knew further pleading would be in vain.

As for Anatole, he merely winked at Beth and took his punishment like a man, much to Emma's amusement, nodding his farewell and striding for the gate. The somewhat arrogant wink of course further enraged her husband and Emma had to beg his pardon. She pushed him into the garden and there his temper cooled as she knew it would.

"*Emma, he had Edna worried to death, don't you see? He really needs to conform to school discipline.*"

Beth rushed into the garden after eavesdropping from the doorway. She was still dressed in her school uniform, white blouse and navy tie intact, though her chestnut curls were by now tangled and dishevelled, her navy pinafore dress pulled up over her knees, her woolly tights wrinkled and untidy from her haste. Her blue eyes gleamed as she protested on Anatole's behalf.

"Daddy, I loved seeing Anatole at the school gates. It was such a treat for me to have a companion on Turton's bus. Please don't be too cross with him."

Philip's face softened along with his temper, and he allowed Emma and Beth to push him back inside, where the little family sat down to their sandwiches and cakes with a recovered harmony.

But that night, the news from the wireless of Germany horrified them all. Ernst Röhm, SA leader of the Brownshirt storm troopers, was murdered along with four hundred of his men and members of Hindenburg's governing party, and there began a terrifying purge of Jewish properties. It was to be known hereafter as the Night of the Long Knives, and afterwards, the way became clear for Hitler's own bodyguards, the vicious SS under Himmler's direction, to take power while the SA—much weakened, now under Viktor Lutze—continued the work of purging the country of Jews. Himmler was to become Hitler's most ruthless right-hand man.

It wasn't long before Philip and Emma heard a knock at the door, and Emma rushed to open it. James and Will were standing there, having both arrived separately but needing to discuss the events.

"Come in," Emma said, immediately stepping aside. She closed the door behind them and led them to the parlour, where the walls were home to many of

the books Philip had brought from his study. Philip was already in there, sitting beside the roaring fire in the grate. Two comfortable old armchairs stood either side of the fireplace, and he gestured to them to come and sit as Emma made her way to stand beside her husband.

"*I assume you're here because you heard the same as us.*" Philip pulled the blanket around his leg tighter, then rested his hands on his lap. "*I can't quite believe it. I hoped and prayed it wouldn't happen, but...*"

"*You know what this means, Philip,*" exclaimed Will, his hands shaking. "*There is no one to stand in the way of the SS now. And Hindenburg is simply not strong enough to withstand them.* God, Mother, *I'm afraid we are looking into a very dark abyss.*"

James nodded in agreement.

Philip sighed with something approaching despair. "*The implications, as you say, Will, are huge, not least for the Jewish population. And the worst of it is that we are completely helpless in the light of it. What on Earth can we do? My heart goes out to the owners of the properties that have been destroyed, and I can't help but think of Pieter and Anatole's family. Frank Jacques will be beside himself.*"

"*Philip, we need to get more children to safety in England as soon as we can,*" Emma decided. "*But our hands are tied if the government won't act to back it.*"

It was midnight before Will and James took their leave, and in that time, they didn't resolve anything. Their hearts were heavy, and they were surprised to find that the night was outstandingly beautiful. There was a crescent moon ringed by stars high in the azure firmament and no cloud to be seen. A nightingale had taken its favourite place on Emma's willow tree and was singing without a care at full throttle.

Once the door of Holt House was closed behind them, James turned to Will. He took his arm, almost as if he needed to steady his nerves.

"*Oh, Will, I wonder what we are in for? I can hardly bear to think that we might be heading for another war.*"

"*Don't say it, James. Don't.*" Will held up both his hands in a gesture of desperation.

Emma glanced at Will and James still talking on the garden path before she drew the curtains and helped Philip up the stairs. They peeped in at their beloved Elizabeth fast asleep in her bed, then made their way to their own.

"*Have no fear, my darling. We must put this to God in our prayers. That's enough for one night.*"

Chapter 13

1934

As that terrible night passed and the world became used to the horrors reported from Germany, Pieter and Anatole found themselves immersed in the School Certificate Exams.

Pieter had great ambitions to get a scholarship to Oxford, where he would be reunited with George. The Freiston Scholarship was purely for boys from Cranston Boys' School, so Pieter had to perform exceptionally well in the Higher Certificate to get the offer of a scholarship directly as a result of his exam grades.

Anatole's behaviour in school and constant absence from classes were still causing deep concern as the Lower School Certificate Exams approached. Despite many reprimands in Philip's study, Anatole remained determined to please himself and would sneak out of lessons in the afternoon to catch the bus to Cranston to meet Elizabeth whenever he saw the opportunity. The tall, slim, dark-haired figure of the young man next to the much smaller figure skipping along delightedly beside him raised many a smile on the lips of the Cranston passersby. Elizabeth would be sharing all her day's encounters with him while he strode along listening with one ear and his mind on something entirely different. Nevertheless, he gave her all the encouragement she needed as she reported her day.

These adventures roused Edna, who was his head of house, to fury, and she tried every possible means of checking on him, always ending up in Philip's study fuming.

"He is beyond belief, Philip. He is so arrogant. It's as though he hasn't a care for anybody or what anybody thinks of him."

"Edna, I'm so sorry. He seems to deal with his fears for his parents by taking this cocksure attitude. But, Edna, you know what he is facing, as is Pieter. News from Germany and the way things are developing there is very nerve-racking even for us. You know Mr Jacques. He is desperate for us to try to get children and Jewish families to safety."

"Forgive me, Philip. It's just that I too want to see him do well in the exams and I do dislike his insolent manner towards school rules."

These discussions always ended with Philip intervening in Anatole's classes and taking him off to his study. Anatole invariably apologised to him and begged him not to punish him too hard. And Philip was torn. He would always accompany the lad to the school chapel, where they would sit quietly until Anatole shared the feelings that were deeply submerged most of the time. At last, Philip would say a very quiet prayer before they went back to class. There, Anatole would become the perfect student until the next time.

***

The time to take the important exams came and went. Results were expected in August, and they were results that made everyone very proud. Pieter had surpassed himself and was awarded a scholarship not to Oxford but to Cambridge. Anatole had three credits and three distinctions in his Certificate and could now move into the sixth form to study for his Highers.

Indeed, the Quaker School in Shadworth resounded with congratulations as many boys received excellent results that summer. Philip's staff had excelled themselves, and he shared his delight with Emma.

But the news of Hindenburg's death on the second of August took everyone's attention away from their pleasure, for it was no mere death of a statesman. With his death, Germany no longer had its firewall to protect from Hitler's power moves. Hitler now pronounced himself president, chancellor of Germany and head of the army. He became the "Führer", to whom all must swear allegiance.

Once more, Will, James and George, fresh home from Oxford, spent many hours in discussion late into the evenings at Holt House. They knew Himmler's SS could now have free rein in ridding Germany of its Jews and its critics. Camps had been created to which many were transported never to be heard from again. Pieter, fresh from his successes, often walked down from school to stay close by them in their discussions, for his place as a family member was now secure. Once again, they landed in the armchairs or on the rug beside the fire in the parlour.

"*Philip, what on Earth can we do? How can the people of Germany succumb to this dictator? Where are the protesters?*" Will was struggling hugely with dread of another war.

Philip was not able to offer them even a crumb of comfort. "*My dear friends, they have all been silenced, protests quashed and the propaganda machine is undermining everything they can do. Goebbels is highly intelligent and is advertising Hitler's popularity and asserting his ambitions to make Germany the greatest country in Europe. Frank Jacques fears for justice. He tells me that the concept of justice and democracy has been drowned in nationalistic fervour. And meanwhile, Pieter, he fears very much for your mother and for Anatole's family.*"

Pieter gave a cry of agony, rising to his feet and beginning to pace the floor as Emma stepped in.

"*Come now, my dears, enough. Philip, stop now. You must not shed fear into these hearts no matter what horrors we are talking about. Such talk is no good for Pieter.*" She took Pieter's arm. "*Pieter, come with me and help me get the cakes out I baked this afternoon.*"

Pieter accompanied her into the warm kitchen, redolent with the scent of her baking. The kitchen was spacious, with a large wooden table in its centre and open shelves displaying all Emma's workaday pans. A huge airer on a pulley hung from the ceiling covered in drying clothes. She knelt to open the cooker and reached in to check her cakes. Pieter's eyes flitted around the room, hardly noticing Emma's hard work, as his mind remained focused on what he could only imagine his family was going through.

"*Emma, what about Anatole?*" Pieter suddenly said. "*He is lonely up in Fox House, I think. He dreads the news from Frankfurt just as much as I do. And those boys who are Mosley disciples don't help. Why, oh why do people hate us Jews so much, Emma?*"

"*Pieter, my dear, I don't understand it either. It's as if the Jews are scapegoats for all that's gone wrong in the world and Hitler uses that to try to make out they are monsters. But, Pieter, he himself is the monster, along with his ghastly sidekicks.*"

Emma turned from her cakes and embraced the boy. Neither of them had seen Beth creeping very quietly down the back stairs that led to the kitchen, and she had heard everything.

"*Mother.*" Beth rushed barefoot across the wooden floor and threw herself into Emma's arms. "*Mother, we have to do something for our boys. Why can't Daddy get their families out of Germany?*" She hid her tears in Emma's apron.

"*My darling, Daddy will do everything he can, along with Will and James. We have to be very, very brave ourselves for the sake of Anatole and for Pieter. Isn't that right, Pieter?*"

"*Of course we must, my little Bethy.*"

Pieter brushed away one of his tears and placed his hand gently on Beth's quivering shoulder. "*Please don't cry any more. It's bad enough without me having to see you crying. Let's try and remember all the good things we have here and say our prayers for them all in Germany. That's what I try to do.*"

Emma smiled, a sliver of happiness amongst all the fear.

"*Oh, my dear Pieter, Philip would be proud of you. He has taught you well to trust God and take each day as it comes. Beth, you must learn Daddy's lesson too.*"

Philip appeared in the kitchen doorway on his crutches and took everything in with one glance. *"Beth, my darling, you mustn't cry. We must stand up for all that's good and help Pieter and Anatole to bear this. Come, my sweetheart, come back into the parlour and have a cuddle with Will and James. You too, Pieter."*

He took her hand and smiled down at her, leading her gently to Will, who put her on his lap.

"I shall try to speak to Frank Jacques and get word to Baldwin, whom MacDonald, I suspect, relies on as a member of the National Government. Perhaps we can persuade Baldwin to allow children leave to come through to Britain," said Philip. *"But I'm afraid it's a long shot."*

As the evening drew on, they continued their discussion, but there was a despondency in the air and they had no solutions save for Philip's promise to talk to Frank Jacques.

"Come now, all of you, we are just going round in circles. Time for bed," Emma began, putting a close to the seemingly endless conversation that was leading them nowhere. *"Pieter, let James run you back up to school, and please tell Anatole he can come with you next time. Philip, would that be alright with Edna?"*

"I'll talk to her, love. Goodnight, my dears. Let's pray for God's blessing on all we have shared tonight."

And so they parted with what felt like the weight of the world on their shoulders.

Late as it was, Philip began to write a letter to Frank Jacques in London the second they all left.

Holt House,
Shadworth
25th August, 1934

My dear Frank,

As you know only too well, the news is very bleak. We have two very anxious boys here in our care, and I wondered if you had any more news of the Staabs and the Czerniks? As I write, I already know the answer and feel something approaching despair.

We really must try to get more children over here. But while Chamberlain is refusing to allow children entry, I believe we are going to have to be patient. I actually think Chamberlain has some sort of flat battery where Herr Hitler is concerned. He just won't see what is happening before his very eyes! It will rest on Baldwin.

Frank, is there anything at all we can do in the meantime? Let me know when you can. Bertha Bracey seems very capable and was appointed as secretary of our Quaker German Emergency Committee last year. She could help us if there is any opportunity to actually rescue these Jewish children.

I am as ever,
Yours,
Philip

Frank's reply was no less despairing. He had received no further news of his cousin, Franz, and his wife, Esther, Pieter's parents. The news of the Czernik family confirmed that Otto had been taken to Dachau, while his wife had fled back to her parents. The fact that Anatole had heard nothing from his mother seemed to point either to her letters being censored or, worse, that she too had been taken to a camp.

Yet Philip and Emma knew they must maintain a calm and patient exterior for the sake of the boys, not to mention Beth, but the truth was they were not really managing to keep their whole family from terrible anxiety over the events in Europe.

Chapter 14

Elizabeth May – Hopes and Fears, Summer 1934 - 1936

I suppose at first it was just a schoolgirl crush that hit me as I turned twelve going on thirteen, but it didn't feel like that, and Anatole frequented my dreams. I was always pushing back the dark lop of hair from his forehead in those dreams so as to look better at his determined face, that face smiling at me as I saw him waiting for me at the school gates. My heart would lurch with the pleasure of it.

I told Mother I was in love. She listened very seriously, but then she said that I didn't really know what love was because I was still a bit young and must wait a while. There would be lots of other boys I would see and like, so I should just enjoy those feelings without getting too overcome by them.

Father was tearing his hair out over Anatole, I know. It didn't help at all when I confided my so-called crush on him. I remember so well the way he looked when I told him—a mixture of shock, horror and then a smile, that gentle smile of his.

That was the summer of 1934, when Hindenburg died and Hitler took full power. However, George's homecoming from Oxford was nevertheless a joy for us all. Daisy reverted to her happy-go-lucky self, and George's father, my older brother Harry, came to Holt House nearly every day to feast his eyes on him, as he put it. Mummy excelled herself with all the suppers she provided for the family, though my dear sister Florence took her share, so we sometimes found ourselves all sitting round the table at Tempests' Farm.

I wish I could recapture those summer days of 1934. It was a glorious summer, so we picnicked out in Tempests' fields nearly every day. We would spread the old pink blanket out, and George, Pieter and Anatole would get into a huddle for serious discussion, sprawled out on it. I can still see in my mind's eye their awfully sad faces anxiously sharing the latest news. Daisy and I were shut out of those sessions and left to organise the sandwiches. I suppose they thought we were too young and only girls. We played with Ralphie and Teddy while the boys simply forgot we were there. But in my heart, as I played "What's the Time, Mr Wolf?", I was really watching Anatole and I suspect Daisy was watching George. In the cloudless sky, the summer sun shone down as the skylarks in the neighbouring field rose from ground level and sang their cascading song in full throat, careless of the troubles of Europe.

The so-called "crush" never went away no matter how many other boys I met from Father's school. In the next two years, as 1934 turned to 1936, Anatole had jumped school many times to come and meet me at the school gates and we shared many talks about his country. I had no chance of getting over my feelings for him as we shared these most personal discussions, yet I knew he was confiding in me as his little sister and no more than that. Nevertheless, I allowed myself the luxury of simply being with him as we sat on Turton's bus together. As I look back on those almost idyllic times with him, I know I should have kept a better hold on my emotions and taken his confidences in the proper way, simply to allow him to get things off his chest as a kind of relief. I should have realised that his preoccupation with thoughts of his missing parents was building in him and, quite simply, I should have told my father for understanding and comfort. But I didn't—it was my own special relationship, which I held very dear. It pains me to think of it now.

I began to dread that moment when Anatole would take his Highers and hope for a scholarship to Oxford or Cambridge. I knew Daddy wanted that for him as Pieter moved into his final year. George had achieved First-Class Honours, much to Daddy and Mother's joy, and now was set on joining the Royal Air Force. That worried my parents, I know, for they were always conscious of the threat from Hitler and were working hard to save the children of Jewish families. But George would not listen and felt called to be a part of a force that might one day be needed to fight against the evils the Nazis were perpetrating—a subject much-debated between the boys.

The trouble was that all our boys had grown up through these tough times, with the detailed discussions that continued between my brothers and parents in our parlour. They were almost too aware of all the dangers that were building up to crisis point as Baldwin became prime minister. And, of course, I knew that Anatole would never let go of his fears for his beloved family in Germany. While Pieter somehow managed his fears, Anatole was boiling up inside.

***

In August of 1936, Anatole heard that he had gained high honours in his Highers and could now at last take up a scholarship in Cambridge. Oh God, I still feel the cold hand of dread that clutched my heart when we heard that news. How was I to bear his going? I knew I was just his little sister as far as he was aware, but I felt a very grown-up emotion though I was only going to be fourteen.

He was due to leave for Cambridge with Pieter as October dawned. But before we had to face that parting, something else happened that took it from our minds.

One morning, a gang of thugs invaded the school grounds and threw stones at the windows of Fox House, Edna's house, where Anatole still had his study room. Their black shirts identified them as Mosley's supporters. Anatole guessed they had been egged on by some of the sixth formers returning at autumn term because they had already been brought before Daddy for their fascist leanings. He watched them as they began cutting at James' beloved rhododendrons using shovels and screamed slogans.

"This school has a Jew boy staying here. Jews have no place in our country. Get him!"

Anatole knew it was him they were speaking of, but some of the other boys had already raised the alarm and my father had been called.

My father was absolutely horrified. He phoned the police and then called the whole staff out into the grounds to chase them away. As Daddy told Mother later, the Shadworth police were only a village force and arrived late with their bells ringing the alarm. So, it was actually Daddy and Alan Lorimer who confronted the bullies face to face, Daddy on his crutches and Alan next to him, while the other staff stood supportively behind them.

Anatole told me that Daddy yelled out, "*You will leave my school now. These are private premises. Get out.*"

And that was when one of them tried to punch Daddy in the chest. I'm glad Mother wasn't there, as I don't think she would have been able to keep even a sliver of calmness in the already heated situation. And I would have been so enraged had they hurt him. But he wasn't hurt, as he leaned away just in time, and Anatole saw him almost lose his balance. James and the three male members of staff grabbed the villain by the shoulders and marched him off. The other thugs then began to drift away just as the police arrived.

As Father told Mother later, he was very relieved to see them making arrests. As for the sixth formers involved, Daddy knew exactly who the culprits were. Their parents were contacted and they were all expelled from the school.

"*There is no place for Oswald Mosley's sycophants here,*" fumed my father as James and Will sat round the tea table. "*I do believe we are going to end up using force against the Nazis ourselves one day soon, though it goes against all Quaker tradition. Meanwhile, we must protect Pieter and Anatole from such appalling abuse. We've got to affirm them and their Jewish roots and make sure our students respect those values that we simply take for granted here. God knows, I cannot understand where such ugly prejudice can come from, and I pray that Anatole will not find such prejudice in Cambridge."*

Daddy wheeled himself around the corner and frowned as he caught me listening from the top of the stairs. He always had a sixth sense about my whereabouts. I remember he was frustrated with me that evening. He desperately wanted to protect me from all the evil that was bubbling up in the world, but he couldn't do it.

He knew how much I cared for the two boys who had made their home here in Shadworth, whose parents, as far as we were aware, had been taken away to the dreaded SS camps, and he himself wanted so much to rescue others from the dangers they were facing simply because of their Jewish roots. He and Frank Jacques were constantly in touch with people on the German Emergency Committee, who kept them informed of the progress being made to bring Jewish children over to safety in Britain.

Oh God, as I lie here in my lonely room, it all comes back to me in its enormity, for it was that night that Anatole broke the news that shocked my mother and father and broke my heart.

"Philip, I've had enough. I am not taking up the place in Cambridge. I am going to London to join the Quaker Emergency Committee so I can go back and find where my parents are."

Chapter 15

1936

The lad's decision to give up a place at Cambridge and leave for Frankfurt lay heavy on Philip and Emma's hearts. But they were helpless to do anything. There had been a blazing row with Anatole when he announced his intention, the sort of row that challenged all Philip's much-cherished Quaker principles.

Nor would Philip ever forget his beloved daughter's reaction. Emma could not comfort her that night as she lay sobbing on her bed.

"*Mother, how could he be so stupid? He is so wrongheaded, so stubborn, and he thinks he can walk into Germany in the teeth of the evil that is happening there. He, a Jew and only eighteen years old. He will surely be taken and put into one of their horrific camps, Mother.*"

In the end, Emma had simply sat beside her, stroking her hair and praying silently for her to pick up her courage.

Anatole had planned to stay with Frank and his wife in London in November 1936. From there, they would arrange for his journey to Germany. Philip and Emma stood on the platform at Shadworth Station watching as Beth hugged Anatole.

"Anatole, I cannot bear for you to go. Please, Anatole, think carefully. How can you be sure it will achieve anything? Won't you change your mind?"

She looked up at him with tearful, pleading eyes, his shirt bunched into her fists around his chest as she struggled to prevent his going. He reached for her hands to release himself from her grasp and held them gently as he stepped back.

"My dear little Beth, I'm sorry, but you really can't stop me. I must go because I simply must try everything possible to find my parents."

"Oh, Anatole, you are taking all my hope away with you."

But he firmly buttoned up his dark overcoat and picked up his haversack as the train entered the station. Beth felt as if her heart had been pulled violently out of her chest, leaving an aching space as he smiled sadly and stepped onto the train, without a second glance in her direction.

Emma looked at her very dear husband, and they both remembered those times when parting had been so difficult for them. Philip felt his heart full of pain at the memory. But his concern was now for Beth. She watched as Anatole's train pulled out of the station, waving her handkerchief till the train was out of sight, then she turned to her father and shrugged tearlessly.

"So, he's gone and what on Earth can we do about it, Daddy?"

"My darling, at least he will be staying with Mr Jacques, who will help smooth his way over there. And we will hold him tight in our prayers all the time, Beth. Don't forget what I have taught you about trusting God. Come, sweetheart, you must let your family cheer

you now. You have George and Pieter and Daisy and the babies to help you. And you must be brave."

Emma took Beth's hand and led the way out to the waiting taxi. Her despair was palpable.

Since that night, Beth turned from the happy child they had known into a very serious and grown-up teenager. James and Philip often shared their anxieties over her as James drove him up to school each day.

"*She'll be sixteen next September, Philip, and she's being very strong, but I think she's bottling it up. We must somehow help her to keep her courage up. Do you think it's getting in the way of her schoolwork?*"

"*No, James. That's one thing we can be thankful for. She excels in all her subjects and is happiest when she has her head in her books.*"

Chapter 16

1937

Philip sat in his office at the school, horrified by the news he was hearing of events in Germany that morning of February 1937. He had just heard from Bertha Bracey that Chamberlain, newly promoted to the office of Prime Minister, had refused permission for Jewish children to come to Britain unaccompanied.

Philip had worked tirelessly with Bertha Bracey and Frank Jacques, his friend and colleague in Parliament, to put the plan for rescue into action. His school had become a key Quaker base for the transportation and resettling of the children in such imminent danger from Hitler's thugs' plans, and he was bitterly disappointed at Chamberlain's response.

Spring term was well underway and with it a letter from Frank Jacques. Kath Hanson hurried with it to Philip's office, his usual cup of coffee in her other hand. She impatiently waited as he ripped it open and read it. She knew he was hoping for news of Anatole, as were they all.

"*Philip, has he heard anything*?" she finally blurted as he folded the letter and placed it back in the envelope.

"*Oh, Kath, this is as difficult a time as we have ever gone through.*" He interlocked his fingers on his desk.

"Frank seems to think Bertha Bracey has made contact with her people in Berlin on the Quaker Emergency Committee to ask for news. We hope Anatole has at least joined them instead of trying to go it alone. But we must simply wait and see.

"Meanwhile, Frank writes that Pieter is feeling a bit lost. I need Emma to get him to come home from Cambridge; he's finished his degree and just needs some time to..."

Philip stopped talking, his eyes flitting to his study door as he heard a knock upon it. Before he could respond, the door opened.

"May I come in, Uncle Philip?"

There stood a young man with very familiar blue eyes and an earnest expression, his whole demeanour expressive of the anxiety that was oppressing him. He was dressed smartly but had taken no care with his looks, his hair uncombed.

Philip rose on his crutches to greet Pieter with a delighted cry of pleasure. Pieter went to Philip and embraced him as Kath surreptitiously wiped a tear from her eye.

"My *dear boy. We were only saying we must get you home from Cambridge. And here you are."* He grinned while he looked him up and down, as if to check it was really him. "*You've done so brilliantly in your exams, and you can decide how you want to go forward. But for now, you need to get home to Emma and relax."*

As he spoke, however, he realised that Pieter's face was not registering the pleasure he had expected. Some dread had its clutch on his heartstrings.

"My *dear Pieter, what is it? Sit down and tell me what the matter is. You're home. Nothing can hurt you here."*

As Kath rushed to get him a steaming mug of tea, it all came tumbling out.

"*Philip, my passport is a German one, and I've been warned that German people here in England will be interned as aliens if war is declared. My God, this frightens me beyond belief. I am hoping to join George as he trains for the RAF, but how will I be able to do that with this appalling threat hanging over me?*"

Pieter hid his face in his hands as the tears began to fall, his next words just about audible between his sobs. "*I feel so helpless in the face of such red tape, and no first-class degree will protect me from it. And then I think of my dear cousin, and we have no idea where he is now.*"

Philip sat in horrified silence, then wheeled his chair to where Pieter wept and simply put his hand on his head. "*Pieter, my dear, do not be afraid. We will sort this thing out, believe me. No one can hurt you. Why, Emma will personally go to war to prevent them, as you can imagine, not to mention Beth.*"

Pieter smiled a wan smile at this.

"*Let's get James and get you home.*" Philip gave Kath a subtle wink as she placed two cups of tea on his desk and nodded in response. "*We need to check this thing out and also see what George has to say. He is already in the throes of the training and finding it tough, I gather, but enjoying it, nonetheless. But clearly you two friends have already discussed it. George has the idea that this will mean he is ready for whatever Hitler throws at us when the time comes, if he has already got his wings.*"

"*And that is what I thought could be my best way forward. But now, Philip, I feel very confused about my future.*"

But Kath had already fetched James from the school garden to come to the study. James took one look at Pieter, and all the dread he had personally felt so heavily after the last war surfaced again. He struggled to let it go and to focus instead on Pieter's lost expression, his sagging shoulders and the drip of a tear hanging off his nose. He felt very sad for the young man, whose look was of utter wretchedness.

"*I shouldn't really leave my desk yet, James,*" Philip explained, "*but this young man should get home to Holt House. I must teach my sixth formers before I leave, but then I'll get off as soon as I can if you can come back for me.*"

James nodded. "*You're coming with me, Pieter, and on the way, you can stop to admire my budding daffodils. Even Wordsworth would be impressed by them. Maybe they will restore your perspective as they do mine, every day.*"

Philip smiled at this comment and even Pieter managed a glimmer of one. But Kath, listening at her desk next door, knew the costliness of the anxiety Philip and Emma were carrying every day as they held all the family in their constant care.

James landed at Holt House's door just as Elizabeth was getting off Turton's bus. She ran towards them, dumping her heavy satchel on the path in total disregard for it.

"*Pieter, Pieter. What a wonderful sight.*" She flung her arms round him in delight.

Emma opened the door and looked in amazement at them while James stood by smiling.

Beth stepped back, Pieter's embrace not quite as tight and warming as it used to be. "*But why are you so sad, Pieter? What's wrong?*"

It was as if Pieter had frozen where he stood, and James and Emma had to help him inside to an armchair by the fire while Beth looked on aghast. James immediately left to get Philip and bring him home for tea.

"*Is it about Anatole?*" Beth asked very anxiously, but Pieter shook his head.

"*Emma, Beth, I am so afraid. I want to join George to train like him to fly, but I have been warned that I will be considered an alien. Ugh. It's my German passport that stands in my way and will, I fear, mean they intern me if I stay in England.*"

Emma hastened to comfort the distraught boy from her own desperate hope that Hitler would not become a threat to Britain, though Philip and her two sons had warned her it was drawing closer and closer. "*Pieter, we will never let anyone take you in that way. We are anticipating something that, I pray, will never happen. And in any case, you are safe here with us.*"

"*But, Emma, they will not allow me to apply for training while this hangs over me. And that makes me feel so worthless and without purpose.*"

Pieter looked across at Elizabeth, who was looking at him in horror. "*Bethy, don't look at me like that.*"

She took his hand and squeezed it hard while her mother hurried into the kitchen to make tea—her eternal remedy. Pieter at last relaxed his head back against the old armchair.

"*God knows what Philip can do, but I do hope my dread of this will all be better soon. Oh, my Bethy, if only we knew where Anatole is. You know how headstrong he is. I pray he is not in any danger.*"

Beth gave a little cry of pain but shrugged the comment off as she turned back to him. "*My father and Frank Jacques are trying to make contact, Pieter. Frank knows someone called Wilfrid Israel who is based in Berlin. He owns a store with a reputation with the wealthy Berliners. He is Jewish himself and is behind lots of rescue efforts for endangered Jews. Daddy is hoping for his help.*"

Emma, listening to Beth's offer of comfort, felt very unconvinced. Philip had told her about this man, Israel, but she felt it could be a very forlorn hope. And she also knew how much this conversation meant for Beth, for Beth had shared with her mother her feelings for Anatole and Emma was wise enough to know that this young love was holding firm and could not be dismissed as just a crush. She busied herself with her baking, half an ear to the conversation between the young people.

Then, at last, the door opened and Philip wheeled himself into the room, James behind him. Emma, delighted that he had come home so quickly, appeared at the kitchen door with a tray of goodies and a cup of tea, prescribed to cheer Pieter up, whilst Beth flung herself at her father.

"*Daddy, my daddy, Pieter is so worried.*"

"*My dears, I've left my sixth formers all working very hard at Dickens, but now let's all try to relax and think our way forward. Nothing is the end of the world despite our worst forebodings. But, Pieter, I do believe we have to put a hold on your entering into RAF training till I can sort this passport issue out,*" he spoke regretfully, shaking his head.

"Daddy, he can stay here with us, can't he? I would love that and so would Daisy." Beth desperately wanted to be able to cheer Pieter, and she looked pleadingly at her father, her eyes full of tears, her hands clasped together almost in prayer.

Philip felt his heart almost miss a beat as he saw the huge love Beth was feeling as she pleaded. "*My little love, of course he can. Here's the idea I have been thinking up as I finished off at school. There are other very worthwhile things you, Pieter, can do here for the time being. For a start, I need to fill in with a teacher who can teach some of the more junior classes some French and German. Their teacher has gone off sick with recurring headaches. She's a tutor in Edna's house, Fox, and Edna will welcome you with open arms if you feel you could bear to do this.*"

Pieter swallowed hard as he encountered such a new idea, but he nodded silently and felt a wave of hopefulness flowing through him. How could he ever thank Philip?

"*My dear boy, no one is going to touch you. Frank and I will sort this out, but in the meantime, unwind and look forward a little to better things and a challenge with those classes.*"

Beth took Pieter's hand. "*We're off to Tempests' Farm now to see Daisy before it gets completely dark.*" She knew that Mary and Ron Tempest would give them a warm welcome and Florence and Ned would do all that they could to help cheer Pieter up.

"*Darling, it's exactly the right thing to do, but, my dear, watch the time because the night comes in quickly now. At least there's a full moon to accompany you home,*" said Emma, and Philip nodded his agreement.

Sure enough, the moon was up as Beth and Pieter trod their way down Long Lane. It was very clear and cold and the stars were coming out in the dusky sky. The starlings were gathering in their multitudes on the telegraph wires and the rooks were calling to each other as they were gathering to roost.

Beth shivered in her thin school coat, but the two of them made a happy pair as they walked along, in a way that Pieter would not have thought possible earlier in the day.

No one could have been more delighted than Daisy and the little family at the farm as they arrived. They were welcomed into the lounge, where Teddy was having his bedtime story with Ned, thumb in mouth in the old rocking chair. Florence motioned to Ned to let Pieter take over the reading, which he did, with a pat on Pieter's back. Mary Tempest watched over the scene as Beth recounted the fears that had brought Pieter home to Shadworth.

Mary turned to Ron. "*Oh, Ron, what troubles gather round us all as the news from Germany gets more and more scary. And what of our young Anatole? I know Emma is worried sick about him.*"

Beth gave an inward shudder. Even Daisy did not know the depth of her feelings for the boy with whom she had travelled home from school so many times. Very special times for Beth, and even so for Anatole, who had found it a pleasurable excuse to cut classes and enjoy his adopted sister's company instead of studying.

Ron and Mary insisted the two should set off back home, as it was, by now, very dark, so Pieter and Beth took their farewells and, holding hands, hurried home to one of Emma's delicious hot suppers. Pieter felt much relieved as they tucked in. Somehow, the atmosphere in the relaxed lounge at Tempests' Farm had put things back into perspective for him, and he suddenly felt sure that all would resolve itself in Philip's hands.

Chapter 17

1937

To Emma's delight, a letter arrived at Holt House from George four months after Pieter's return. She shut herself away in her well-stocked pantry to ensure a bit of privacy as she hurried to open the envelope and take out the letter.

RAF Training Centre,
Parliament Road,
Torquay
Devon
8th August, 1937

Mr & Mrs P Manners
Holt House,
Low Shadworth,
Yorkshire

My dear grandparents,

First, an apology. I have been so oppressed with all the heavy training here, not to mention the summer exams that I've had to take to reach my more senior level here. It's meant I've been unable to get home to you all. Dad is unhappy with me, I know. Please forgive me. I do hope you are all staying well.

Daisy has written to me to tell me the news of Pieter. I do envy him a bit, I must confess. Lucky man being cossetted by you, Grandma, and able to teach at your school, Philip. But

I wouldn't really swap places, as I know his heart continues to feel shattered at the terrors he has for his parents. And, in any case, I do love my training although it is gruelling. At least I will feel ready for any encroachment on our country by that piece of evil in Germany. Which doesn't make Pieter feel any better, I'm sure. Pray God he is allowed to train as soon as the German passport has been proved a non-issue.

We still have no news of Anatole, I suppose. All Beth's letters are full of her fears for him. I worry about her and hope her anxieties are not spoiling what should be such a happy time, as she has a good chance to do well in her school exams if only she can settle to work.

Oh, my dear Philip and Grandma, growing up is not easy. I will try to get home at least for a week at the end of this month. I love you both so much and our little Beth. Not so little now, I know.

I'm closing now and sending my dearest love. Please tell Father I shall aim to make it up to him when I can. I've a feeling he is getting on very well with a lady he's met at The White Swan. Has he told you about her? I certainly hope so. I do want him to find happiness again.

Your loving grandson, George

Emma was enjoying her little bit of peace entrenched in her pantry. It was nearly six in the evening, but Philip was not yet home and Beth was entertaining Ralph and Teddy in the lounge. She left her sanctuary in the pantry and, sitting at the kitchen table, wrote straight back.

Holt House
Low Shadworth
Yorkshire
12th August, 1937

Mr George Holt
RAF Training Centre
Parliament Road
Torquay

Our dear George,

It was lovely to hear from you and to hear that you are enjoying your training. It does my heart good to think of you becoming expert in the air though the idea is quite frightening. Nevertheless, I know it will stand you in good stead as you pass out and get your wings. Who knows what the next years will bring, given the news from Germany? And Pieter is wishing he could join you yet is really enjoying his teaching. I think he has a natural talent for it, and he has the younger boys eating out of his hand.

Now, of course, it's summer holiday time and we are very busy looking after little Ralph and Teddy to give Laura and Florence time to themselves. Laura is very preoccupied with Will, who still has black days remembering all he lived through and, moreover, fretting that he relies on Laura's pay to keep the family going. His pay from the cobbler's shop is dire, and he really detests that. You can imagine.

My darling boy, do please try to get home at the end of this month if you can. Beth will be pleased to see you. She is studying for her exams, which are still a long way off, but she is determined to do well, and I think it keeps her from fretting about Anatole. We still have no news of him, but Philip reckons that no news is hopefully good news.

Meanwhile, your father is about his work as usual. Cooking for The White Swan is a godsend because you will remember how he loved cooking for the French troops all those years ago in Verdun. So, he's back doing what he loves. And yes, the lady is called Milly and is an in-house housekeeper for the hotel. She is very charming and hard-working. Philip thinks she's lovely, so we all hope this may be a real opportunity for him. We shall see.

I must close now, as little Teddy and Ralph are shouting for attention. Come home soon.

Your loving grandma

Emma had hardly concluded her letter when she heard James' car drawing up and Beth ran out to greet her father and help James with the wheelchair. Philip, after greeting the youngsters, relaxed by the fire in the lounge, keen to read George's letter.

"*I do believe the boy is coming into his own, darling*," said Philip as he came to the end of the letter. "*He sounds as if he is taking hold of the training and making a good job of it. I know he sounds just a touch homesick, but I actually think he has taken the challenge well. And I'm glad he's so positive about Harry.*"

"*I hope you're right, Philip. I love him so much and hate the thought that all this may lead him into untold dangers if things deteriorate with Germany. I hope Chamberlain can make peace with Hitler, though I'm afraid that we may end up having to go to war.*" Emma's face portrayed her fear as she reflected again on the thought of another war.

"*Emma, you know how difficult it would be for me to condone any such thing as a Quaker, yet I fear that we may be faced with alternative evils. Can war possibly be the lesser evil? But let's not worry about that now or allow it to cloud our pleasure that our boy is doing well.*" He pulled her onto his knee and kissed her very gently.

Chapter 18
Letters

Houses of Parliament
Westminster
10th September, 1937

Philip Manners
Holt House
Shadworth
My dear Philip and Emma,

I at last have some good news. I have been in contact with Bertha Bracey, who is soldiering on as ever in London but with close contacts in Berlin and Frankfurt. She has been in touch with the owner of an apparently extremely up-market store in Berlin, something like Harrods here. His name is Wilfrid Israel. He is himself a Jew and very aware of the dangerous position he and all other Jews are in under this vile government. All his employees are Jewish, and Bertha tells me he cares very much for each one of them. He is as keen as we are to get the children to safety over here and is working with Bertha to that end.

My dear friends, he has found our reprobate, Anatole. The lad is now safe under his wing but turned up at his store as a very sick young man. I believe he fell over the doorstep, with a high temperature and thin as a rail. Wilfrid took him straight to his doctor friend, who sent him to the hospital, where he slowly recovered. You can see now why you have heard nothing from him.

He had been desperately trying to track down his mother, Hilke, knowing his father had indeed been taken to Dachau. He had lived on the streets, keeping out of the way of the Nazi thugs until he was mugged by some of them outside his old home. The Czernik apartment was empty, and the neighbours told him that Hilke had been taken by the SS. Then he realised that his search was over, for he could do no more for his mother or his father. You can imagine the state he was in. This does not make the news of his parents any less unbearable, but Anatole himself is alive and recovered.

Fear not now, Philip and Emma. He has been given a job in the shop and is getting back on his feet albeit slowly. I thank God for this news and cannot thank Bertha enough for her efforts on our behalf. I'm sure he will write to you when he feels he can. I am enclosing the address of the emporium in Berlin.

We will talk soon, and, in the meantime, I send you and the family my very best wishes.

Yours,

Frank

This letter, as school term was just getting underway, filled the whole family with relief and joy that their other boy had been found and secured, though in a very different place from George. Emma immediately set about writing to Anatole, in the care of Wilfrid Israel's establishment, knowing how deeply hurt he would be at the ghastly news of both his parents. She wanted him to come straight back home, but in her heart, she knew he was in a good place and might be able to help Mr Israel gather together the children to be rescued.

Meanwhile, Philip prayed quietly for the boy and for the unknown man in Berlin. Neither could he ignore the tears of joy that Beth was shedding. But he couldn't help a quiet smile as he thought of the daredevil Anatole he knew of old working in a luxury shop like the English Harrods.

"*Oh God, keep him from betraying his Jewish identity and help him to see his safety depends on keeping his head down and obeying Wilfrid Israel.*" He turned to look at his beloved Emma as she tried to mop up Beth's tears with her hanky.

"*Bethy, my Bethy, steady now. We must hold him in our prayers and thank God that he is alright. Why don't you write him a letter to post with Mother's? I'm sure that will be a comfort to him.*"

Accordingly, Beth sat down at the desk Philip had set up for her, close to his own, and set about her task.

Holt House
Shadworth
13th September, 1937

Mr Anatole Czernik
c/o Mr Wilfrid Israel
'N.Israel'
Unter den Linden
Berlin

My dearest Anatole,

Beth here. I am so relieved to hear you are in a safe place now, but my heart is bleeding for you after all you've been through. I do wish you would come home, but Daddy says it's good that you are with this man because he is known for his work with the Germany Emergency Committee. So I won't beg you to return yet, I'll just say you must take great care. And we are all thinking of your mum and your dad.

Anatole, I miss you so. I am working for my School Certificate now but want to go on to the Higher Certificate in the sixth form, like you did. I would dearly love to get a place at university, but that is in the future. How I wish you could be standing at the school gates as you used to so we could catch Turton's bus home.

Sorry for behaving like a baby.

I send you all my love, dear Anatole,

Yours,

Beth

She carefully folded her letter and added it to Emma's envelope. Now it was to be a waiting game. Beth retreated to her room and lay down on her bed, praying for help in the fearful circumstances Anatole found himself in.

Emma made as if to go after her, but Philip held her back.

"*Let her go, Emma. Let her find her own peace about this thing. God, Emma, I would have her back as the little toddler she was without a care in the world. But I have no magic wand, darling. We've got to let her do her growing up.*"

"*I know, my love. But it's very hard.*" Emma knelt by his wheelchair and laid her head on his lap.

Chapter 19

1937

New boys were taking up their places in the first year as term was once again in full swing. Pieter found himself promoted to housemaster in Fox House under Edna's care. Daisy and Beth celebrated their sixteenth birthdays together with a family dinner at the farm, where Pieter found himself enjoying a warm welcome in the fellowship they all shared. He flourished at school, having a gentle and sympathetic touch for the youngsters, who were only just leaving home to board.

He often walked home with Laura at the end of the school day and shared his anxieties over his parents with her. As they approached the house, little eight-year-old Ralph would run to meet them at the gate and hug his mother. It gave him a stab of pain as he remembered his own mother's embraces, but he was always comforted by Emma's appearance at the door greeting the two of them.

"The kettle's boiled and I have baked us some fresh scones for teatime. Beth is due any time from Cranston. She'll be very pleased to see you. You've beaten her home."

The door swung open, and Beth walked in, hot and pink from carrying her heavy satchel.

"*Any letters, Mother?*" were inevitably her first words on arrival, and with a shake of Emma's head, she was disappointed yet again. No letter from Anatole. But she had become an expert at hiding her disappointment from them all.

Ralphie started pulling her towards the garden door. "*Come out and see what Grandma and I have made. It's a bird bath, and we've hung up some nuts to attract the little birds. Come, Mummy, come, Beth.*"

Outside, it was one of those September days that folks like to call an Indian summer—hot and hazy, humming with the sound of bees busily gathering pollen from Emma's sunflowers. Laura loved to see Ralphie so content, and she relaxed and smiled at Pieter as she soaked up the warmth, enjoying the evening sunshine that lit up the glorious yellow of the flowers.

Beth took Ralph's hand, and he skipped beside her to the chicken pen.

"*Can I feed them, Beth? Grandma said I had to wait for you.*"

Beth nodded, and together they scattered the seed as the chickens clucked and pecked.

They heard James' car drawing up, and Beth hastened to the front of the house to watch her father as he emerged from the car, into his chair, with James behind him. Emma had heard from the kitchen and appeared at the front door, her face beaming with pleasure at seeing him.

"*Daddy, James, Ralphie will want to show you his bird bath. Come out into the garden,*" said Beth.

"*Well, my love, I think you should first see what was delivered to school in this afternoon's post. Why not bring Pieter inside with you for a minute?*" Philip smiled as he held up an envelope.

Beth gave a squeal of wonderment and shouted for Pieter from where she stood, who soon appeared beside her. She had been waiting and praying for news of Anatole, and now she could hardly bear to look at the writing on it. Was it really from Berlin?

Emma looked across at James, who nodded at her as Philip tore open the letter. One could almost feel the held breath of each one standing there.

"*Yes, my dears. It's from Anatole, thank God.*"

They all exhaled as one.

"*Shall I read it out so everyone can hear it?*"

"*Daddy, read it quickly. This is unbearable.*"

"*Alright, my Bethy. Here goes.*" He looked away from his beaming daughter, focusing instead on the words on the letter.

"*Dear Philip and all at Shadworth,*

Thank you so much for my letters. My little sister, Beth, I loved yours especially. The letters made me better in my spirit. But I know I have been very slow at writing to you, and I beg your forgiveness. I have been overwhelmed by all that has happened.

" *that the trail to find my mother led only to Dachau, that evil place where I knew my father and aunt and uncle had already been sent, was almost too much to bear. I think I had some kind of breakdown and ended up on the streets of the city, caring little for life. That's how I got really sick. They say it was pneumonia, and it's only for the kindness of the Friends Service Council here in Berlin that I got picked up off the streets and avoided arrest by the SS.*

"*The doctors in the hospital were wonderful, and Mr Israel took me to his home after. There, he treated me to such amazing hospitality and listened to my sad account of all that's happened. I told him about you all and about our school and your hope that we could rescue Jewish children from danger and bring them to England. I'm afraid I boasted that I knew that you, Philip, would be sure to welcome the children to Shadworth if it could be made possible."*

"*I knew he'd have faith in you, Daddy.*" Beth moved from foot to foot as she struggled to contain her pride and excitement.

Philip brought his forefinger to his lips in a shushing motion so he could continue reading, silently pleased by the complete trust Anatole had in him.

"*Now he has given me a job alongside his other employees in his shop, who are all Jewish, like him. Oh, my Bethy, if you could see the shop. It's magnificent, and the clients who come to it are very wealthy German ladies. I wish I had money to buy Emma and you some of the jewellery that's on the counters here. A dream, of course. But Wilfrid is about the business of rescue under cover of it all, and he has asked me to help and to liaise with you when the time comes for the rescue operation. He says we must wait a while yet.*

"*I shall close this letter with a promise to write again and a promise to hold you all in my heart as I work. You can see, my dear Emma, that I have found my old self again. Please reassure my little sister that I love her and tell Pieter that I wish he were here with me. But I know he is doing well working for the school.*

"*With my love.*

"*Yours, Anatole.*"

Beth ran into the garden, picked a surprised Ralphie up and swung him round in her relief at this wonderful news. Laura had been playing hide-and-seek with him, and she watched wonderingly at Beth's sudden exuberance. And just at that moment, the garden gate opened and in strode Will. Ralphie ran up to him, and Will picked him up and swung him onto his shoulders.

Laura went to him and put her arms around him. She could see how weary he was from his hard work at the cobbler's shop. His hair was greyer than when he had arrived at her school that day long ago when he was demobbed. She still remembered vividly how he had described the way that his dear friend, her husband, had died on the battlefield, to his utmost grief. Now the lines of tiredness were inscribed heavily on his face, but she loved him for it.

Beth couldn't wait to tell Will the news of the letter from Anatole and spilled it all out to him as he walked along patiently, his smile holding the great news she was sharing plus some news of his own.

"We have something special to cheer us all up soon." He winked at Beth, then called out to the house, *"Mother, Philip, come out here."* There was an urgency in his tone that exposed his excitement. Emma and Philip, followed by James and Pieter, all appeared at the kitchen door. They could see he was thrilled about something.

"I've had a visit at the shop from our Harry, and he is going to get married to Milly if you will all give him your blessing. Guess who he wants to be his best man?" He pointed to himself and grinned, not that any of them would have needed the clarification.

The news and the fact that Will was so pleased to be his brother's best man set each of the listeners to different reactions of delight. Beth took hold of James' hands and danced him round in a ring, much to his astonished pleasure. Emma plonked down on Philip's lap and kissed him. Laura tossed little Ralphie up in the air and Pieter stood in pleased wonderment. They had all met Milly and were truly delighted to hear that, after all the years since Maggie's death, Harry was to find a new happiness at last.

Philip sat back in his wheelchair in real contentment at the two pieces of news that meant so much to each of them. He could see the great sense of relief in Beth's face, and that meant a lot to him. He was particularly anxious that she should be able to enjoy her last two years of school without the fears she carried for Anatole. And he knew how Pieter too would be able to feel reassured that all was well with his cousin, though Philip was perfectly well aware that the shadow of Hitler and his minions was looming larger and larger.

"*Well, my lovely family, we will enjoy our good news tonight. Emma, what were you going to cook for supper, my love? Can it keep till tomorrow? Then we could all go up to The White Swan and eat there together. What do you say?*"

Emma simply laughed. She knew his delight at the thought of having them all together, which matched her own. "*Of course it will keep. I shall ring Harry and make sure they can cater for us all, and I might ring Florence and get the Tempests along too.*"

Chapter 20

Elizabeth May – Family Joys, 1937

I shall always remember the day that we had news of dear Anatole. At last, we knew he had been picked up by the good people of the Quaker Emergency Committee and was alive. He had a purpose doing worthwhile work on behalf of his beloved parents, work that would have made them very proud. I thanked God for Mr Wilfrid Israel that day.

And on top of that news, of course, was my brother Harry's marriage. Ever since his wife Maggie died so tragically of Spanish flu many years earlier, he had stumbled along as best he could, and this had troubled his son, George. George had grown up with us at Holt House but always remained very close to his dad. A wedding would bring George home on leave from his training for a little while, and both Daisy and I were thrilled at the thought.

Another family milestone was passed in December, when my dearest mother reached seventy years. We all threw ourselves into making Mother's birthday memorable. Daddy had arranged a service of thanksgiving in the chapel. He invited the school staff, family and friends to attend, and after leading in prayer, the chapel fell into silence in the Quaker tradition. Philip finally broke the silence as he voiced his thanks for Emma's seventy years. But the most touching moment was when he took her hand and very gently placed a beautiful ring on her finger.

"*James and I sneaked off to Mr Moreton's jeweller's shop in Cranston the other day to find a ring to fit your tiny finger, my love. The ring from Scarborough served us very well those years ago, but now I want this diamond to mark a marriage that I, once upon a time, thought could never be. And you, Emma, have always been and are everything in the world to me.*"

As he spoke, Mother put her hands over her face, overwhelmed at his words, then she stood up beside his wheelchair and found words to respond.

"*Oh, my beloved Philip, thank you. It's beautiful, oh my. But let me say with this thank you that my heart belongs to you and always will.*" She took the folded hands in his lap and kissed them tenderly.

There were tears in James' eyes as Will, Harry and Florence gathered round my mother to hug her. As for me, tears were streaming down my face as I waited my turn to embrace her. Then Pieter, Daisy and George gave three cheers, shedding all our fears for the future for that moment.

Yet such a joyful end to 1937 led to a devastating 1938.

Chapter 21

Elizabeth May – Growing anxieties, 1938

1938 arrived with more and more anxiety as to what Hitler was going to do next. We were all so furious with Chamberlain, who continued trying to appease him and who, to my father's especial fury, refused to allow permission for endangered children to come over to England. I knew Anatole was working hard with Mr Israel to make it possible. He wrote to us when he could, sometimes to my father at school and sometimes to Holt House, to Mother and me.

I was a sixth former and I was trying my utmost to get good exam results following my distinction in the School Certificate Exams. I do remember how Mother and Father rejoiced at that result, and Father was so proud he could hardly contain himself from telling everyone at his school about it. I was determined to try for a place at Oxford, as George had. A few boys from Daddy's school asked me out during that time, but I had only one boy in my heart, and his letters still called me his "little sister". Oh God, it was a difficult time.

Frank Jacques came to visit us in great distress in March. We could tell he needed to get away from London and share his horror at events in Germany. It was becoming clearer and clearer that Hitler had no intention of keeping peace, and now he had annexed Austria to the Reich, to sustain and fulfil his nationalist ambitions, keeping Austria under his control as part of Germany. Even so, he was completely ignoring the Treaty of Versailles, which had been signed to end the war. What Frank detested was the way his colleagues in the British Parliament were just standing by as Hitler pleased himself.

Father and he, along with my dear brothers and James, talked into the night during his visit, and when he left, it was with great sadness. As I tried to concentrate on my studies, I couldn't help sharing their dread of what would come next. Mother maintained an atmosphere of calm throughout, but I knew she was earnestly holding Daddy and the others in her prayers. Florence knew it too and often called in during the afternoons to see Mother and help her with managing everyone's needs.

Then some things happened that we could never have anticipated. It was the end of spring term and we were hoping to celebrate Easter together down at Tempests' Farm. Florence and Daisy had been hiding chocolate eggs in the garden because we all kept up the pretence that the Easter rabbit would be hiding eggs for Easter Sunday. Though Teddy and Ralph were nine years old, they were still our babies.

Daisy told me after the Easter egg hunt on Easter Sunday how her father had run into the farm kitchen that Maundy Thursday with a face as white as a sheet and had just managed to spit out the grim words, to his mother and to Florence, that his father was dead. He had found Ron lying out in the field where he had been planting an early crop of barley and his breath had gone from him. Ned's father had died, as he would have wished, working in his beloved fields. But Ned was quite beside himself and his mum was speechless with horror, unable to believe that her husband of many years was gone. Daisy said it was her mother, my sister Florence, who took charge of all that was needed now.

We had received the news that Thursday at Holt House and sat appalled. I shall never forget my mother's face as she turned to Daddy and asked him to say a prayer for them all before we set off down to the farm together. Ron had always been a steady rock of strength through all the vicissitudes we had shared. We had taken that for granted. Now there was a new reality.

Easter passed with a much quieter celebration under the shadow of this death. Mary Tempest became her usual resolute self in the weeks that followed, often comforting young Teddy with words of assurance. Daddy admired her courage very much, I know, because he spent time with her and with Ned before the funeral to lead her through her grief to a faith that Ron would always be close to her.

Just as we were emerging from this shock, Hitler began his new campaign to take Czechoslovakia into his control. It was now May time and summer was upon us. I was taking school exams and revising hard. I needed to keep up my test results in preparation for my final year at school, when I would be taking my Higher School Certificate.

It was very difficult to concentrate. We had very few letters from Anatole at this time and we were watching with mounting anxiety what Hitler might do next. Daddy and Frank Jacques were constantly in touch. It was Pieter who explained it all to me. There were three million Germans living in the Sudetenland area of Czechoslovakia and their leader, Konrad Henlein, was complaining that they were being persecuted. This was all the excuse Hitler needed. That May, he set in motion plans to take Czechoslovakia. Pieter told Daisy and me that his uncle Frank was desperate for Neville Chamberlain to act against all of it, but that Chamberlain just wanted to keep the peace at any price.

Then we were notified of another death, and this left us all bereft, most especially my dear James. He drove Daddy to school that morning in May, and as Daddy wheeled himself into his study, the phone was ringing. It was Mother, and she was crying. James and Daddy looked at each other in alarm, and Daddy hushed her so she could tell him what was wrong.

"Philip. It's Leonard. He has been in an accident and he's very badly injured. He was driving to a patient in Cranston and a lorry pulled out of a side road and hit him. An onlooker called an ambulance because he was just slumped at the wheel. He's been taken to the hospital.

"Philip. Is James with you? I'm with his mum now. He must return home as fast as he can to get her to the hospital. Oh, my love, send him home."

James had looked on aghast and wasted no time. He ran back to the car and drove straight to his home, picked up his mum and drove her, with my mother beside her, as quickly as he could.

But it was no use. Leonard had died on the way to the hospital. I can hardly bear to think of the look on James' face when he brought his mother back to Holt House. This loss was a towering one for us all. Our doctor, and our very dear friend, James' wise and loving father. After all, he had brought me into the world as well as Daisy and Teddy and Ralph, and he had stood beside Mother when Father woke up without his leg all those years earlier.

Tears could not quite touch the pain that was overwhelming us all. I simply found myself sitting as close to James as I could get, holding his hand in both of mine as Mother talked so gently and soothingly to Sheila Thomson and made pots and more pots of tea for us all.

Chapter 22

1938

It was late when Philip and Emma left Sheila Thomson's home. The stars were out, bright pinpricks in the dark sky, and the crescent moon shone down on them as Emma pushed his chair along.

"Thank God James is at home with her and thank God he is holding it together. I was afraid he might revert to the stammer with the shock, but, Emma, he has grown into such a steady and peaceful presence in everything he does. The school garden is flourishing and, truthfully, darling, I don't know what I'd do without him. I know Beth relies on him too."

"I hope she's been able to finish the essay she was writing without our distracting her," said Emma. *"We've had no news of Anatole for a while, and I know she frets about him."*

Emma's frown showed her anxiety for her beloved daughter. Philip understood this only too well. He himself often wished he could wrap Beth in cotton wool to protect her from the world's ills.

"Two deaths in such a short space of time have been bitterly painful, my love. How can the whole village manage without Leonard looking after everyone?" Philip shook his head with great sadness, for Leonard had accompanied him through his worst suffering

and he couldn't imagine how anyone else would be able to step into his shoes.

"*There are so many that make up the fabric of our lives, Philip. I sometimes feel that I am trying to hold the world up for them all. And then I remember what's going on in Germany, and I can do nothing.*"

Philip reached his hand back to squeeze Emma's as she guided his chair. "*Emma, you must let it all be simply in God's hands. Easier said than done, sweetheart, I know. I'm talking to myself now. I am busy fighting for Pieter to receive permission to remain in school despite the question of his German passport. And I feel so much for Will and Laura. She always looks so tired and Will slaves in the cobbler's shop to make ends meet for them. And then I pray Anatole is safe with Wilfrid Israel and watch Beth's face when there is no letter.*

"*And, oh, my Emma, what will Hitler do next? He has made his play for the Sudetenland, and Chamberlain has been unable to stop him. Appeasement at all costs, and my Quaker conscience aches because I know we must confront him soon.*"

Emma stopped the wheelchair and stood in front of him. They were still on Long Lane, in the silence of the evening. She took his hands in hers and leaned down to kiss his forehead.

"*Philip, we must do what you have taught me—one day at a time and patience in all these anxieties. Our love is very strong and you enlighten my life every day. I can't bear your uncertainty. Let's look forward to the good thing that will be Harry's marriage. We shall have George home, even though it will be only for a short time, and he will talk to Pieter about how he views his next step.*"

"And I shall write another letter tomorrow to plead for Pieter to be allowed to stay as tutor at the school, with our reference."

Philip sighed heavily. "*Do you remember, my love, those meetings at the station? Such tender memories. And see how we came through all the agonies we faced to this moment now. Here you are, my darling, and I love you so very much. Let's go home to them all and face whatever Hitler has in store.*"

Chapter 23

1938

It took Philip a long time on the morning of Leonard's funeral to feel he had the energy to rise out of his bed and heave himself into his wheelchair. He was due to give the eulogy for his old friend in the service at the Methodist chapel, and he was still searching for words to express his huge respect and love for the man who had cared for him in his worst moments and encouraged him to recover himself and return to his job at the school.

Emma had already left to stay with Sheila, to be able to accompany her in the funeral car with James. Will and Laura were to take Philip, with Beth and Harry following the car. It was a beautiful summer's day, and as he waited for Will, he looked up at the tall elms in their effulgent summer green. Emma's roses were in full bloom and the occasional sparrow lighted on a stem and rocked it as it delved for insects in the heart of the rose. Butterflies were skimming the heads of the lavender bushes and, somewhere, a bumble bee was humming its way through the pollen-bearing flowers. Philip reminded himself that he should be more thankful for these blessings. Such beauty should remind him it was God's world and that Leonard was now at peace.

How can we keep faith in this troubled world? And how can we all manage without our dear friend?

But his reverie was interrupted by Will's arrival and by Beth running out to him to see if he was ready to leave for the chapel.

"*Daddy, come on. Don't look so sad. You have to help us all to keep our courage up. James needs us. Come on, Daddy.*"

And indeed, he arrived at the chapel some twenty minutes later, and as he sat before the gathered mourners who filled the space to overflowing, he found the words to celebrate Leonard and comfort those who were wiping their tears as he talked. His own wife was amongst them, sitting close to Sheila Thomson, and James was listening to his every word as if everything hung on them. His dear Beth was sitting next to James and holding his hand.

Philip never failed to be astonished at how God gave him the words he needed when he asked for help, and he was truly thankful. "*We celebrate today one who is irreplaceable, yet we have to go on living as we know Leonard would have us do. We can only rely on God's grace to strengthen us to carry on and serve all those whom Leonard himself served. I do not believe he is far away, but very close to us all in our grief. We must believe that and live in its light and assurance. May God hold us all in the palm of His hand today.*"

Afterwards, as he relaxed at home after the busy and emotional day, he told Emma about it, and she smiled and nodded.

"*Darling, do you remember the words of the hymn you wrote to me long ago from Scarborough? They are still true today:*

'Father, hear the prayer we offer, not for ease that prayer shall be,

but for strength that we may ever live our lives courageously.'

"Darling, you did well."

It was the end of June, and Harry's wedding to Milly was to be in two days at the parish church in Shadworth, which stood on the hill just above The White Swan. Milly had chosen this church, as she had been baptised there and had occasionally worshipped there with Harry.

For Emma, it was an especial delight, as, at last, her beloved Harry was to have a new wife. The death of his first wife, Maggie, was engraved on her heart, for Emma had stayed with her as she died painfully so many years earlier, barely able to breathe, but always full of the love she had felt for Harry.

As Emma was breathing in the joyous feeling of the upcoming occasion, putting the finishing touches to the spread she had prepared in her kitchen for the wedding breakfast, the front door was flung open and a voice bellowed out, "Is *anyone home?*"

Emma held the hem of her skirt up and hurried to the door, her heart hammering with excitement. "*My dear boy, I've missed you so much.*"

"*Grandma, are you* OK?" George hugged her and lifted her off her feet with the pleasure of seeing her. "Is *everyone well and all set for this great event?*"

"*George, let me feast my eyes on you.*" She stepped back and held his hands in hers as she looked at him and smiled, for he hadn't changed at all except in height. "*They are all dying to see you. Pieter is coming home with Philip in James' car and Beth will be on Turton's bus hastening home. Mary Tempest is in charge of dinner tonight at the farm—she is bearing up very well—and as for Daisy, she is desperate to see you. I must put the kettle on for all our arrivals to have a cuppa.*"

At that moment, the door opened, and Beth flew in, straight into George's arms.

"*George. Welcome home, my own best friend. Oh Lord, you have gotten so tall. Is everything going smoothly? Oh, you must tell us all about it.*"

Emma chuckled. "*Beth, let the lad have some air, my darling. You can catch it all up degree by degree. I am so pleased Mary is cooking for us all tonight, as I'll be able to sit back with Daddy and listen to all your adventures, George.*"

"*You know, Grandma, it's very tough discipline and the timetable leaves no room at all for leisure. And yet, I am actually loving it.*" George laughed, almost in disbelief at his delight. "*The feeling when you finally have your hands on the joystick and the plane is yours is difficult to describe.*"

They were interrupted by the sound of a car drawing up to the gate. Beth and George rushed to open the door to enjoy the welcome sight of Philip being helped into his chair by Pieter and James.

George grinned, hands on his hips. "*Uncle Philip, words can't describe my delight in seeing you and Pieter, my dear friend.*"

Pieter's face was wreathed in smiles as he saw George, and Philip opened his arms to him.

"*My dearest boy, you are more than welcome. Thank God your father has chosen to make us all such a special day as an excuse for being together.*"

He looked across at the doorway where Emma stood watching with James beside her. "*And is that my wife I see? Emma, how glad are we to receive this very tall and upright young man?"*

Emma giggled and, hurrying over to him, bent and kissed him.

"*Come on, everyone. I've made a cuppa, then we should make our way down to the farm. Mary Tempest and Florence will be hard at work, and I don't think Daisy should be made to wait much longer for the sight of you, George. And Will and Laura will be arriving with Ralphie.*"

It was a very happy gathering that night in the old farmhouse kitchen around the huge table laden with delicious savouries and cakes, though some moments of sadness could not be disguised amongst the revelry. Mary and Ned felt Ron's absence very keenly and Beth sensed the shadow of the grief that all felt for Leonard—a shadow that darkened James' brow more than most. Beth stayed very close to him that night as Daisy cavorted with George, closely followed by Ralph and Teddy. And Pieter was very thoughtful as he joined in, a point not lost on Philip, who took him to one side quietly to share his thoughts about his parents, Franz and Esther, and about his aunt Hilke and uncle Otto. Philip felt Pieter's anguish like a knife in his own heart. Nevertheless, the evening was a great success, and all agreed that Harry's marriage on Saturday was to be a glorious affair.

And indeed it was. Milly was no longer a young and blushing twenty-something as she walked up the aisle with a sweet expression and enormous dignity. She wore a suit of cream linen and clutched a posy of lilies and anemones. Harry greeted her, his expression full of love. Just as proud as Harry, there stood Will, his best man, handing his brother the ring with aplomb. Laura, watching Will, squeezed Ralph's hand with the emotion of seeing him so handsome and so gratified at his role.

That night, as Philip and Emma lay together in the big bed at Holt House, he drew her to him and, with his old, tender touch, reminded her of how thankful he still felt after all their years together, that she indeed belonged to him. And she, in his arms, gasped with pleasure.

Chapter 24

1938

It was the start of a new term, and Philip gathered his senior staff together to sit around his desk. He wanted to share his ideas for the rescue of threatened Jewish children and the potential role of his school in accommodating them. He was also very conscious of his age, as he too was approaching seventy years, and so the discussion that morning led to his announcement that he would step down as head at the end of the year.

"*It really is your time, Alan.*" He smiled. "*I know everyone will be delighted for you to take over the management of our school; after all, you already carried the burden of it during my illness and convalescence.*"

He could see that a frowning Alan was about to object, so he held his hand up to stop him, appealing to Beatrice and Edna and to Pieter and Laura.

"*My dears, you know I won't be far away.* What *I would dearly like is to be able to support those children who will, I hope, come to us and find comfort and love here.* With Emma's *help, we can help them to adapt to their surroundings.* That *way, I will still have a room here, though not my study—that will be yours, Alan. How does all this sound?*" He looked around at them enquiringly.

"*I do believe this way will be an excellent compromise for us all,*" Laura said. "*We cannot bear for you not to be your peaceable presence in the school, and those children will be absolutely in need of such a guide.*"

Beatrice looked at Alan and smiled reassuringly across at him. She turned to Philip. "*I know no better man to replace you, Philip.*"

Edna nodded. "*You will be able to use the school chapel as you did in those awful years during the war, Philip. I am with you.*"

Philip sat back in his chair with a sigh. "*Pieter, I believe we will need you to help those youngsters with their English. You have already proved how well you can do it. Thank you, my friends. Can we retire to the chapel after we've discussed the business of the new term? I feel very keenly that we should ask God for the help we shall certainly need in these coming days.*"

Mere days after Philip's decision to step down as head at the end of the year, a letter came from Frank.

Westminster
20th September, 1938

Mr P Manners
Headteacher
Quaker School
Shadworth

My dear Philip,

I find myself more and more frustrated by Chamberlain's behaviour. He is determined to keep peace with Hitler, but it seems it's at all costs. He plans to go over to Germany shortly to speak to the leader of the Czechs, Beneš, to persuade him to hand over the Sudetenland completely to Germany's control.

Philip, what can we do? Parliament seems totally helpless to prevent him going his own way over the issue; meanwhile, he continues to refuse to allow any unaccompanied children to come over to us. Something has to give.

Can I ask you to be prepared in case he changes his mind and we can act for those children? And please, my friend, maintain your prayers for us to find a way forward in this vexed situation.

Please pass on my regards to Emma. I am very relieved Pieter has enjoyed teaching in the school. It has given him new confidence. He is so very grateful that you have settled his passport issue on the grounds of his role in the school. Give him my love.

As for Anatole, I gather Wilfrid Israel is using him in the shop, and for this, much thanks.

Best regards,
Frank

Sure enough, days after Frank's letter arrived, on the twenty-ninth of September, Beneš handed power over to Hitler, and in Munich, Chamberlain signed the agreement along with Italy and France that the Sudetenland would become German. Chamberlain claimed he had achieved "*Peace for our time*" as he returned to Britain triumphant. Philip, in his study, shook his head sadly at this, utterly frustrated.

That afternoon, Pieter walked down to Holt House with Laura and landed in Emma's kitchen in a paroxysm of grief. Emma was glad when Beth arrived home from school to help her calm him down. Beth proceeded, as she always did, to take his hand and lead him to the farm, where he could breathe in the scent of the fields and get to work helping Ned with the harvesting. Ned was a wonderful steadying influence on them all and, without words, set Pieter the task of baling up the sheaves of corn.

Beth and Daisy at last had the chance for a little bit of time to themselves, and they enjoyed gossiping about the wedding, Milly's outfit and Will's pride in being best man. The two girls made a charming summer picture as they laughed together.

Pieter and Beth walked home together later that night, with Pieter somewhat revived from his anxieties by the supper of ham, eggs and mushrooms Mary had given them. They took in the scent of the evening air as the starlings were settling along the telegraph wires and the glowworms were shining out their pure, clear pearls of light in the hedgerows.

"It is very beautiful, is it not, Beth?"

Beth nodded. *"We are very lucky to live here in this peaceful sanctuary, Pieter, but I am so afraid it can't last forever. I know Daddy, who is such a man of peace, believes that Chamberlain will have to act to stop Hitler before too long. I have heard him say to Mother how naive Chamberlain is to even think he can persuade Hitler from what he's doing."*

"He is of course absolutely right, Beth. God help us all."

As they opened the door of Holt House, they found Philip musing in his chair and Emma sitting at his foot. They both looked up delighted to see the two young ones as ever, but they had been quietly considering what must be the next step.

"I'm making us hot cocoa, my dears," said Emma, *"and then we should retire to our beds. We all have work awaiting us tomorrow. Beth, my love, have you really done all your homework?"*

"Emma, let her be." Philip laughed. *"You can trust her to be on top of it all. Am I right, my darling?"*

"Of course you are, Daddy. I can't afford to let my work slip if I am to get into Oxford."

"I have a busy day with my young second years tomorrow," interrupted Pieter. *"I must get back to school. I shall say goodnight and thank you all as always for everything."*

He slipped away quietly despite the huge anguish they were all feeling. As he walked, he tried to analyse what it was he'd been feeling as he watched Daisy's delight at George's presence. Perhaps it was a kind of envy that she was so wrapped up in George, yet he knew what pleasure it gave him whenever he and she spent time together and Daisy threw herself into companionship with him.

It dawned on him that he would very much like to claim a corner of Daisy's delight for himself. But he shrugged and let the feeling go, looking forward once more to his students and his role in school.

Chapter 25

Late 1938

On the ninth of November, their worst fears were realised. In Germany, the violence that had been building within the ranks of Hitler's SS now surfaced in the horrors of Kristallnacht. Violence had found many vicious opportunities to express itself with the permission of its leaders, but it was not only paramilitaries that were taking part. Civilians had soaked up the evil propaganda around the Jews and believed it to be perfectly legitimate to think of them as second-class citizens, no better than dogs.

Will, James and Ned arrived at Holt House on the night of the tenth of November. They found Emma stoking up the fire in the parlour. They were all appalled at what they were reading of events in Berlin and across Germany and had come for words of wisdom and comfort from Philip, needing to share with him and Emma their horror that such events could ever happen. Jewish premises were being smashed up, indeed torn apart, without compunction.

"*My dear boys, hate is stalking the streets of the German cities, I'm afraid,*" said Philip, "*and there has never been the like ever before. We are in new territory now. German citizens are even joining in.*"

"*I am so afraid for Pieter's family and especially for Anatole working as he does for the N. Israel store, but what can we do?*" reiterated Emma.

Beth's face turned pale as she sat quietly on the floor next to her father.

James hurried to her side and, kneeling next to her, took her hand. "*Bethy, keep steady. Our people cannot stand by doing nothing for much longer.*"

There was a sudden, hasty rapping on the door, and Pieter strode in, trembling violently.

"*I've run all the way. Philip, it's horrific. The employees at Wilfrid Israel's shop are being rounded up by the SS. Uncle Frank has been in touch with me, and he has it on good authority that the N. Israel store has been ransacked and goods slashed and smashed.*" He leaned back against the wall and ran his hand through his blonde hair. "*Oh God, we are so helpless to save them all.*"

Philip looked at his wife with great sadness as they both felt the anguish of the young ones. Emma stood up, knowing it was important for her to recover her composure for the sake of them all. Beth had slid to a foetal position on the floor and hidden her face in her hands.

"*My dears, we must never lose heart. I shall make tea, and we shall find a comfort in the very everyday routine that keeps us from descending into despair. We must trust that God is still close to us and will be caring for those who are in the middle of this evil.*" She crouched next to Beth and stroked her arm gently. "*Beth, come and help me.*"

Philip smiled at her as she scurried into the kitchen to get them all drinks and biscuits. Elizabeth pushed herself up weakly from the floor and followed her.

Her mother hugged her close, though she felt a sense that a cold hand was gripping her heart.

"*Let's be quiet for a minute,*" Philip said.

Will, James and Ned closed their eyes. Pieter stood by the door to the kitchen and gripped the doorframe for support. He dropped his head and closed his eyes, his legs feeling as if they would give out at any second.

"*Dear Lord, we have no answer to the horrors perpetrated in Germany at this time, but we ask for your guiding hand to show us what we can do to aid the situation. We ask you to draw very close to those in the midst of this evil and to give them your Spirit of courage to maintain their steadfastness despite the terrors that enfold them.*

"*In the quiet, Lord, we would ask you to remind each of us of your promise to be with us always to the end of time. Amen.*"

News only came through slowly, much to Beth's anguish, but Philip was in constant touch with Frank and, through him, with Bertha Bracey and the Germany Emergency Committee. Chamberlain, having refused to allow children to enter Britain, now found himself approached from all sides thanks to these events that so shocked the family in Shadworth. The home secretary, Sir Samuel Hoare, lobbied mercilessly by Bertha, at last persuaded Chamberlain to accept the aching need for rescue to reach the Jewish families and their children.

"*Listen to this, Emma,*" said Philip as he sat in the garden of Holt House, though it was already approaching a November dusk of misty grey. "*There has been an edict announcing that, at last, children may come to us. It reads, 'They will be labelled* TRANSMIGRANTS *with a £50 bond required per child, certified as an interim measure.'*"

Philip put the newspaper down and looked at the sky. "Oh God, Emma, *this world is a cruel one. The costs will have to be met by the families of the children themselves unless charities can help them. And the Nazis have threatened to cancel outgoing trains altogether if those who bring them attempt to stay with them. And yet, my love, at least it is good news at its heart, I suppose.*"

He sat back in his chair as if he were utterly weary, and Emma had an acute stab of fear as she looked at him.

He has to be so strong for the school and for all of our children, and I am afraid for him. Will we be able to meet all these dangerous requirements and satisfy the demands they will put on us? Thank God Beth hasn't seen him like this. We have to maintain such a brave face for them all.

The afternoon was wearing on and nearing Beth's return home from the Cranston study group, where she was studying hard to achieve the scholarship she needed for Oxford. Her mother wanted her to keep her faith and optimism alive not only for herself but also for Pieter. At least James was keeping a careful eye on her, and Daisy was her usual irrepressible self who kept Beth from too much introspection.

"*Beth'll be home soon, Philip, and you must put your courage back to greet her.*"

"*Darling, of course I will, but I pray Anatole has not been arrested. I really wish he would write to us so we can be assured he is still under the shelter of this man Israel.*"

A robin landed on a nearby branch and began to sing. The November gloom was already gathering now, but the little bird cocked its head to one side, as if to remind Philip that the garden and the peace engendered there had not deserted him.

And just at that moment, Pieter appeared at the garden gate, holding a letter. His mouth had lost its grim, set look and there was a smile on his face.

"*Emma, Philip, I've had a letter from Anatole, and he is still safe with Wilfrid Israel, though many of the shop employees have been gathered up by SS guards and taken to a camp. Do read it for yourselves. Is Beth home yet? I might walk back up the hill to meet her if not, and you two can peruse it.*"

"*Pieter, my dear,*" exclaimed Emma, giving him a hug. "*That's more than we could hope for. Wait till Beth hears this news. I'm expecting her to walk in at any minute. I'll get you a drink while you wait.*" She looked across at Philip, who had leaned back against his headrest and breathed a sigh of relief. She bent over him and kissed his forehead, mightily relieved herself that Anatole was at least, for the time being, safe.

Pieter didn't have long to wait. As he sipped his homemade ginger beer, the gate banged and a voice called, "*Mother, Daddy, I'm home.*"

"*Welcome, darling,*" said Emma. "*And here is Pieter. Guess what he has brought us?*"

"*A letter?*" She slung her bag onto the floor, eyes widening. "*Is it from Anatole? Oh, let me see it quick. Is he safe?*"

Philip looked across at her before handing her the letter. She took it quickly and began to read it to herself.

Berlin,
20th November,

My dear Pieter,

I write to let you know I am safe and, so far, have managed to keep from being taken to Sachsenhausen camp, like many of Wilfrid's employees. Please, Pieter, let them all at Holt House know this.

It has been a nightmare like no nightmare ever was. The whole shop has been smashed apart and the jewellery I told you about all stolen. All the properties around this Jewish sector are in ruins and huge star signs have been scrawled all over the people's shops with horrid and insulting words about us Jews.

But Mr Israel has refused to be intimidated by it and is using his huge influence and wealth to persuade the commandant at Sachsenhausen to set them free. This has cost him huge amounts of bribe money but, fortunately, the commandant is open to corruption and the hierarchy of the SS has not intervened, so he has been able to release them on the quiet.

Because I have been lodging at the Israel house, I have kept clear, and I cannot tell you how grateful I am to him for his incredible kindness to me and to all the others. Now he is paying for them to leave the country with salaries included.

But another matter of great urgency is preoccupying Wilfrid. He knows the desperate need for the Jewish children to get out of Germany as soon as they are able. Pieter, I feel sure that our school at Shadworth with Philip at the helm will be sure to help with such a rescue. Uncle Frank and Philip are such good friends and they are in touch with Bertha Bracey, I know. She has been in Berlin at great danger to herself, but she is helping organise the gathering of the families to persuade them of the real need to sign for their children to travel on the transports. Wilfrid believes I should act as a chaperone for the children and bring some of them back to our school. It will all have to be planned in minute detail, but if we can pull it off, think what a rescue would mean.

Pieter, I think of them all in Shadworth and long to see you.

For now, in faith that there is hope somewhere in all this,

Your cousin Anatole

Beth shrieked with a mixture of relief and horror at what she was reading. "*Daddy, Daddy, do you think we can do all he wishes? And this means Anatole will come back with the children. Oh, my Daddy, that would be so wonderful.*"

"*Hush, Beth. Of course we will do everything in our power to bring this about. Emma, my love, this is good news, isn't it? Alan, Beatrice and the staff have discussed how we are open to taking as many children as needed into our care, so we are and will be ready.*

"*The dangers of all this lie with others. I pray hard for Wilfrid Israel every night, and Bertha Bracey is also stepping close to the edge of real danger out in Berlin, with all her efforts to persuade the Jewish Women's organisations. As for Anatole, let us hope and pray he manages to accompany them and get home to us.*"

Seeing the streams of tears making their way down Beth's face, Emma hurried to Philip's chair and whispered to him, "*We must keep Beth from despairing and try not to talk so much of the dangers, my darling. Let's try to keep things as normal and steady as we can.*"

He reached up and took her hand, smiling despite his sense of the grim reality of it all. "*Emma, what on Earth would I do without you?*"

Chapter 26

Elizabeth May – A Planned Rescue, 1938

The day Pieter brought us the letter from Anatole will live in my memory for ever. There was such a contrast between my happy home and the pleasure we all took in each other in the peace of Shadworth's fields whilst the sword of Damocles hung over us and those we loved.

The thought of Anatole sharing in the perils of the Jewish people in the home of this Wilfrid Israel and planning to escape to England on one of the trains being allowed grudgingly by the Nazis to leave truly horrified me.

I don't know how I managed to study for my exams for Oxford with very little heart for the project. And yet, I suppose my books were a kind of refuge. Pieter, Daisy and dear James kept me from giving way to my feelings, and Teddy and Ralphie would insist we all played cricket down at the farm at every opportunity.

There came an announcement on the wireless on the twenty-fifth of November that told us of the urgent need for the rescue of the children of the Jewish communities in Europe. It came from Baldwin, who was second to Chamberlain in the coalition government. Father thought he was as guilty as Chamberlain for the appeasement policy, but he did, at least, try for the country to wake up to the glaring needs of the children.

"*I ask you all to come to the aid of victims, not of any catastrophe in the natural world... but of an explosion of man's inhumanity to man.*"

Following this appeal, Viscount Samuel then went on to ask for foster homes for the expected children, and I believe that made it easier for Bertha Bracey to persuade parents to register their children for the transports. At last, the government was waking up to what the Central British Fund for German Jewry was urging them to. And I am very proud that Daddy's school was one of twelve Quaker schools that offered to take the little ones.

As I look back now on those early days of persuasion and preparation, I am told that the number that apparently came through the transports was some 10,000 Jewish children from not only Germany and Austria, but also Czechoslovakia and Poland.

At that time in our lives, it was acutely painful at every turn of the planning. My heart felt there was a leaden weight resting on it from which there was no escape.

And so, November rolled into December, and Daddy heard from Frank that the first train would be leaving from Berlin on the first of December for the Hook of Holland where the children would board ships for Harwich. Once in Harwich, they would be met by volunteers who would accompany them to their various new homes.

That was our moment. I can still see the look on Mother's face as she realised that nothing could ever be quite the same again. It had all been arranged. James and Pieter were to go with Alan Lorimer to meet the travellers from the ship. I desperately wanted to go with them, and I know Daddy found it really difficult to be left behind at school. That was when he felt his disability the worst, and he and I hugged each other very close as we waved them all off.

But my steadfast mother would not allow us to sit fretting, and she sent us to help Beatrice and Edna with the reorganizing of the dormitories so that the kinder could all be together in Ayton House. For those few hours, time went quickly, and then we were back at Holt House.

As I pushed Father through the front door, Mother came to stand before us, her cheeks red from baking cakes all afternoon in preparation for the new visitors.

"There is still a lot to do to make it all ready, and we should try to get down to the farm as soon as we can to help Mary and Florence with the wonderful supper I've no doubt Mary will be preparing for them. We have no idea exactly how many will arrive, but we've counted on thirty. I presume you helped make thirty beds up in Ayton dormitory. Kath is going to hold fort there with Beatrice and Edna."

The rest of the day dragged as no other ever had before. Each minute crawled round, and still it was only three o'clock and no word from James—we were awaiting a call from him from a phone box. Daddy, I know, was beside himself with the waiting. He looked pale and exhausted, and Mother pushed him into the garden to find some rest from the anxiety hanging on us.

Then, at long, long last, the telephone rang.

"*Philip*," James said, "*we are catching the seven-thirty train out of St Pancras, due to arrive at Shadworth around eleven. The children are in our hands, safe and sound but absolutely exhausted and some inconsolable. Philip, God help us in this last leg. I look forward to when we unload them all into your and Emma's hands. I must hasten back to Alan and Pieter. Please be there, my friend."*

I cannot describe the way I felt as the evening drew closer and closer to the time to go down to Shadworth Station to meet them all. How would it be? What would the children be feeling? How would they understand our English? I knew Pieter would be there to translate and I had a smattering of German from earlier language classes, but it was very little. I had not realised that Daddy knew a little German from some of his friends at university.

The worst was the way my teeth kept chattering with anxiety and my legs felt as if they didn't belong to me. And yet, I put on my favourite skirt and the jumper Kath had given me for my birthday.

Mother rang the school to let Beatrice know they would be soon with us as 11 p.m. drew nearer. Kath and Edna were to await the young ones back at school. These children were to be warmly welcomed at the farm, though Mother was afraid they would be too exhausted to take it all in or even to eat. And of course, of great importance was Ned, who was to drive the farm charabanc to collect everyone.

"Come, my love. Let's trust God to be with us and to give us courage and a little bit of wisdom in greeting these blessed youngsters."

Daddy smiled at me, and I knew he was admiring the way I looked. Then he took Mother's hand, and she bent and kissed him as she turned to push his wheelchair down to the station.

The sky was a clear azure and there were myriads of stars up there, twinkling down on us as a benediction on all of it. My teeth stopped chattering, and I looked up, reassured somehow that all would be well.

Chapter 27

1938

On the station platform, Philip looked up at his wife. "*Emma, it is a wonderful thing that those who disembark the train will now be making special new memories of this place. But now, let's welcome all those who will gather here tonight.*"

Philip and Emma shared a look as they thought back to their own special memories of this place.

"*And, Emma*"—he beckoned for her to come closer, and she leaned down so that he could whisper in her ear—"*I did not say what else James told me so as to keep it a surprise for Beth, but Anatole is with them.*" Philip's voice rose with excitement. "*He hid in the luggage compartment of the guard's van, undetected in Berlin, and then boarded ship at Hook of Holland as just another traveller. Now, at last, he can relax and enjoy his homecoming.*"

"*Philip, Philip,*" Emma said, struggling to keep her voice quiet due to the happy news. "*That's just wonderful. How could you not tell me? That dear, brave young man. And to think he will be with us soon.*" She clapped her hands as Beth turned to look at them enquiringly.

"*Hush, darling. Keep the surprise for her.*"

They heard the train chuffing slowly over the points just outside the station, and the steam from its funnel drifted gently towards them. Then, with a surge, the huge engine pulled into the platform with a hiss of heat. They watched as windows within the train slid down and some heads hung out. James was peering out and waving at the group on the platform and then Alan's head appeared. Faces were looking out of the window—some with tired eyes drooping closed, others with eager looks.

Philip turned to greet Alan and Pieter as they stepped from the train, Pieter with a little one each side holding tight to him. At the same moment, James stepped out over the high step, and behind him, a tall dark-haired man appeared, slender and handsome.

"*Beth*," shouted James. "*Look who I've brought home to you*."

James and the young man walked together towards the little group awaiting them, and Beth's eyes were suddenly blurred with tears as she gasped.

"*Anatole, oh, Anatole. Is it truly you?*"

James' companion began to run towards them. He swung Beth off her feet and whirled her round as if she were still a little girl. "*My little sister. Beth, how glad I am to see you all.*"

She hid her face in his shoulder and took in the familiar smell of him that she somehow still found comforting despite the tinge of sweat from his travelling. He put her back down onto her feet and turned to greet Philip and Emma.

"*My dear boy*," said Philip as Anatole bent to grasp his hand.

Emma simply opened her arms to him and embraced him with all the love she had held in her heart for so long, in the weary breadth of time that had passed since he left.

Ned strode onto the platform and looked with wonder at the gathered assembly. "*Taxi*," he called out, smiling.

Suddenly, it was as if the tired children woke up to the realisation that here was indeed someone whom everyone on the platform was greeting with joy. At last, they felt that they had reached a place of safety. The big man, the taxi driver, was grinning and the man in the funny wheeled chair was lovingly smiling at them. The girl and the lady seemed to know their companion, Anatole, so it must be alright.

Pieter led each child to Philip, and Emma and Beth counted them as they gave their names. Twenty-two children in all with some very young ones who were clinging to James' hands, some no older than Ralphie or Teddy and some already nearing their teenage years. Beth felt for each one as they clutched their teddies and their toys, their bags slung over their shoulders and their names pinned on them.

At least they've got warm coats, thought Emma. She was pleased, for it was a winter's night and getting very late and colder by the minute. Then sadness hit her, as she could see these children were loved and it must have felt impossible for their parents to send them on their way despite knowing the need to.

"*Come, everyone, onto the charabanc now*," called out Alan Lorimer, and one by one, they climbed up onto the old farm vehicle. "*Time to get some food into you.*"

He heaved Philip's chair up onto the truck, and Ned, at the wheel, opened the throttle, and the engine lurched back into life.

Beth squeezed in beside Anatole, and he looked down at her with a look of relief, but also of some puzzlement. Something had changed, and he sat very still as he considered it and contemplated exactly what that was. Beth looked back at him, enjoying the ride and wishing she could simply stay there on the charabanc, soaking up the sense of his presence at last after so long.

When they reached the farm, there stood Mary with Florence, Daisy and Teddy close beside her.

"*Welcome to you all*," said Daisy.

Ned leapt off the driver's seat to embrace his daughter and wife. Beatrice cried out with relief to see Alan safe at last and home to her after his rescue mission. Pieter ran to Daisy, and she hugged him with a loving smile.

"*Here they all are, Florence*," said Ned. "*They are exhausted after the long journey, so let's get them fed as soon as we can, then I can drive them up to their new home at school. Your father is very weary but just as determined as ever.*"

Emma made her way to Mary's side. "*Let's go, Mary. Have you made soup? They're so tired, I reckon that's all they'll need till tomorrow. Bless them, so bereft of their parents. We have so much work to do to make them happy again.*"

And so, the supper proceeded despite the fact that it was already well past midnight. Alan, James and Pieter wolfed down the delicious steaming hot tomato soup, but the children and Anatole dipped the chunks of homemade bread delicately into their bowls.

"*Don't worry, my loves*," said Philip, noticing Emma and Beth's anxious faces, "*you'll see the difference when they wake up for breakfast.*"

And at that, he clapped for attention and spoke to the gathered party, Pieter, beside him, translating as he went. "*Children—kinder—you are so welcome to our home here. Do not be afraid anymore; you will find only kindness awaits you and we are so very pleased to have you.*"

Two of the older children began to clap him, and they all let out a somewhat tired cheer. Philip looked across at Emma, who was clapping him too, and he smiled an embarrassed smile.

"*But now, we must beg our friend* Ned *to escort you all to your waiting beds. Can you line up and each thank* Mary *and* Florence *for the delicious supper? Then we should get you to the charabanc and on.*"

Anatole was watching Beth's face curiously. He turned towards her intently as she pushed a stray chestnut curl behind her ear.

"*What is it,* Anatole?" she whispered.

"*Only that, Beth, you have transformed in my absence. I am meeting tonight not my dear little sister, but such a lovely, grown-up girl. I have to allow my thinking to refigure. Beth, let me look at you properly.*" Anatole took her face in both hands, pushed away the wayward curls that were falling over her face and very gently kissed her forehead.

Beth smiled and looked into his gaunt, dark face. A surge of pride, unexpected and new, surprised her and thrilled her with a quiet joy.

"*While I've been missing you,* Anatole, *I seem to have grown up a good deal. But to see you now safe and really here is something like a dream that I don't want to wake up from.*"

"*My dear girl, you need not wake up yet. Let's walk up the lane and let the charabanc go ahead. Let's pretend I've just met you out of school.*"

"*But,* Anatole, *we can't.*" She shook her head and looked at all the new faces. "*You really must accompany the children to school. They know you, as well as James, Alan and Pieter, much better than all of us. You can't just leave them with the others."*

"Beth, my Beth, I had forgotten your almighty conscience. And you are, of course, right. Forgive me." He remained staring into her eyes, seemingly impressed with her morals rather than disappointed. Then he looked over her shoulder and leaned back. *"And here is Emma come to take you away from me."*

Emma had been anxiously watching the two of them and could see the latent, unspoken emotion that was aching to emerge. Philip had gone ahead to get the children onto the carriage, so she could not share this rather special realisation with him at that moment, but she knew she must help them to be more patient and to take time to explore what was happening. She was aware that her beloved Beth was still only seventeen, while Anatole was twenty. She also knew the passion Beth had felt for him for so long.

James strode up to them and hustled them to follow him to the waiting charabanc. *"Come on, Anatole, the children are looking for you. Beth, your father is waiting for you."*

As he spoke, he saw the look on Emma's face and, smiling reassuringly at her, took her arm and led them to the bus. Emma was relieved and made up her mind to leave this new situation until tomorrow.

Beth watched as Anatole got on, the children all cheering him. She had to smile at seeing how much the children had learned to rely on him as their chaperone all the way from Berlin.

"Mother, I am so happy that he is safely here."

"Let's talk about this tomorrow, Beth."

Beth threw herself into the care of the newcomers, but James stopped the Manners family from boarding.

"No, *you need not come this last stretch. Trust us to get them safely stored up at school. You are done in and should sleep. Philip, you mustn't overdo your strength. Please don't object. It's best you three stay.*"

"*James, let me come,*" begged Beth, looking past him at Anatole, who winked at her as he boarded the bus and raised his hand in a mock salute.

But James shook his head firmly at her. "*Look at your father, Beth, he is absolutely exhausted. You and Mother must get him home to his rest. Can't you trust me to look after them all till tomorrow?*"

He turned from them and climbed up to where Ned, at the wheel, was waiting for him. To Beth, this seemed painfully ruthless.

Philip, with a resigned sigh, looked up at his wife and nodded. "He's *right, my dears. Tomorrow is another day.*"

Many of the children had fallen fast asleep, so it was a heavy task to wake them sufficiently to unload them into Kath and Edna's waiting arms. One by one, they followed sleepily as Beatrice led the way with Alan close beside her. She herself was so very glad to see him safely returned from the long journey back from Harwich and had confided in Kath that she felt somewhat overawed at the huge responsibility the school was embarking on.

"*I have to say, though it's the last thing I would have wanted to, Kath, that it's a very good job Alan and I couldn't have children. At least I can now consider these young ones as our family, and God help us to make this thing work.*"

Kath smiled with sad understanding and squeezed Beatrice's hand. They at last reached the dormitory in Ayton House where, between them, they helped each child into their own bed. There was much sorting out to do during the next few days—the children's ages varied, so they would need to be divided into ages before finally getting their own sleeping spaces—but at that moment, late in the night as it now was, the dormitory's beds looked white and pristine, so neatly prepared by Edna and the others. There was something very satisfactory about the sight of the tousled heads on the clean pillows safe at last.

The three women and Alan left them asleep and shooed the others to go home themselves and try to sleep for the little time that was left of the night. Pieter took Anatole's arm and led him to his own bedroom, where he soon managed to make up an impromptu bed for him on his sofa. Finally, Ned and James rumbled home on the empty charabanc.

Chapter 28

Elizabeth May – My Changing World, December 1938

As I look back now, I see the task we had set ourselves in all its dimensions, all these children, unknown as yet to us.

I felt keenly how *they* must be feeling, bereft of all they had known up to that time. And such a time—a time of fearful terror, as the Nazi brigades of hate terrorised the streets and dragged many of their Jewish neighbours out of their houses, smashing their way with ruthless violence. What if they came for their home next? What if they dragged their parents away? And who could save them?

But now, after the long journey by rail and sea and, at last, by the funny old tractor in which the kindly man had picked them up, they found themselves in such clean, white rows of beds with gentle people showing them their new home. They must have almost thought they were dreaming.

But equally, I felt for my beloved friends, for Beatrice and Alan, in charge still at school with all the other pupils to teach and manage. We had undertaken an overwhelming task and yet we were rejoicing that we had achieved the great journey. My darling daddy and mother were so proud that we all would now share in making them feel the pleasure of freedom and safety here with us.

But best of all for me was the sight of Anatole and the amazing joy that woke in me as he kissed me. I had loved him for so long in the depths of my youthful heart. There he was, safe at last, but then I saw the dark shadows under his eyes, his too-slender waist, how tall he had grown in that fearful adventure he had survived. And all I wanted was to walk with him, hear all about it and hold his hand once again.

Yet I thought I had noticed a new understanding in his eyes as he kissed my forehead. Oh my, I could hardly wait for the morning to come.

James arrived to pick Daddy and Mother up early. He grinned at me as I leapt onto the back seat beside Mother. He knew me far too well and understood, I think, what was going on in my head.

We pulled up in the school drive and immediately saw the lines of children all being sorted into age groups by Beatrice and Pieter. It struck me how little some of them were, and I felt a huge pang of sympathy for them, for they still looked forlorn, clutching their cuddly toys.

Anatole was with them, checking their names, and he was holding a little one in his arms. He brought her over to me, smiling the smile I know he reserved for me. How I loved him then.

"Beth, this is Suzi. She's only four years old. Her twin, Heinz, is with Kath over there. Can you retrieve him for me? Suzi is fretting for him." I ran over to Kath, who was wiping the little boy's tears away with her hanky and talking gently to him.

"Heinz, will you come with me to find your sister?" I held out my hand to him, and he took it so trustingly

that my heart melted. I had no clue whether it was my words he understood or the gesture. He was such a dear, gentle little soul, and as his sister saw him, she let go of Anatole's hand and ran to us. Anatole smiled at me but had no choice but to continue collecting the children and delivering them to Alan. Daddy was by now next to Alan in his wheelchair and greeting each child as they came up to them both. He spoke to them haltingly in German. I could see their pleasure that this was their own language.

It was a marathon task, but by lunchtime, all the children had been allotted to their different dormitories. Edna took charge of the seven older ones to go with her to Fox House, while Beatrice was to be a mother to the six eight- and nine-year-olds. I cannot tell you how relieved I was to see my sister Florence with Laura and Daisy. They had all cycled up to school to find us.

I hurried over to Florence as she leaned her bike against a wall. "*Oh, Florrie, it feels a bit overwhelming. How can we manage to make them happy? I cannot bear for them to be afraid or to sicken for home.*"

"*Beth, you must trust Mother and Philip to have it all in hand. We are to take the four six-year-olds back with us to the farm, and Mother is all set to take the littlest ones home with you to Holt House. You will have those dear little twins with you and three others, who are all five. I can't think of anywhere better for them but with Mother, and the farm will be a place of pleasure and safety for everyone. You can be sure Grandma Tempest and I will look after those six-year-olds.*"

My father wheeled his chair up to us and took both my hands in his. I'm sure he must have been eavesdropping.

"My darling Beth, don't look so anxious. We have placed them all in safe keeping and we will make a sanctuary for them. I'm going to gather them all into the chapel with Alan after lunch and reassure them there that they are most welcome. I've asked Pieter to say a Jewish prayer for them there, one that will be familiar to them and remind them they are part of God's house whenever they come into our school meeting house. Our Quaker silence will make this easy for them."

Daddy's very calm and quiet authority reassured me, and together, we all filed into the school canteen. There, of course, lunch was proceeding as usual with throngs of the ordinary students tucking into the hearty winter casserole prepared by Cook. They were very curious to see the newcomers, whose arrival Daddy had already prepared them for. He had warned them not to stare and to be as welcoming as they could, to make this advent comfortable. They were true to his instruction, much to my inner relief, and some of the sixth formers came up to the children and shook their hands, offering warm smiles.

Daddy told me that night how proud he was of his students. Now it was up to Beatrice, Edna and Laura, with the other more junior staff, to enfold them into the life of the school, though they were too young to have lessons like the older ones. Pieter and Laura had outlined a programme of learning for them, including the vastly important language learning. I especially thanked God for Pieter that day. I knew his capabilities would not let him down, and with Laura by his side, he would manage the challenge.

I had hardly been able to get a word with Anatole all through this long day; he had been taken over by the twins, who were so attached to him. But, when at last the afternoon wore on, Mother and Daddy gathered the littlest ones, who were coming home with us. James, by some miracle, got them all in the back of his car with Mother, with Daddy in the front.

"*Beth, do you mind walking home, my dear? Maybe Anatole can walk down with you.*" James smiled as he got into the driver's seat. Dear James, he knew me oh so well.

As they drove away, I found Anatole by my side.

"*Shall we pretend you are still being met out of school, Bethy? Let's take a walk down memory lane, shall we?*"

He took my hand tightly in his as we made our way through the school gates to the fingerpost that led to Low Shadworth. It was a winter afternoon and the sky had already darkened. The streetlamps were flickering and the rooks were gathering in the tall elms as we walked. As we approached home, Anatole walked on past the house and onto Long Lane.

"*Beth, I can see you have grown up while I have been away. Oh, Beth, I have seen so much terror, so much horror, such unspeakable things the Nazis have done, yet here you are, like a calm and quiet haven, all turned into a woman.*"

He stopped short and turned to look at my face. I think the tears were running down it as I looked back at him. He tilted my chin and suddenly, very gently, kissed my lips. I could hardly believe my dream of him actually coming true. I'd felt butterflies before, but it was as if each butterfly inside me had gained extra wings.

"Anatole, words can't quite frame what I feel. I have prayed and prayed for you to come back safely, and now here you are at last. Anatole, are you sure about this?"

He laughed at me in the old teasing way he used to have, then grasped hold of me tightly and kissed me again, not so gently, and I, Elizabeth May, returned his kiss with all the fervour of the years of longing.

"My God, Beth, you really have grown up."

Once again, he took my hand and strode off further down the lane, as if he had to register what had happened as he walked. He was full of energy and almost skipped along with me in his wake.

"Look, Beth, look. Even the glowworms in the hedgerows are twinkling at us, and see, the stars are out. The night is clear and the world belongs to you and me, my dear sweet Beth."

As we walked, he told me all about what had happened to him. He slowed down and shivered as he told how he had found that his parents had been sent off to Dachau and had tried to find a way to see them there, only to be stopped by the guards who patrolled the outskirts of it with pistols at the ready. He had returned to the city, completely bereft, hungry and desperate, moreover in huge danger as a Jew on the streets.

I stopped and clasped him tightly to myself, lifting my head to kiss him again. For me, such sweet and incredible delight, though his whole body was shaking with the memory.

"My dear, you must not give up hope that they will survive and be returned to you. Surely Hitler's henchmen cannot get away with their evil much longer."

"My Bethy, things are far further on than you can dream of. Your father and Uncle Frank know the score, I believe, and that's why Philip has tried so hard to help Bertha Bracey and the others to get the Jewish children to safety."

Then he told me about how ill he had been, in hospital with pneumonia, and how he had been rescued from it all by this man, Wilfrid Israel. As he named him, he stopped short and looked at me again.

"Beth, such a wonderful man. He took me in and put me back on my feet. His kindness was so very like that of your mother and daddy. And when I was strong enough, he gave me a job in his amazing emporium, the N. Israel store, so famous in Berlin, in the face of the Nazi threat. Beth, I wrote you all about it. Did you get the letter?"

"I did indeed, my dear, and cannot thank the man enough for what he did. But, Anatole, surely he himself must be in danger at every minute. You wrote that all his staff were Jewish by his deliberate choice. How can this be?"

"They are safe, Beth. He bribed the corrupt Nazis with large amounts of his money and then packed his people off to safety out of Germany. And now he has worked with Bertha Bracey to enable the Kindertransport to go ahead. And here I am, sent by Wilfrid, to accompany them. Beth, my dear, I shall never be out of his debt."

We were alone on the quiet country lane but for a silent fox who crept past us as we stood. The darkness was lit up by the stars above us, and I shivered with the icy cold of the winter evening.

Anatole took off his coat and wrapped it round my shoulders. "*We must head back, sweetheart. Philip and Emma will be anxious about you, wondering where you have got to. But they know you are with me."*

"You're right, I mustn't frighten them. Daddy won't be comfortable till he sees me, and Mother will be keeping busy in the kitchen. But they will have been working hard to settle the little ones in. Oh God, Anatole, I pray we can manage this incredible challenge that lies ahead."

Anatole laughed, put his arm around me and we strode off together back up Long Lane.

At last, we saw the lights of Holt House ahead and then finally we saw Father's wheelchair at the gate. He was watching for us, his hands gripping the sides of his chair.

"Beth, Anatole, you had us worried. You'll catch your death of cold, Anatole, without your coat. Come in, the two of you, this minute," said Father, frowning at me before wheeling himself to the door. My heart missed a beat.

"Daddy, Daddy, please don't be angry. You knew we had a lot to catch up on, so we just carried on up Long Lane for a little while."

Mother appeared at the door and held it open for Daddy, and we followed. Daddy shook his head at Mother as she folded her arms and looked at the two of us.

"Philip, calm down, they are perfectly safe, and, Philip, have you forgotten how it was for us all those years ago? Come and get warm now, you two."

Anatole looked at Father then and knelt beside his chair. *"Philip, forgive me. You know what an irresponsible wretch I am and how many times you have had me beg your pardon. But this time, I know you'll forgive me because Beth and I needed the chance to be together and talk together. And you know how much I have always cared for her. Philip?"*

Daddy sighed and simply put his hand on Anatole's bent head. "*Anatole, you haven't changed since the days when you climbed the school tower and did any number of irresponsible things. But I know and can see in Beth's face that she is the happiest I have seen her for months. She has awaited your return so anxiously, and who am I, her poor father, to spoil that reunion? You can see my wife is so much more at peace with this, as I should be. But, Anatole, remember she's only seventeen, so treat her very gently, please.*"

Daddy had tears in his eyes, and Mother and I hurried to his side as Anatole rose to his feet. I couldn't bear for Father to hurt on my behalf; I wanted him to know my happiness. Mother just took my hand and pressed it hard before bending down to kiss Father's forehead. Anatole gazed at me, smiling. There was a memory inside us both that couldn't be repressed. Our kiss had sealed a bargain between us that was irrevocable.

And so the night drew on, and Anatole, having received the affirmation he needed from my father, knew he must head back to school to sleep. Mother made him a hot cocoa to set him on the way, and I walked him to the gate to say goodbye. My dear daddy had given me a reassuring nod as I looked at him for his approval.

Anatole took me in his arms at the gate and kissed me again in such a tender, loving way.

"*Goodnight, my sweet Beth. Let's make every moment count now that we are at last back together.*"

And with that, he strode off up the hill back towards school. I turned to find Mother beside me, and she gave me one of her loving hugs and led me back indoors to Daddy, whose arms were open to us both. The adventure had truly begun.

Chapter 29

1938

Philip gazed at Emma ruefully, and she gazed back, sighing. The fire flickered and lit up the photographs she had arranged on the old dresser, the inviting armchair with its stacked cushions, the mantlepiece and the candlesticks on it that Emma polished to a sheen every week. It was a room redolent with memories, comforting and welcoming. The two were at last able to share their feelings about the hugely busy day they had just lived through and the new responsibility of the five little ones asleep upstairs.

Elizabeth had retired to bed, not without peeping in at the large upper room where the five little ones were sleeping soundly. She had to smile at the five neat beds all in a row, so neatly made up for them by her mother. Soon, she herself was fast asleep, exhausted by the wonderful excitement of her reunion with Anatole.

"*My darling wife, how are we to protect our daughter from the pain she will have to bear now they have acknowledged their feelings? I know that eventually, when things have calmed down a little, Anatole will feel called back to Berlin and Bethy will find that terribly hard.*"

"Philip, we can't be forever worrying about what might happen. Dearest, you remember how you and I learned to take one day at a time?"

"I do, and how agonising it was, Emma. I know you're right and I must let be. But nothing I have ever had to endure can have been any worse than what I'm feeling now for Beth."

Emma knelt by Philip's chair and laid her head on his knee. He stroked her hair and smiled down at her.

"My love, I know between us we can do this. We have to see it through, and I know we cannot legislate for her. But, Emma, I dearly want her to pass her Highers and perhaps get a place at Oxford. Though with all the news from Frank about Hitler's evil intentions, who knows what the summer will bring."

"Philip, we've got an enormous challenge in front of us to look after these youngsters. Let's try now to make a Christmas for everyone in the old-fashioned way. Darling, it's my birthday just before and then George's just after. I pray George can come home for it. Let all this help us to forget our fears and look to better things."

Philip laughed. *"Emma, what would I be without you?"*

And so they retired to sleep and soon awoke to the cries of one of the twins, who had woken early and begun to fret for her mother. That put courage afresh into them both as they took the little one down to the cosy parlour and wiped her tears to assure her that she was safe with them. Philip thanked God he could speak a little German to them.

Little Suzi looked up at Philip. *"Why do you ride in your chair? Why don't you just stand up?"* she spoke in German.

Philip was able to explain in halting German what had happened to his leg.

She cheered up and reached up to sit on his knee. "*I shall tell my brother all about it*," she said, suddenly bright and alert.

This wakefulness from the little ones was to last well into the new year. At some point in the following weeks, every child woke like Suzi, fresh from nightmares about their departure, pulled from the arms of their mothers and into the waiting train, overlooked by Nazi soldiers with guns. The Kindertransports were watched very carefully by Hitler's minions.

But, of course, the implications of this for the Holt household were wearisome. Emma sometimes simply brought them into her big bed to snuggle beside herself and Philip until they soothed back to sleep. Sometimes Beth took a turn when she could see her parents were exhausted and brought them down to the warm kitchen, sitting them on her lap and singing to them. Very gradually, they all began to feel comfortable and confident in their new home, their English developed and the Manners took them to their hearts. But the strain of the interrupted nights told on Emma, and Philip worried about her increasingly.

"*One day at a time, Lord Jesus*," he would say to her as she strove to fulfil every duty at top speed.

James and he would drive off up to school each morning as December took hold and the end of school term drew nearer. Philip hated that he had to leave her. Beth would hurry off to Cranston after studying into the early hours for her Highers and then share in the night watches with whichever child needed reassurance.

But Emma had to get them into their clothes and have them breakfasted ready for the short walk to the little school, to which, in earlier days, she had accompanied George and then Elizabeth. The head there was kindness itself in dealing with the situation, and Emma knew she was delivering them into safe and loving hands. They vied with each other to be the two who held Emma's hands as they walked in a little cluster and, as time went on, began lifting their little faces for Emma's kiss before letting go and following the head through the school door.

Teddy, now aged ten, had won them over very quickly, and they had got over their initial fears. Laura would appear with Ralph, also ten, and the two big boys would scamper into school, leading the way delightedly.

That always left Emma with Florence and Laura to share their inmost feelings, albeit briefly, for Laura was hastening up to her post at Philip's school and Florence back to the hard graft awaiting her at the farm.

Florence noticed the shadows that were darkening each day under Emma's eyes and the wrinkles that looked as though they were deepening in her face. "*Mother, how are you? You look done in.*"

"*Emma, let the children come to tea with Will and me tonight so you and Philip can have some quiet time,*" Laura added.

"*Oh, my dears, I'm alright. These nights will get easier as they settle in with us. You have quite enough to do, my dear Laura, dealing with the bigger ones up at school. How is Pieter doing?*"

Laura smiled at the question. "*Emma, he thrives on the task. He is loving teaching them our language and he cares for them all so well. I don't know how I would manage without him. But I must hurry now, or I shall be late.*" She blew a kiss at them as she hastened off with a wave.

They waved back.

"*What I dearly want is for us all to celebrate Christmas at Holt House,*" said Emma. "*I am determined these dear souls will enjoy an English Christmas despite everything.*"

"*Do you think George will be able to make it, Mum?*" asked Florence. "*Our girls would be enchanted if he came.*"

"*We are praying he can, my love. But we must be patient.*"

Chapter 30

Christmas 1938

Emma's birthday, just before Christmas, was a quiet affair down at Tempests' Farm, presided over by Mary and Florence. The children from Holt House joined with the little ones in the care of the farm, and Teddy and Ralph organised games to occupy them while the grownups celebrated Emma's day around the laden kitchen table. Daisy had baked a delicious chocolate cake in Emma's honour and James was there too as part of the little family. Emma blushed with pleasure and relief as Philip raised a toast to her as the one who was his most dear companion and comforter of them all. Beth whisked away a thankful tear at her father's words, hiding her face in his shoulder.

But Christmas, of course, coincided with George's twenty-fourth birthday, and every member of the Manners family held its breath in anticipation of Christmas day, with the hope of George's homecoming. Ned had provided the turkey and all the stuffings had been cooked in advance. The kitchen at Holt House was redolent with the aroma of Christmas preparations.

Pieter had brought the little German children from school, and they were now under Beth's care. They had each taken a turn at stirring the pudding and making their wishes, so they were taking an especial interest in the steaming pan that contained it.

Anatole had arrived early on Christmas Eve to join in with the festivities and entertain the little ones. Anatole took Beth's hand and led her to the Christmas tree, adorned so beautifully by Laura, with Ralph and Will, for, as Will proclaimed, "*The Christmas tree must be decorated by me, as it's always been my job since the world began.*"

Emma and Laura had hugged each other at these words, seeing a glimpse of the old relaxed Will they loved.

"*Look, Beth,*" whispered Anatole as they stood looking up at its splendour, "*the star on the top is reflecting the light and shining out almost as if it is lit up from within. Beth, you are the star that is reflecting the light for me, to keep me strong, to keep me hopeful despite all we are facing. You, my Beth, are lit up from within with all the love your parents have given you, and I can't believe you're now allowing me to share it.*"

Beth gasped at the huge and awesome responsibility she had to fulfil to keep this vision alive for Anatole, to return his love so wonderfully given, and to which she had given her love. He bent and kissed her, though he knew quite well they were being observed by everyone. And she returned the kiss very sweetly, then hurried over to her father, who was sitting in his wheelchair quietly enjoying all the proceedings.

"*Daddy, is it alright with you?*"

"*My darling, you need not ask. You know Mother and I only want what makes you happy. All I ask is for you to take care and tread softly, for the times are dangerous ones.*"

Beth leaned down and kissed his forehead. James, watching, smiled to himself, then, suddenly and surprisingly, found himself shivering.

But at that, there was a knock at the door and a very loud voice called out, "Is *anyone here expecting anyone else tonight?*"

"*George*," screamed Emma and Daisy. "*George*." And in strode their dearly beloved boy, smart as paint in his RAF uniform, now a fully-fledged officer.

Each of them hugged him whilst the little German children looked on in awe.

Little Suzi, already best of friends with Philip, ran to him. "*Who could this be?*"

"*Why, darling, this is the rather splendid young officer who once snuggled in my bed when he was as small as you. This is our grandson, George, and you can see how pleased everyone is to greet him.*"

Philip called the other little ones to come and be introduced to this newcomer. They all gathered round George, and he grinned at Daisy, who was thrilled to have him home. Then, solemnly, he shook hands with each of them as they squealed with pleasure.

"*George*." Emma smiled. "*You have made our Christmas complete and you have so much to catch up with us all. Sit down here on the old settee and tell your family all about it.*"

And so Christmas at Holt House was celebrated. It was a very happy gathering that sat around the huge dining table with both leaves extended, covered in a holly-embroidered cloth. The little ones had their own table at the side, where they sat entranced, hardly believing the spread that Emma with Mary and Laura had prepared. Turkey and chestnut and sage stuffings, baby sausages, roasted potatoes, delicious turkey gravy and shiny green sprouts, followed by Christmas pudding in flames from the rum all lit up. Throughout it all, Daisy sat as close to George as she could.

As for Beth, Anatole made sure he was right beside her at dinner and surreptitiously took her hand under the table. She slid her fingers in between his so they were locked together, though even they had to let go when the turkey feast appeared on the plates before them. George regarded this finger paddling with some astonishment, for he had missed the impact that Anatole's return had caused.

Later, Philip took him to one side to explain what had happened between them.

"*Philip*," answered George, "*we must let them be free to explore their relationship. It was brewing, I know, the minute Beth set eyes on the young scamp who came back with you all those years ago.*" He stood in a pondering silence for a moment and then gasped. "*Was it really four years ago? Oh, Philip, how time moves us on. And here I am, fully fledged at last and ready, I do believe, for whatever Hitler may have in store for us. And remember, Philip, Beth knows she is surrounded by love, and your love for her keeps her secure and confident.*"

"*My dear boy, wise words from you and a timely word for this over-protective father. Thank you for them. Emma holds me fast, you know, and won't let me cage Beth in. Your grandma has always been the guiding light for me.*"

"*I know it, and for me too. But, Philip, whatever would I do without you both?*"

Philip laughed, and the two returned from their tete-a-tete to join in with the party. Pieter had noticed their absence and he too took George to one side to share his own feelings with him. The two of them leaned into each other as they talked, Pieter spilling out some of his thoughts and fears for his family so far away. The two of them had grown together through the years, and George had been very pleased that Pieter had found his own niche, teaching at Philip's school. He knew Pieter had wanted to take up training in the RAF, as he had done, but could now feel very glad that Pieter was happy.

"*The arrival of the kinder has been transformational for me, George*," confided Pieter. "*I love teaching the teenagers anyway at school and working with Will's Laura is a real pleasure, but to have these much younger ones in my care is quite special. I can speak my own language with them, though I am their English teacher. Ironic, isn't it? They are doing so well, George, and I can see a new hope coming into their eyes as they settle and learn. I am very grateful for this chance to do some good for them.*"

"*I am so pleased for you, Pieter. I do believe the children have helped Philip too. He really feels now he is playing a worthwhile part in all the grim reality of our time. Who knows, Pieter, what will happen next?*" George looked around the room, so beloved by him through all his growing up and knew he could and did rely on it always being, for him, the place of safety and comfort, whatever lay ahead. "*But also, Pieter, remember I am relying on you to make sure Anatole does not break my dear Beth's heart.*"

"*Have no fear, George, I will. And I have James at my side in this. No one adores her more than James.*"

They returned to the festivities, relieved and pleased that their old comradeship was not lost. And so at last, the evening came to a close.

Anatole and Beth tucked the little ones into bed whilst Philip and Emma saw off all the other family members, all laden with the leftover goodies to take back to their various homes. George retired to his old bedroom at the house, with a huge sigh of nostalgia. Anatole was last to leave for the school with Pieter, but he took Beth into the garden to give her his goodbye kiss. She clung to him as if she would never let him go, and he tilted her chin up to him with a smile on his lips as he pushed the wisps of hair from her forehead and hugged her close in return.

As the old year turned into the new and 1939 dawned, none of them knew how different the world would look before another new year came in.

Chapter 31

1939

In the ensuing weeks, term rolled on as the older boys began serious study for School Certificate and Highers, though to the accompaniment of echoing laughter from the Kindertransport children enjoying outdoor sports. The winter snows made snowballing and snowman building a particular pleasure as January and February brought the winter storms. Beth struggled to catch Turton's bus through deepening snow and often stayed late into the dark afternoons, studying hard for her Highers. Her ambition to get a place at Oxford had not died, and this gave her parents relief and pleasure.

For that short time, whilst Anatole was acting as helper with the children, she blossomed. Her cheeks grew rosier, her work improved, her eyes shone with the anticipation of Anatole once more waiting for her at the bus stop for home before accompanying her on a slow walk to Holt House. This was, of course, after his childcare duties and language teaching with Pieter. Emma invariably made him join them with the little ones around the tea table, always laden with her baking. Of course, the youngsters all greeted him with delight and gathered round him to show him what they had drawn or written that day.

James would bring Philip home later, after the day teaching the upper school classes his beloved literature, whilst Alan took them through the exigencies of calculus in the next classroom. Emma would always greet them both with joy, as if the very sight of Philip restored her energy day by day. He never commented on Anatole's presence; instead, he had determined to let Beth savour the love she was sharing with him despite his fears for her youth. He and Emma had struggled so much in the long years of abstinence, maintaining their care for Jack and indeed also for Harriet, so he could not bear to spoil the sweetness of love given and returned for Beth.

But into this idyll of day-by-day pleasures came letters to draw them all back to the dangers and indeed horrors of the outside world.

After Beth had left for Cranston and the little ones had gone to their school, Emma and Philip were left alone as the early mail arrived.

Houses of Parliament,
Westminster
15th March, 1939

Philip Manners
Holt House
Shadworth
My dear Philip and Emma,

I almost hesitate to write to you to interrupt the invaluable work you are doing in Shadworth for the children, not to mention Pieter and Anatole.

On that personal note, I must tell you that I have heard news that does not come as a surprise but reduces me to despair. Franz has written to tell me that his beloved Esther, her father and her brother, Otto, with his wife Hilke, have all been taken from Dachau to another concentration camp near

Weimar, named Buchenwald. Here, many Jews were brought after Kristallnacht and it has a record of being a most brutal regime. Philip, this is heart-breaking news for the two boys, as it is for me. You will have to break it to them as gently as I know you will.

Furthermore, you will have watched with increasing horror, I know, Hitler's seizure of the Sudetenland. But he is not stopping there. It is believed he now has his sights on the rest of Czechoslovakia. Chamberlain's bit of paper is rendered meaningless, as we already anticipated. This is unconscionable, my friends.

Philip stopped and gave out a cry of fury.

"*Philip, what will it mean? And for our boys, Philip?*"

Emma could hardly bear to hear yet another piece of damaging news. Indeed her hand was trembling so much she could barely take the letter from him.

"*My darling, we must read the rest. But this will threaten Poland, and our people cannot ignore this blatant aggression.*"

They returned to Frank's letter.

You and I know this puts Poland very much at risk. Our government has joined with France to issue Herr Hitler with an ultimatum. If he advances his troops any further, we guarantee armed assistance to the Poles.

You can see why I do not enjoy writing to you today. My dear friends, we shall speak further on this matter.

As ever, I send you my very best wishes and love. My heart goes out to the boys. And who knows what is happening at this very moment to the kinder's parents.

I am, yours sincerely,

Frank

Philip groaned and pushed his hair back from his forehead in despair—a gesture Emma was used to seeing whenever he was overwrought with troubles. "*I will call the two boys into my study today. I must break this news to them very, very gently. My dear, this is appalling news, and God knows how they will take it.*"

"*That sounds like the best way to deal with it, and you could take them to school chapel and pray with them afterwards, my love. Shall I come with you?*"

"*We will frighten them if we both appear, I suspect. Sweetheart, can you bear to be on standby here?*"

"*Of course, and I shall ring Frank up and see how he is in himself.*"

The plan was made, but another letter had also arrived that same day, addressed to Anatole. Emma had left the letter waiting in the hallway to be given to Anatole when he brought Beth home, but as she dusted the hall stand, she couldn't help but keep looking at it. She bit her lip and fingered the corner of the envelope, feeling the sharp edge against her fingertip. She recognised the handwriting as being Wilfrid's. No, she told herself. *Leave it.* But as she carried on dusting, it remained in her eyesight, tempting her. Eventually, in a moment that was very unlike her, she gave in to the impulse.

North Israel Store,
Unter den Linden,
Berlin
13th March 1939

Dear Anatole,

Things are getting more and more difficult here, and I find myself besieged by the cries of my fellow Jews for my help in getting them to safety. My dear boy, I could do with your assistance in the to-and-fro business here in the store.

Could you find it in yourself to return to this risk-laden place to help me in this process? I know it is asking so much of you to leave your safe haven in England, but I know you care as deeply as I do for these wretched victims.

It won't be for too long, as I know my days are numbered here. The Nazi hierarchy is at my heels and Bertha Bracey is telling me to get out. But, Anatole, with your help, there is more we could do.

Yours in hope,
Wilfrid

Emma gasped in horror and dropped the letter.

"*Emma, what are you doing?*" Philip demanded to know as she hastened to pick it up off the floor and put it back in the envelope. He already knew the answer but couldn't quite believe Emma would do such a thing.

"Oh God, *Philip. He wants* Anatole *to go back to* Berlin. *Look at it yourself,* Philip. *It will break* Beth's *heart.*"

Philip felt a flame of fury at Emma's improper intervention rising in his chest as he regarded her, and she saw his anger.

"*Sorry, oh, sorry, Philip. Forgive me. It was a moment of aberration, but, my dear, I just knew it carried danger to* Beth." Emma collapsed onto Philip's lap in the wheelchair and hid her face in his chest.

"*Emma, it is improper, it is wrong.*"

"*I know, my love, I know, and I truly am sorry.*" Her tears started to fall, and Philip could hear her sniffling. "*Oh, Philip, I hate it when you're angry at me. But I know I deserve it.*"

One tear from Emma was enough to pull Philip back to himself.

"*Emma, it's alright. Don't cry, darling.*" He stroked her hair as she continued to cry. "*What's done is done, and we have to deal with its consequences. How can we put this together with what I must tell the boys and then watch as Anatole discovers Mr Israel's plea? Emma, my Emma, what a tangled web we weave.*"

Emma sat up and looked down at him. "*I love you so much and I don't deserve you, my dear. But thank God you and I belong to each other, and nothing can ever take that away.*"

He smiled despite his awkward conscience, and still the tears dripped down her cheeks such that the only remedy was to kiss her in the old tender way. They were interrupted by James' knock on the door. James pushed the door open, having heard nothing from Philip in the normal way. He strode in looking perturbed.

"*Is the headteacher intending to come to his study today? His chauffeur awaits,*" said James, though he stepped back as he saw there had been tears.

"*I'm coming, of course, and on the way, I'll tell you why Emma is in tears. Oh, James, what on Earth will the future hold?*"

And so James ferried Philip to school, as he always did, parting with him at his study door, both men with very heavy hearts.

"*I'm only too glad I can attend to my planting in the kitchen garden this morning. Let me know if you need me.*" James touched Philip's shoulder as he left.

Kath was waiting for Philip, and as she emerged from her own room, she saw the lines of weariness etched on his forehead.

"*Kath, can you send a message for Pieter and Anatole to come to my study, please?*" Philip sighed. "*I have news to give them of the worst kind. Oh, Kath, why are we again facing a terrible threat from Germany? We thought we had finished with the war—how did they put it?—*'to *end all wars*'. *Kath, I'm not sure I can still hold to a strict pacifist view,*" he said in a tone of heightened anxiety.

"*Philip, you must not allow yourself to give up the hope you have held so dear throughout all you've faced. My dear friend, we all rely on your strength. I'll go and fetch them now.*"

Sure enough, she returned very quickly with the young men and closed the door of his study very quietly. She heard, with sorrow, their cries as Philip told them the news. The study door opened, and Pieter pushed past her, tears pouring down his face. He left the door wide open, and Philip caught her eye pleadingly.

"*Kath, call James to catch him and bring him back, will you? Can we have tea, do you think?*"

She took in the sight of Anatole on his knees in front of Philip's chair, head resting on Philip's lap, and hurried to call James to find Pieter. Anatole was wordlessly drinking in the information that his parents had gone to the vicious camp at Buchenwald, and he found himself unable to stop shaking.

Philip stroked the dark head, feeling the agony of the moment. He prayed James would find Pieter and return him. He bit his lip before delivering the next piece of news. He drew the letter from his inside pocket.

"Anatole, there is more. I have another letter for you. It's from Wilfrid, and I must apologise, my dear boy. Emma and I were so overcome with anxiety that we opened it. Please forgive us."

Anatole sat up, still trembling. He took the letter, his eyes quickly glancing from left to right over and over as he took in its contents.

"Philip, he wants me to go back and help him. I must answer this and make plans to go." Anatole's shaking stopped as he pushed himself to his feet, determination and drive already coursing through him. *"I love and respect Wilfrid and he is clearly in trouble. This is a cruel blow, but if I go, maybe I can find my parents, though God knows how."*

It was at this point that James half carried, half helped Pieter back into the room and landed him on a chair. Kath followed with a tray of tea. Philip, musing to himself in the anguish of the moment, wished with all his heart that he could avoid the reality that faced him.

"Bless you, Kath. We'll drink this and calm ourselves down. I know it's all a terrible shock, so I feel we should go to the chapel and be quiet with God. Kath, will you close my study down now for today?"

"Of course, Philip. Tell Emma I'm here if she needs me."

Anatole grasped Pieter's hand and smiled at him, trying to reassure him. *"Can you push Philip's chair, Pieter?"* It was a clear action to help Pieter remain steady on his feet.

"James, will you come too? I feel we need all the support we can get."

James nodded sadly. The morning had brought back many memories to him that he usually kept stored away. Philip, very conscious of this, hastened them all to the chapel, so long a place of comfort for many boys through the years. He himself was missing Emma's presence, as she had often been at his side in the many times of prayer with distressed boys.

They sat silently in the peace of the beautiful Quaker chapel, heads bowed. Pieter could not restrain himself from sobbing quietly at the thought of his beloved mother, Esther, now suffering at the hands of the SS. Anatole was keeping a strict grip on himself, torn between the longing to leave immediately for Berlin, with thoughts of his parents, and the thought of what all this would do to the girl whose love he had only just discovered.

As for Philip, he could hardly bear to think of Beth, his darling daughter, whom, he knew, would be completely devastated to lose Anatole to Wilfrid Israel after such a short time with him. At last, Philip wheeled himself to the front of the chapel and bent his head in prayer.

"*Lord God, we ask simply for your strength and courage as we face this hour. We know you will guide us in the coming days, and we ask your especial blessing on those in so much peril in the hands of wicked men. We let go now into your hands. Amen.*"

With a huge sigh, Anatole led Pieter out of the chapel. James followed closely, pushing Philip.

"*Let's go home to Emma, James,*" said Philip.

And so they did.

Chapter 32

Elizabeth May – Time to Let Go, 1939

The dreadful day the war turned real for me, I ran out of the school gate, delighted to see Anatole waiting at the bus stop, as he so often did. But at the sight of his face, my foot faltered. There was no welcoming smile.

"*What is it, Anatole? Why are you looking so sad? Is everything alright at home?*"

I was revived a little at the sight of Turton's bus pulling up beside us. This was part of my own, homely world. We climbed onto the bus, and he put his arm around me as we found a seat. I was fearful that something had happened to Mother or Daddy, but I never dreamed what it really was.

"*I've had a letter from Wilfrid, Beth. He has sent for me to go over and help him. It means I must go back to Berlin.*"

I felt a shudder of horror go through me and looked at him in despair.

"*Uncle Frank has sent to tell us that Mother, Father and Aunt Esther have been taken away to another brutal camp where many Jews have now been sent. Oh my, Beth, you mustn't look at me like that.*"

I swear I could feel the blood leaving my face as an overwhelming sense of weakness drained the strength out of my arms and legs. I leaned against him as he gently held me from slouching in my seat.

I had only just discovered the joy of giving love and being loved in return, and the agony was intense. He too was feeling it. And yet he would go, I knew, without any compunction, for he was loyal and faithful to his friend and mentor and his mother and father were most beloved. How could I protest? Would I not do the same if it were my mother and father?

Turton's bus rattled its way towards Shadworth, and the truth forced me to discover resources I didn't know I had: I had to grow up in that moment. It was a dark and dank March day, no birds sang, rain spattered the windscreen and my soul was desolate.

Anatole hugged me to him as we descended the bus steps and did not let go of me until we reached my garden gate. There sat my beloved father in his chair, watching out for us.

"Beth, come on in, my sweetheart. Come in, Anatole. Mum has made scones, and James and Pieter are already enjoying them as they wait for you two. Beth, stand firm, my darling; you know how resilient Anatole is."

He wheeled into the kitchen, and Mother greeted us there with outstretched arms. Pieter and James were beside her, regarding us with sombre looks, yet their very presence gave me courage I didn't know I had.

"Philip, Emma, you know what Mr Israel has asked, and I cannot refuse to go back. Pieter, you must stay here though," said Anatole. *"I truly believe what you are doing here is so important. Those children need you to stay."*

Those children need you to stay too, I wanted to say, but the truth was it was me who needed him to stay. And how could I be so selfish with him?

"*I couldn't agree more*," said my father. "*But, Anatole, it falls to you to manage the journey back and see how you can assist him in his incredible work in getting the refugees to safety. And, of course, there may be a chance to find your family.*"

How I loved Anatole then. He was so determined and so strong, and I knew I had to match him.

"*Philip*," continued Anatole, "*may I ring Uncle Frank and arrange for my journey across? I guess I should make plans straightaway.*"

Before Daddy could reply, I appealed to Mother, "*Mother, you will have to give me a small token of the courage you had when Daddy was away sick for so long in Scarborough.*"

James looked across at Mother then and smiled at her. He knew what she'd gone through those years ago. Father smiled too.

"*Beth, you have all your mother's strength, I know. Anatole will know that you are supporting him every inch of the way and that you are behind him in it.*"

Anatole nodded grimly and shook Daddy's hand.

"*Enough, everyone*," James said, trying to temporarily take some pain from the conversation. "*Let's eat Emma's delicious tea and put our sorrows to rest. The motto you yourself taught me, Philip, is to treat one day at a time. That is, I'm afraid, what we must all do under the threat the world now faces, though we must prepare ourselves for what lies ahead. And we must not forget the kinder. Daisy has picked them all up and taken them to tea at the farm. But we must keep our brave face here for them.*"

Frank Jacques arrived in Shadworth the next day, ready to accompany Anatole down to London and thence to board the ship that would set him on his journey for Germany. We barely had time to grieve or say our goodbyes, which might have been more protracted and oh so much more tearful if it weren't for Mr Jacques standing by.

When I look back, I can hardly believe that I managed it and somehow let him go even with many a reassurance of my prayers and steadfast love.

Chapter 33

Spring 1939

Shadworth was quiet as Easter came and went that year, spring appearing gently. The weather was mild, and the snowdrops made a bank of white on the terraces in James' garden up at school. The daffodils and primroses popped their heads from the soil, the whole garden becoming a tapestry of colour.

The young ones all blossomed too as they settled more and more into life in the village. Some helped James with his planting and some spent time at the farm enthralled with the lambing that Ned and Daisy were busy with. Teddy had become an expert in helping the ewes give birth, much to Florence's delight. However, on hearing Teddy boasting of his prowess to Ralph, she was furious with him and invited Will to bring Ralph down to the farm at every opportunity. Teddy was duly chastised and both boys shared in the enterprise after that.

Beth buried herself in her books at this time, much to her mother's anxiety, but Philip reassured Emma that it was good for Beth to keep her mind from fretting for Anatole, especially now that the exams were close.

News from him came in fits and starts. He was busy helping Wilfrid in the dangerous but relentless process of saving the Jewish families from arrest by the Nazis, but he was also desperately searching for news of the camp at Buchenwald where he knew his beloved parents had been taken.

Unfortunately, remaining in Berlin was feeling more and more impossible by the day, and finally, a defeated Wilfrid shared a big decision he'd made one morning as he and Anatole sat at the kitchen table, eating toast and drinking orange juice.

"*Anatole, I know this is so far from what you want to hear, but...*" He shook his head sadly. "*I need to leave Berlin.*"

"No, *Wilfrid.*" Anatole shook his head too, though with naïve determination. "No. *You are needed here. How can we do the work required without you?*"

"*Anatole, listen to me,*" Wilfrid gently spoke. He put down his remaining slice of toast that he'd only taken two bites from, nerves and fear playing with his appetite. "*If you stay, you will be in mortal danger. But if you come with me, we can both work with Bertha Bracey and her relief work for the Jewish refugees. Time is running out for me. The SS's power is growing every day and it becomes more and more dangerous.*

"*You have a choice, my friend. Will you come with me and work from London assisting those refugees who manage to get away?*"

Wilfrid waited for a response, but Anatole just looked down silently at his plate.

"*If you choose to stay, you can of course remain lodging here, working at the store and rescuing as many more folk as you can safely do. But the end approaches for the shop. It could be vandalised and smashed up, possibly quite soon.*"

Anatole gasped, completely torn. He longed to return to Beth and his loving home in Shadworth. Yet he felt he should try even harder to locate his family and bring them to safety if that were at all possible. He poured all this out in a letter to Philip and Emma with a note inside for his Beth. She wept when she received it and hid her face in her father's lap. Once again, Philip felt the old agony of helplessness in the face of tragedy.

He knew Anatole would choose to stay, in the hope of finding and rescuing Otto and Hilke, and equally he knew it was probably futile.

He rang Frank up to discuss the problem, and Frank could only say that he would use all his power to bring Anatole back as soon as he could persuade him.

Then something else happened in late April that put everything else out of their immediate thoughts, though Beth cried herself to sleep each night.

Philip could usually hear even small sounds from Kath's study, but the bump he just heard from there was especially loud.

"*Kath, is everything alright?*"

On getting no response, he hurriedly wheeled himself into her study. There, he found her on the floor next to her desk, paperwork still clutched in her hand. She was as pale as a ghost, eyes closed.

"*Kath?*" he said loudly, hoping to bring her round, but there wasn't so much as an eye flicker.

"*James? Alan?*" he called out. "*I need help.*"

With much effort, he managed to heave himself out of his chair and onto the floor beside her, feeling for her pulse on her wrist. There was one, though it was weak. "*Kath, can you hear me? My dear friend, come back to us. We cannot do without you.*" He didn't realise he was crying until one of his tears made a plip noise on the wooden boards beneath him.

"*Philip, what is—*" Alan stepped into the room and froze. "*Oh God, Philip, poor Kath. We need an ambulance straight away.*" He picked up Kath's phone and made the request.

"*Philip?*" Kath said weakly.

Philip cradled her head. "*Kath, my dear, what happened?*"

"*Philip, it's alright. Don't look so worried. I just feel a little strange. Perhaps the hospital will be able to sort me out.*"

And with that, her head rolled back and she fell once more back into an unconscious state.

James came running in with two ambulance men carrying a stretcher. He took one look at the scene and hauled Philip up, extremely carefully, back into his chair.

"*Can I follow you in my car?*" James asked the men, and they nodded.

"*Her pulse is very thready,*" the one said to the other. "*We should put the blue light on.*"

Philip looked at James and Alan in utter dismay.

"*Let's get you into the car,*" James said to Philip, whose colour had also drained from his face.

"*Alan, will you ring Emma and Beatrice and hold the fort here?*"

With bells and blue lights flashing, the ambulance roared its way along the quiet country road out of Shadworth and onto the Cranston road. It reached Cranston Infirmary and unloaded the stretcher into the open doors and arms of the waiting emergency nurse.

Philip was truly beside himself with impatience as James found a parking space at the back of the hospital and then they made their way through corridor after corridor to the emergency department. There at last they found Kath already lying flat, tucked into a pristine white bed but with her eyes open, much to their relief. She sounded very weak and looked so frail that Philip could feel the tears pricking behind his eyes. Imagine his pleasure when he heard Emma and Beatrice's voices drawing near to the room where Kath lay.

Kath looked straight at Emma as she entered the room and beckoned her over. Emma leaned over her to catch the barely audible words.

"*Emma, I've been bleeding heavily this last week. I thought I could manage it, but it won't stop. Emma, I am just a little afraid. Don't mention this to the others. It's so embarrassing.*"

Emma covered Kath's hand with her own. "*Kath, I am right here with you, my dear friend. Not a word. But the doctors will need to examine you and decide what must be done. Be strong, my dear, as I know you will.*"

Philip, watching this whispered conversation, wheeled himself to beside Emma. "*No secrets to be kept, Kath. We are past the point of polite decorum. You and I have shared everything.*"

The little party of Kath's dearest friends stepped back as the doctor entered, and very soon, Kath was being wheeled to the operating theatre as they all made their way to the waiting room.

It was one of the longest days any of them had ever lived through. Emma, practical as ever, rang both Holt House and the farm to tell them what was happening, and Florence immediately promised to meet all the school homecomers to take them all with her back to Tempests' Farm. Beatrice, meanwhile, rustled up sandwiches from the hospital canteen, but Philip found he could not eat them.

Emma made him force one down, seeing how drawn and pale he was. She had begun to dread the outcome of such a lengthy operation.

When at last the surgeon appeared in the waiting room, no expression on his face, struggling to meet their eyes, they all knew the news was bad.

"*Are you her next of kin?*" he asked Philip.

"*She has no next of kin, but I am her closest friend and colleague.*"

"*Then can I speak to you and perhaps your wife?*"

He took them to one side in the waiting room.

"*The lady has a massive tumour in her womb that we have not been able to remove successfully. She shows signs that it has spread internally, and there is very little that can be done, I'm afraid. I am so very sorry.*"

Philip was speechless, unable to comprehend, the shock preventing any sort of immediate reaction.

"*Will she be able to come home for us to care for her or at least find her a place in a convalescent home?*" Emma asked, holding back the tears that were making her voice quiver.

"*She has not long. We should keep her here under sedation.*"

"*Oh God, how can this be?*" Philip wheeled himself back to James and Beatrice and clutched James' hand for support as his tears started to fall out of direct view of the doctor.

This was to be the last time they could share with their dear friend, who had steadfastly cared for them all through many vicissitudes over many years. Her death came after two more days as Philip and Emma stood guard by her bed. It was peaceful and gentle at the end, as they would all have wished, but it devastated Philip in particular. He shut himself away in the conservatory at Holt House to pray on his own.

This action was uncharacteristic, but the sadness of losing Kath had completely overwhelmed him.

Emma understood Philip's need to be alone with God, so she simply kissed his forehead and pushed him back into the kitchen once he emerged, where she plied him with tea and reassurance. As time wore on, she was much relieved to see him returning to his old self when he welcomed the little ones home from school and then waited at the gate to greet his daughter.

She whispered to James one afternoon after he'd brought Philip back from the school that he sometimes gave her heart-wrenching moments.

James laughed and hugged her. "*It's because you belong to him, heart and soul, Emma. There is a cost that comes with that.*"

Chapter 34

1939 – War

May dawned with events in Germany preoccupying Philip and the whole Holt family. They knew Hitler was not to be trusted for any of his promises. When he signed a pact with the Italian fascist leader, Mussolini, the "Pact of Steel", the warning signals were flashing.

One balmy evening, the family gathered in the garden of Holt House. The sun was still high and the little ones were playing hide-and-seek. Chickens were clucking away, as Beth had just fed them. The camellia was in fullness of bloom, already shedding its glowing dark pink petals onto the grass, while the rose buds, tightly folded still, promised an effulgence of colour.

Philip and Emma were relaxing in the late sunshine when the gate clicked and Beth ran to see who was there to visit.

"*Why, my boys*," Emma cried out as four old friends appeared. Harry embraced his mother, while Will sat down beside Philip on the old rustic garden seat. James and Ned waited and were soon drawn into the circle by Beth, who felt her heart lifting at the sight of them.

Yet they were unsmiling as they shared their sense of the fear and urgency of the moment.

"Philip, I can hardly bear to think what all this means. If they conscript us, I don't know how I'll cope. I can't live through the violence and killings again," said Will.

"Will," interrupted Harry, *"don't think like that. You are the bravest man I know, and besides that, you are forty-three and may be exempt because of your age."*

Ned, stoical as ever, just nodded his agreement, but James felt a wave of deep anxiety pressing in on him.

Philip saw his face and wheeled round to him, holding out his hands. *"James, it will all work itself out, but we must pray for common sense to prevail. Don't allow yourselves to panic, my dear friends. Prayer and patience must now be our watchword, though we may have to face the worst."*

Beth listened to their discussion as she played with the little ones. She knew they must not hear the fear that was creeping into the men's words and made her mind up to take them off to bath and bed. Her heart was beating very fast, for all her thoughts were with Anatole and how he was coping out in Berlin.

That night, they all slept fitfully, conscious of the dangers that awaited but somehow strengthened by their mutual fellowship. Emma lay close to Philip and spoke aloud her fervent prayers for everyone's safekeeping while he simply held her hand very tightly in reassurance.

With the morning came a call from Frank.

"Philip, I have had a message from Bertha Bracey. Wilfrid Israel has had to leave Berlin in haste, as the Nazis are closing in on him. There was no mention of Anatole in the dispatch, so I'm very much afraid he has chosen to stay. Expect to greet Wilfrid on his arrival in London. Bertha has promised to bring him to meet me and, Philip, he has asked to come to Shadworth to

see your 'kinder' and meet Beth. What do you think? I would certainly love to see you all and trust it won't be too much for Emma."

"You would offend my wife if she heard your anxiety for her," Philip replied. *"She is just as strong as she has ever been, Frank. God knows what we would all do without her. Of course, come with him as soon as you wish."*

When Philip ended the call, he noticed Beth lingering in the doorway.

"Daddy, what does this mean for Anatole? I feel so afraid for him." She knelt and put her head on Philip's lap in the age-old way. He smiled and stroked her hair.

"Chin up, my Beth. Let's enjoy meeting Anatole's rescuer and find out what we can do to help."

The day of Wilfrid's arrival dawned, and James took Philip down to the station to meet this man who had played such a part in the rescue of so many Jewish refugees. They greeted each other warmly, and Frank embraced his old friend. Back at Holt House, Emma shook him by the hand and gave him a very warm welcome.

He relished the delicious meal she put before him and was clearly very hungry. He finished before anyone else and sat back truly contented. "I *thank you very much for sending Anatole back out to help me. We have been able to reach more folk than would have been possible without him, and we have managed to send many to safety. He has worked terribly hard for me and I am very grateful."*

He went on, "*Mrs Manners, what a truly wonderful meal. Thank you very much.*"

"*You are very welcome, Mr Israel.*" Emma blushed with pleasure.

"*Beth will be home from school desperately anxious to meet you, Wilfrid.*" Philip smiled. "*In the meantime, let's take you up to school to see my colleagues who are caring for the older children alongside the normal running of the school.*"

As they reached school, Alan and Beatrice were waiting for them in Philip's study, and, minutes later, Edna hurried in. They greeted Wilfrid warmly and explained their roles in school to him, but also in caring for the older refugee children.

"*I am so much in your debt, my friends,*" said Wilfrid. "*The group of Quaker schools have been more than generous in helping bring these children to a safe haven. I have been and still am so very anxious for them all. Your school has been a relief to me, and I am so pleased to meet you all. Your headmaster has entertained me to a most delicious lunch, and I look forward now to seeing your work at close hand.*"

They all laughed at the mention of lunch, knowing how Emma would have provided for him.

Frank nodded, very glad to have brought this meeting to fruition. Philip could not help but sigh as he looked across at Kath's open door and her desk standing empty. His heart was still raw with that loss.

They led Wilfrid to the various classrooms to see the students at work. All stood up as he entered their rooms, and he was quietly impressed by the atmosphere of study engendered there.

At last, he came to a hallway where he could see into Laura and Pieter's classrooms. The older German children were being led through their maths by Pieter, who was managing to maintain the lesson in a mix of German and English. Laura, on the other hand, was teaching from a book of English grammar to show her students the nuances of English speaking. Wilfrid could see that both Pieter and Laura were committed to the children and the children were fully responsive to them.

But Pieter stopped his lesson when he saw who the visitors were.

"*Children,*" said Pieter, "*we have a special visitor today who has been working on your behalf for a long time making all the arrangements to bring you safely to this school. Please stand to greet him.*" The class rose as one. "*And now let's give him a clap to thank him for all his help.*" And the class joined with him in giving Wilfred a joyful acknowledgement.

Then he turned to Wilfred. "*Sir, I am so glad to meet you. You saved my cousin Anatole from the streets, and I cannot tell you how grateful I am for that. And you can see from the children how grateful we all are.*" He shook his hand warmly.

"*Why, you must be Pieter Staab,*" Wilfrid replied. "*I knew your parents well in the old days in Berlin and am so very sorry they have fallen into the hands of the Nazis. My dear boy, your cousin is striving with all his might to find them and return them to safety. But it may be a forlorn hope, I'm afraid.*"

Pieter's eyes filled with tears, and Laura, watching through the window of her classroom, stopped her teaching. She quickly took her place at Pieter's side and squeezed his hand. He silently mouthed his thank you.

"*We never give up hope, sir. We pray daily in our chapel here for the safekeeping of the parents of all these youngsters,*" *said Laura.* "*Your work here is admirable, and I thank you for it.*" Wilfrid bent down to look at the students more closely, speaking to them in fluent German. They all looked up in astonishment and pleasure at the use of their language. For those of the upper age group, this was a reassurance.

Pieter looked across at Philip then, his eyes full of admiration for the man who had made his school so much a sanctuary.

"Well, Frank," said Philip, "*we should be returning to Holt House now, I believe. Beth will be home very soon, and she deserves to speak with Wilfrid before you take him away again. And maybe my wife will have been baking afternoon tea scones for us.*"

The little party left the others with many heartfelt thanks and promises, on the staff's part, to care for Wilfrid's children. In James' car, Wilfrid thanked Frank for giving him such an opportunity.

As they drove down the hill back to Low Shadworth, Philip spotted Beth walking quickly on her way home, her heavy satchel over her shoulder, weighing her down. Her chestnut curls were flying in the wind, her long school skirt wrapping round her ankles. "*Stop, James. There is my Beth on her way down from the bus. Stop, and let's give her a lift home.*"

Beth saw the car just as it was drawing up and ran to greet them. She squeezed in beside Frank and Wilfrid as James headed for home.

"*So, this is your daughter, Philip? And this is the young lady that Anatole never stops talking about?*"

He took her hand. She was blushing pink with embarrassment at his words, but she kept her equilibrium.

"*This is indeed my wonderful daughter, Wilfrid, as James and Frank will attest. She's studying for her Highers and hoping to get a place at Oxford for September. But let her tell you how much she thinks of Anatole."*

They drew up outside Holt House, and Beth got out with a certain amount of relief. She whispered to her father as James was helping him into his wheelchair, "*Daddy, stop it. You mustn't boast like that.*"

"*But, my darling, I am allowed to be proud of you. Don't take that away from me.*"

He wheeled himself up to the door and called out, "*Emma, we're home, and here is Beth too. Come on in, Wilfrid. You too, Frank. We've had a busy day.*"

Emma appeared and saw Beth's pink face, realising that Philip had embarrassed her with his praises. She let her be, not wanting to deepen the colour of her cheeks any further. She led them through to the kitchen. "*Mr Israel, can you tell us about Anatole? Beth has been very anxious to hear about him.*"

"*Well, Beth, Anatole is safe, staying in my house for now and still working hard with the refugees. He is very capable and knows how to keep under cover. In truth, he is doing my job with the others, for I dared not stay any longer, as I suspect my name is on the Wanted list.*"

"*Oh, Mr Israel, that makes me feel a lot happier now about Anatole. But tell me, is there a chance he might come back to England to work with you here?*" Beth asked hopefully.

Philip, watching her, felt an anxious pang of pain for her. He looked across at Emma busily serving up her scones and tea, and she looked back reassuringly.

"*We know, sir, that you will help Anatole to return when you feel he has done as much as he can. Beth really misses him. She hopes against hope he may be able to come home soon.*" She smiled at Beth, who was silent, suddenly overcome with shyness. "So *come on now, Beth. Let Mr Israel eat his tea and be assured all will be well.*"

"Yes," said James. "*Fret not, Beth. But let me remind you, Mr Jacques, you have a train to catch. Are you aiming for the ten past seven back to London? If so, we must hurry up. We should set off down to the station in about half an hour.*"

"*Thank you for the reminder, James. We have done well today and I've been glad to see the progress the children are making here in Shadworth. I cannot thank you enough as usual for your hospitality, you dear people. My nearly family,*" exclaimed Frank.

"*Yes indeed. May I reiterate those words to you all?*" said Wilfrid, picking up a scone. He was determined to get a taste after his delicious beef lunch earlier. "*And, Beth, an especial pleasure to have met you. Be patient. Anatole will be back when it becomes possible.*"

Beth had to smile at that, forsaking her embarrassment thanks to his kind words.

So Wilfrid at last began work at Bloomsbury House alongside Bertha Bracey, and the rescue work continued, though now at a distance.

The news on the twenty-sixth of May was no surprise to the "*boys*" so beloved of Emma. The establishment of the Military Training Act ordered all males between twenty and twenty-one to undertake full-time military training before being transferred to the Reserves. The fact that Will and Harry were much older gave them time before the anticipated axe fell.

Philip and his colleagues spent much time now with the sixth formers in lessons, where the whole subject of German aggression was discussed and emotions shared. He occasionally brought them to the school chapel for quiet and prayer, as if to ready them. Emma sometimes joined him there, and they were both reminded of those years in the Great War, when they'd prayed with grieving boys.

Meanwhile, Beth was studying very hard for her Highers alongside the entry exams to Oxford. George, though training in his new-found status as an RAF officer, still found time to write encouraging letters to her, having himself won the coveted Freiston scholarship to Oxford those years ago. These letters encouraged her to look forward to the chance of Oxford honours and, in a small way, helped to soothe her aching and ongoing anxiety for Anatole. There was very little news of him during these days, and they could only commit him to prayer and assure Beth that she must remain patient.

Chapter 35

Elizabeth May – Exam Results, 1939

It was a hot June, too hot to study, and yet I had to.

The young kinder at home were terribly distracting, and Ralph and Teddy entertained them, playing all kinds of chasing games. Prominent of all the games, however, was cricket. Even the youngest ones loved to get hold of the bat Daddy had bought for them, and they would urge me to join them in the station fields on the way down to Tempests' Farm. I am proud to say that I resisted them and studied even harder.

From my bedroom window, the sky was a piercing crystal blue. There were goldfinch nesting in the hedge across the road by the little school, and they feasted on the Brazil nuts Mother had put up for them. They were enchanting, all green and gold and red, quite spectacular in fact. But the blue tits were my favourite, and they sometimes landed on my windowsill, as if to keep me company, the sweet, gentle creatures.

In Mother's garden, near where Daddy loved to sit enjoying the sun, was the rose garden set up for her by James, rich with the loveliest pale pink and creamy yellow flowers. My father loved to pick one before he wheeled himself in for tea and then he would present it to her with a flourish and with the special smile he reserved for her. It made me wish for Anatole to return even more. I would turn back to my revision and stop myself from longing for him.

Daddy's students were sitting for their Highers, just as I was in Cranston. The results would come out in late June, but before that, the results of the entrance exam for Oxford came out. The letter arrived with the morning post as we sat finishing our breakfast. Mother had already taken the young ones to school. I think Daddy recognised the Oxford emblem on the envelope, and he hastily took it from Mother as she gathered the letters up.

"Beth, it's addressed to you. Beth, open it up quickly."

I slit the envelope open with a shaking hand and, to my utter disbelief, saw the letter heading: Lady Margaret Hall, Oxford.

There, in print, was the invitation to take up a place at the university to study English and history as from September. I let out a shriek as I read it, and Daddy seized the paper and read it aloud for Mother to hear, with an exclamation of joy.

"Beth, you've won a place, my darling. And it is well deserved. I am so very proud of you."

Mother simply hugged me wordlessly, hardly able to believe that her child, so late arriving in her life, was all grown up to be a student in Oxford. She had seen her clever grandson George win the Freiston scholarship to go there, she had seen Pieter win the equally special place at Cambridge, but now her own little girl—so astonishingly born to Philip and herself, like some unlikely and unexpected gift from God—was about to step forward into a world far removed from Shadworth.

"Philip, how can I bear to part from her?"

Daddy just laughed at her then and pulled her onto his knee. "*Emma Manners, am I really hearing you, who has been my touchstone in every trial of my life, showing fear at letting our baby try her wings? Surely not, my dearest.*"

She hid her head in his chest and I, watching them, felt a surge of love for them both.

"*Now for the results of our Shadworth students. It won't be long now,*" said Daddy. "*I am hoping they have all done themselves credit because they were all excellent students for me and I know they were for my colleagues. I want speech day at the end of July to be a very special one. They receive their Higher Certificates, and the younger candidates will receive their School Certificates.*"

"*Are you going to give out prizes to our kinder for all they have achieved in learning English, Daddy?*"

"*I am, and I'm leaving the arrangements for that special treat to Pieter and Laura, who have cared for them all so wonderfully. And Mother knows, though I haven't admitted it to you, my darling, I am announcing my retirement then as well.*"

I was very shocked to hear that. The school had been integral to his life. Since his marriage to Mother, he had shared all his problems and his achievements with us all at Holt House. It was hard to imagine he was handing his pride and joy over to Alan Lorimer. So, when he announced his retirement so seriously to us, it almost felt as if the loss was ours as well. "Mother," I said, "*he can't. He's far too young to retire.*"

Mother smiled. "*Beth, he will be seventy in the autumn. You know he will carry on tirelessly in his efforts for Frank and for the kinder. That will never stop, and neither will he stop working for everyone in any kind of need. But as far as the school is concerned, he needs a rest now."*

Daddy's face was very solemn. I knew he was deeply anxious about events in Europe and what they might mean. But he also felt his responsibility to the school and for the kinder very keenly. He took my hands in his and whispered, "Beth, *have no fear for me. I believe this step is the right one. Mother and I will be, as the saying goes, 'holding the world up in prayer' every moment."*

Mother handed me her hanky and I dried my eyes. It was a good job James arrived at that moment, as it meant I was able to stop my tears and greet him with my wonderful news.

"*By all that's perfect, my lady. That's something again. Congratulations, sweetheart,*" cried James. "*Are you really able now to take up the place in Oxford? Beth, this news needs to be shared with everyone. When we all get home tonight, we'll spread this good news and celebrate. What do you say, Emma? But, Philip, we need to head up to school now, and you, Beth, don't miss Turton's bus. We still have a few weeks until the end of term.*"

With a nod, Daddy wheeled himself after James, and I gave Mother a parting hug and left for another school day.

Chapter 36

Summer 1939

The days moved quickly now. Higher and School Certificate results were all Philip, Alan and the Shadworth staff had hoped for. The date of the final speech day drew near, and Philip had moments of regret as he sat quietly in his study that this was indeed to be his last as head. These thoughts were often tinged with terrible nostalgia as he looked over at the empty desk where Kath used to sit. No new secretary had been appointed as yet, and Philip was glad he would be gone by the time Alan was installed there with the new appointee.

Both Frank and Wilfrid had been invited to the day, and Frank was to hand out prizes and certificates. Laura and Pieter were busy training their special group of children to make a presentation in the programme. Emma had worked very hard with Cook to produce a fine afternoon tea for after the proceedings.

The hall became suddenly silent as Philip took centre stage to welcome all the parents, some of whom had travelled many miles to get there.

"Ladies and gentlemen, it is my pleasure to welcome you this afternoon as we celebrate our students' achievements. I have asked Mr Wilfrid Israel to say a few words before we give out the awards. His work

at Bloomsbury House is of great significance, as many refugees are being helped at this very time to reach safety in England. You will all know how proud we are that, as a school, we have been able to welcome our group of children, secured from Berlin on the Kindertransport. Indeed, we have shared in giving shelter to these refugees with other Quaker schools.

"*We have encouraged our students to take a positive grasp of the world situation under threat from Nazi Germany, and our prayers go out to all those who will take up places at university, aware of the dangers that may lie ahead. Mr Israel, you are welcome.*"

Wilfrid shook Philip's hand as the audience applauded, and then spoke very movingly of all the work he was undertaking.

Next, it was Frank's turn to give out the pile of certificates and prizes that awaited him on the desk. Philip announced each boy and what they had achieved as Frank shook the hands of each one and awarded the prizes and certificates.

Then Alan Lorimer stood up and took to the stage next to Philip. "*I'm excited but also sad to bring you the news that I will be taking over as head.*" He smiled softly at Philip. "*Philip is retiring, but I'm sure you're all aware of the many amazing things he's done for the school.*"

There was a gasp amongst many parents who had known Philip through the years.

"*It is time,*" Philip confirmed. "*But I can assure you that the school is in safe hands.*" He patted Alan on the back. "*Mr Lorimer's position as head has been unanimously endorsed by the school governors. And I'm sure you will all agree that we couldn't have found a better replacement.*"

The tributes that followed brought Emma to tears where she stood beside Cook in her old place by the refreshments. She loved this man, and to hear him praised to the heavens greatly moved her.

There came another surprise. Laura and Pieter went onto the stage followed by the thirteen children they had been teaching.

Pieter spoke, "*These are some of the German children we have been teaching this year who have escaped the dangers that threatened them in their own country. I am so grateful to all the staff for how everyone has taken them to their hearts and supported them. Our head, Mr Manners, has made all this possible and we are proud to be one of several Quaker schools in the country offering this help to Jewish refugees. The children want to show their gratitude today.*"

Then each child ran towards Philip and hugged him, while the six girls each took a posy from the basket Pieter was holding and, with a curtsey, presented them to Laura and Emma. At this, the school hall was filled with enthusiastic clapping.

Beth was watching with James from a seat near the back, and she could see how overwhelmed her mother and Laura were feeling. She felt most keenly for her beloved daddy.

"*What an afternoon, James,*" she said with a choke in her voice. "*Whatever we have to face in the coming months, we shall never forget this special day.*"

James squeezed her hand and smiled.

That night, as Philip and Emma retired to their bed, he took her in his arms and kissed her tenderly.

"*Now, Emma, we must be ready to face what seems inevitable. I believe Hitler is preparing to invade Poland, regardless of the Munich agreement, which,*

I think, was merely a meaningless gesture to keep Chamberlain happy. If he does, then there is nothing for it but to fulfil the obligation of our guarantee to provide armed assistance to the Polish people."

Emma pulled away from him and shook her head vehemently. "No, *no, Philip, don't spoil this moment. It cannot be; it has implications for our boys' lives. When they came the other night, they were all filled with dread. They can't go out and fight another war. I can't let them go again. God forbid.*"

"*My darling, lie back down and rest. We must keep strong for all of them. There is no one better than you, my Emma, to hold them all in your love and to keep the faith. We shall do so together, and for that, thank God.*"

She smiled, relaxed against him and, in the twinkling of an eye, fell fast asleep, exhausted from all the day's events.

The summer lay before them, and despite the shadow that hung over them, the Manners and the Holts managed to celebrate summer. Elizabeth, knowing her life would change quite drastically when she left for her first term at Oxford, was determined to enjoy the lazy days of August with those she loved most. She spent many happy hours down at Tempests' Farm with Daisy and Pieter, the smaller children and with Ralph and Teddy joining in. She packed picnics with her mother each morning to enable them to stay down in the fields till teatime. Emma rejoiced at the pleasure they were all taking in this peaceful time before everything changed.

She quietly wheeled Philip down to join them for the packed lunch. They spread the old rugs out and lay out watching the young ones. Mary Tempest was never far away and brought out huge jugs of homemade lemonade for the cricketers and hot tea for the more staid grownups. James would appear on cue just in time for lunch and then roll his sleeves up to be part of the team. Laura and Florence had become the best of friends during this time and gossiped together, sharing the joys and tears of motherhood as they watched Ralph and Teddy.

The small German children were by now speaking English as if they had grown up in Shadworth, and this amused Philip and heartened Pieter. They loved to climb all over Philip as he sat observing them.

"He has some sort of magic they cannot resist," Emma said, laughing. *"Goodness knows what stories he's telling them."*

So the long, hot summer refreshed and renewed their hopes and courage. Now perhaps they could be ready to face up to the inevitable.

Chapter 37

September 1939

Things did indeed move swiftly then. Hitler marched into Poland on the first day of September, and Britain and France could do no other than honour the pact they had made earlier in March by which they had guaranteed armed assistance in the event of an advancement of German troops. Philip's fears were realised. James, Ned and the Holt boys saw to their horror that their worst fears were to be enacted and that there was absolutely nothing they could do to change the inevitable course of events.

On the third of September, Britain declared war on Germany. The conscription of all men between the ages of eighteen and forty was put into action. Only Will, aged forty-two, would escape that mandate, but it gave him no pleasure to realise it. The horror he felt remained with him, and he and his old comrade, Frank, sat together in the pub in Cranston and drank the night away whilst Laura, at home with Ralphie, fretted about him.

One painful irony for Emma and Philip in particular was that Daisy and Elizabeth's eighteenth birthdays fell less than a week later on the seventh and eighth of September. Emma's granddaughter and Philip's beloved daughter could not truly celebrate, as a sense of dread hung in the air. Nevertheless, Emma and Florence, never willing to be hostages to fate, held a quiet birthday party for them in the garden of Holt House, and everyone assembled there to assure them that nothing in heaven or on Earth could ever take away the love they all had for each other.

"*Why are Mother and Aunt Florence crying?*" enquired Ralphie. "*And why is Grandma looking so sad?*"

James took his hand then and, with Teddy, picked up the football sitting nearby in the grass and started a rough and tumble game with the kinder children at the back of the garden. Philip, watching them, had to smile. He felt a strange, unanticipated peace about it all and stretched out his hand to Emma standing by him.

"*Whatever happens, my love, we can weather it. I love seeing the children so settled now and so happy, playing with James.*"

But their strength and courage were soon tested as the call-up papers arrived for their boys. Ned felt very keenly that he must leave the farm he had worked and toiled over all his life, except for the fearful time he had spent in the trenches of the First World War. But he knew his wife and his sturdy tomboy daughter, Daisy, were both capable of managing the farm.

His mother, Mary Tempest, longed to be able to share her sorrow with her dear husband Ron, but he was gone, and she knew she had to back up the others now without flinching. She was grateful that she had Philip and Emma close by, and she knew that, between them, they could somehow hold things together.

Meanwhile, Harry Holt was also desperately frustrated that The White Swan, his business, would be left in Milly's lone hands, the woman with whom he had hardly had time to enjoy their new-found happiness. Now, she would be the mainstay of the pub with all the help she could get from the local folk.

Strangely enough, his walk down to Holt House coincided with the moment James walked into the kitchen there and threw his gloves and cap down on the kitchen table.

"*Harry*," he exclaimed as Harry too strode in and went straight to hug his mother.

"*James, can we stand this all over again?*"

"*At this moment*," answered James, "*I feel incapable of anything more than a cup of Emma's coffee. Then I might just go down to the cellar and hide.*"

"*Can I come with you, my friend?*"

Philip, observing all this from his chair, smiled despite the pain he knew was being articulated. He looked across at his wife and nodded to her to put on the kettle. She was standing soundlessly, watching the two boys with a look of terrible sadness.

"*Mother, what about Will?*" asked Harry. "*He doesn't have to go and he'll be relieved, but I reckon he'll feel really torn about it, knowing we have to.*"

"*He may still be called up if things get tougher, but in the meantime, let's encourage him to keep his eye on Florence at the farm and on your Milly at the pub. Laura will keep him calm, if I know Laura*," said Philip.

James looked at his watch as Emma handed him his coffee, which he quaffed in one go. "*Emma, do you want me to get the young ones out of school? It's almost time. Then maybe Harry and I can walk them down to the farm and have a game of cricket?*"

"*That's a very good idea, James. Yes please*," replied Emma. "*You'll find Beth down there with Daisy. She's making every minute count before she is expected in Oxford. She had a letter this morning warning her that things would be a little different now from ordinary times. She has to go quite soon to register and prepare. I believe the girls will be asked to help in the running of the college, doing the basic housekeeping chores, as many of their maintenance staff have been sent to do war work."*

"*I think I'll retreat to the cellar the day she has to go,*" exclaimed Philip. "*It sounds like the best plan, James. I can hardly stand to think about it, if I'm honest.*"

Harry had to smile at this comment, spoken so wryly by his stepfather. Harry knew Philip would be the first to see Beth off with a smile and a prayer of encouragement when the moment came even though his heart would be breaking to part from her.

"*Come on, Harry, let's get those kids. Laura will be there meeting Ralphie and Teddy too. Let's all go and play cricket.*" James picked up his discarded cap and gloves, pecked Emma on the cheek and strode out. Harry followed.

Emma walked slowly to her husband and sat on the kitchen table chair closest to him. "*Philip, I feel so anxious about them all. And what about Anatole? Beth hasn't had a letter from him for a while, and I know she's hoping he will come back to England and content himself by working with Mr Israel in Bloomsbury. I wish Frank would write too. He may have news.*"

"*My darling, I have that same sense of dread, but we really must put a braver face on now. We're back to that 'one day at a time' stuff. I expect a letter from Frank any time, I promise you. Come, sweetheart, let's sit in the garden together and let go of all our fears for a while.*"

Emma pushed him slowly to their favourite spot beside the clucking chickens. The roses were still in their prime—pink, peach and cream—and overhead, a blackbird was singing in the pear tree, its beak at full throttle.

"Emma, I love you very much," he said. *"I am so very thankful that we can face anything together."*

"You will make me cry, Philip Manners. And I really can't afford the luxury. Once my tears start to fall, I lose my courage. And that's what we both must avoid."

"Pray for courage, then. But remember, God might just answer the prayer by sending us something that demands it."

"Oh, my dear. If He does, I expect He'll meet us halfway."

And with that, she left him enjoying the quiet and returned to the kitchen to make hot soup for the hungry cricketers.

Chapter 38

Elizabeth May – Departures, September 1939

Conscription hit us hard as Harry, Ned and James were all sent to join up to the King's Own Yorkshire Light Infantry. They would become part of the British Expeditionary Force, but at first, the three of them were sent to Cranston Barracks to receive basic training before being allotted to whichever battalion they were assigned.

The day they appeared in Holt House in their uniforms—so smart, so brave, so gallant—gave us no pleasure. Will was tormented by the prospect, feeling he should have been with them but glad at the same time to be holding back. Will suspected he would be called up later.

We all knew George was stationed close to an airfield somewhere near the South East coast, but he was not allowed to tell us exactly where because of confidentiality restrictions. He came to see us one afternoon in late September, looking very handsome in his uniform. I could see he was actually excited by the chance to fight Hitler's forces when the time arose.

Daisy clung to him then and longed for him to acknowledge her in the especial way she wanted, but he remained aloof and treated her just like he treated me, his little sister. She confided in me that night that she loved George very much though she knew that, as cousins, close friendship between them might be frowned upon. I felt so very sad for her, and this only made me long for Anatole to return even more.

I had to leave for Oxford at the beginning of October—a terrifying thought. I was desperate for news of Anatole, and you can imagine my relief when Father received a letter from Frank Jacques with news of Wilfrid Israel and Anatole.

Westminster,
12th September, 1939

Philip Manners
Holt House
Shadworth
My dear Philip,

I write with some anxiety particularly in relation to Pieter. I am trusting you to ensure that he will not face internment as the holder of a German passport. And what of the kinder? I pray they are secure in their lodging with you and at the school.

At least I have some good news. Wilfrid is working closely with Bertha Bracey at Bloomsbury House in the process of arranging the rescue of the many Jewish refugees, as you know. But he has persuaded Anatole to join him and leave Berlin behind. The store has now been completely taken over by the Nazis, to his great grief. Its very name has been removed and replaced by a poster announcing the new company, 'Das Haus im Zentrum.'

Moreover, he believes Anatole has faced up to the fact that he can do no more in the search for his parents. They are in the Buchenwald camp, we believe, and it is hopeless to think any rescue from there is possible. Only the defeat of Hitler can make that happen now. And God knows how long that will take.

Anyway, my friend, Anatole is on his way to London as I write and will be of immeasurable help to Wilfrid and Miss Bracey in Bloomsbury.

If I can get to Shadworth, I will, but at present, I am overwhelmed by the work under Chamberlain. He persists in hoping to negotiate with Hitler to end this frightful aggression. Only Churchill is speaking out against him. The word "anxiety" does not really cover it.

I remain your very good friend,

Frank

Daddy went very quiet as he perused this letter. He felt keenly, I think, for his old friend, so obviously deeply troubled by events. The letter had also alerted Daddy to the possible danger in Pieter's situation. His position as tutor at the school had been agreed to much earlier, before the issue of internment had arisen.

My father quickly arranged a meeting with the passport authorities to argue for Pieter's position in school, to avoid any danger of internment. He would fight it on the grounds that, like Alan Lorimer, he was an important and integral part of the running of the school.

He was glad for me of Anatole's arrival in England, I know, but he was also very protective. Mother rejoiced with me at the news but whispered that Daddy was afraid that the careless boy he knew of old might bring me pain.

There was nothing I could do to reassure him, but I promised him that I could take any pain if it meant I could be with Anatole.

He took this announcement calmly and, with a smile, simply said, "*My darling child, take care, that's all I ask from you.*"

Mother wheeled him into the garden and sat on the old garden bench next to him, beckoning me to follow. I could see tears in his eyes as I knelt on the grass beside him to comfort him.

"Daddy, please have no fear for me. You've made me strong and taught me to trust God, and I will."

"Forgive me, Beth. I am very glad for you, and Mother and I will support you in everything, as you know. Now, enough. Let's look forward to his coming."

He wheeled himself back into the kitchen without another word. I stared after the wheelchair's retreating back and knew quite well he was hiding his emotions.

Anatole arrived just three days later, to my utter relief and joy, full of news about his hair-raising adventures in Berlin. He was very proud of all the rescue efforts he had managed to effect, sometimes by the skin of his teeth.

Wilfrid had found him a room in a hostel close to the headquarters of the association and set him to work on the numerous pleas for assistance they received every day. But he took every opportunity he could to head on the train back to Shadworth, usually at the weekends when he had time to himself.

It felt just like the old days, when he had met me off Turton's bus, but now we were deeply immersed in our relationship, and we walked for miles around the country lanes, holding hands and sharing all that we felt and hoped. We lay in the grass of Tempests' fields and embraced. He kissed me so gently, but I returned his kisses with all the fervour I had bottled up for years. Our bodies ached for each other, but it was he who held back, knowing I could not risk becoming pregnant and losing my place at Oxford. He had such respect for my parents and felt keenly the debt he, and Pieter, owed them. And I could not forget my father's words to me, "*Take care.*" Indeed, I think he would have found it difficult to forgive me if I had become pregnant.

The departure date for Oxford was looming, but Anatole assured me that he could get to Oxford from London far more easily than to Shadworth. He planned to come at weekends if he could get away, and that had to be sufficient for us.

I was expected at Lady Margaret Hall on the third of October. Mother helped me pack a trunk with all my belongings and my books. My darling daddy watched these preparations quietly, and I felt so sad knowing they were both dreading my leaving. By this time, my dear brother Harry, James and Ned had already left for the barracks in Cranston, so my last evening was spent with only my parents after lunch at the farm with Florence, Daisy and Mary. I missed the boys terribly.

In the morning, the three of us walked slowly down to the station, Mother pushing Father's wheelchair. We put on a brave face as they set me onto the train. I found a seat, then went to the window to make every last minute count. The train pulled away, and I saw them watching it into the distance. I flopped down into the seat and took a very deep breath. I should have felt thrilled that I had a chance to study literature and follow in Father's footsteps. He had taught me the delights of reading the classics and Mother too had taught me much about the books she had loved. And now I had my chance. I had worked very hard for this moment.

But I admit, I felt sick to my heart that I was leaving them in the midst of the turmoil and threat of the war and leaving the little ones too. I thanked God for the very thought of Anatole, knowing he would find me as often as he could. *Oh, Anatole, you are my only comfort.*

Chapter 39

Christmas 1940

The months that followed Beth's departure were dark ones in Shadworth. Only Christmas brought some respite but without the three men who were 'en route' for France in their allotted battalions.

Emma, Florence and Laura ensured that the growing German children should taste the pleasures of a true Shadworth Christmas. A fat chicken was produced, accompanied by all the delicacies Emma was wont to make. Milly contributed her own homemade Christmas pudding, which she carried flaming to the extended table in the Holt kitchen. Keeping busy was helping to overcome her acute awareness of Harry's absence.

Beth was glad to be back at home, though only briefly. And she was full of pleasure at her successful first term away, excited to tell all about it. She and Anatole entertained the children with Teddy and Ralph's help to all the sweet nonsense of the old-fashioned party games. Blind Man's Bluff and Postman's Knock produced much hilarity and squeals of pleasure. Beth and Daisy had the delight of George arriving unannounced for just one day off duty. He swept them up and swung them round before kissing them under the mistletoe.

Philip looked on, feeling the joy they were all sharing and thanking God for the home he and Emma had been able to make into a haven for them all.

Yet, once Christmas was over and all had to go back to their differing duties, Philip and Emma returned to their perpetual state of anxiety for their loved ones, knowing that Harry, James and Ned were now preparing to be part of an expeditionary force moving forward into France to put a stop to Hitler's ambitions. And there was little or no information forthcoming.

There was something of a lull in the progress of events. The term 'Phoney War' kept appearing in the newspapers, as if the troops were waiting for something that hadn't materialised. Troops were guarding and strengthening forts along the Maginot Line as German troops faced them. But there were few skirmishes between them and there was a kind of unspoken faith that the Maginot Line would hold and that the Germans could never manage an assault through the Ardennes Forest, supposedly impassable to an army. There was a kind of stalemate in which the three Shadworth men, sent out so fearfully, were merely hanging fire.

Nevertheless, the war at sea was fully engaged. Emma and Philip were aware that George was undergoing the training of the RAF aircrews, who had to be ready for whatever Hitler intended. What everyone knew was that Göring had built up the Luftwaffe into a mighty force, whilst the policy of appeasement held sway in the British government. Frank's letters to Philip during this time had been frantic and despairing of Chamberlain.

Even at this stage in the early months of 1940, it was clear that Chamberlain's government was loath to enter the true reality of war. Frank felt his colleagues were sleepwalking into terrible danger unless they realised the magnitude of Hitler's intentions more fully.

For Emma in particular, it was all horribly reminiscent of the days when Will and Harry had been out in the fields of France, and therefore it seemed even more difficult to bear. She could hardly believe she must endure it all again. She was only grateful that she had Philip beside her, carrying the hope and the dread in equal measure, and she felt a pang of nostalgia thinking about how Jack had supported her through all those dreadful days long past.

Philip had fought for Pieter's right to remain as a teacher in the school alongside Alan Lorimer. He had stressed Pieter's important role in caring for the Kindertransport children, and Frank had supported his fight until at last it was all approved.

But Philip missed Beth terribly. Emma watched him anxiously, for he was losing weight, having little to no appetite.

And then she heard the words she'd been praying for.

"*A letter, Emma. Let's read it together.*"

Emma rushed to the hallway, where Philip was sitting in his wheelchair, a letter in his hand. They knew from the handwriting that it was from Beth.

Emma pushed him into the garden to take in the weak spring sunshine and to show him the shoots of snowdrops and crocuses emerging. There, they opened the letter.

Lady Margaret Hall,
7th March, 1940

My dearest mother and father,

It feels like ages since Christmas, and I miss you both terribly. Anatole manages to get up from London whenever he can, and that is the best part of my time here. We are not allowed to have men in our rooms, so he and I have to walk and find ourselves somewhere to sit and rest together. Mother, we've walked miles, it seems! Daddy, you would be proud of me in these times. He and I have shared all our hopes and fears and dreams with each other.

He has suffered greatly knowing the Nazi hatred of Jews. He longs to be able to rescue his parents and has tried so hard to find out their whereabouts. But it is, I'm afraid, hopeless. Yet he is so grateful to Mr Israel, who has been like a father to him. Best of all, he is thankful to both of you for making him so much at home at Holt House. Oh, Daddy, I miss home so much.

Life in college is not easy. Wartime means we have to take a share in the running of college. I find myself scrubbing floors and helping to cook, not to mention helping in the vegetable garden. I truly long for James to appear by magic to grab the spade out of my hands. Thank goodness he has taught me a lot about caring for plants.

We have all been told our time here is curtailed from three years to just two, as the college believes we should be available for working in the outside world.

As for my studies, I just wish I had more time with them. My personal tutor in literature has given me many books to research the work of George Eliot. Daddy, you remember how you made me read 'Middlemarch' before I even started on Jane Austen? That has stood me in good stead now. If I get a degree in the end, half of it will be down to you.

In any case, I must close now and look forward to my next visit from Anatole. Write soon and tell me all the news about our boys. I am your own.
Beth

Philip sighed. "My *darling child, Emma. Oxford ought to do better for its students. I can hardly bear to imagine her feelings about it all.*" He put the letter back in the envelope and then put his head in his hands.

Emma stood up and held him by his shoulders. "*My dearest, we mustn't despair. She trusts us to stay firm so she can throw herself into Oxford life. And, of course, the relationship with Anatole is so important for her. Philip, think how it was for us so long ago now. We must let her enjoy her time with him and trust God to keep her safe.*"

"*You are, my love, right as usual, I know it. Let's go back in and then look forward to the children coming home.*"

Chapter 40

May 1940

At the start of May 1940, the German army began a ruthless and speedy invasion of the Netherlands. Soldiers in the expeditionary force suddenly found themselves facing a massive and rapid onslaught. On the Western Front, the French generals arrived too late to prevent the German army from sweeping into Belgium and through the Ardennes Forest—territory previously thought of as unassailable. The German march forward had begun in earnest as they violated the neutrality of the Low Countries and surged into France. The tenth of May marked the battle for France and the defeat of the French Resistance. The expeditionary force had no choice but to retreat to the Channel beaches and trust in a rescue, as defeat stared them in the face.

One outcome of this disastrous retreat, however, was that Winston Churchill was brought to the forefront of Britain's government. Chamberlain was forced to resign as his hope of 'Peace for our time' was reduced to tatters. Frank rang Philip in great relief at this change of leadership. At last, Frank argued, they had a leader who would act against the Nazi forces with full intent; however, the relief was short-lived, as the news of casualties on the coast grew and grew.

Philip and Emma shuddered with horror as reports came in of the Battle of Arras, which had failed to stop the Nazi onslaught. They watched the newsreels in utter dismay as they saw the British army driven to the beaches around Dunkirk and trapped on every side by the German attackers. The strafing and bombing of the troops were merciless. Not knowing what was happening to her boys was a kind of unlimited anguish for Emma.

Philip was in constant touch with Frank Jacques throughout this dreadful time, but he could not staunch his wife's agony. From Frank, he learned of the small miracle that was happening—many small boats being brought across the channel to help save the shattered troops as they gathered starving and thirsty on the beaches. These small boats bolstered up the efforts of the large troop ships that had to steer as close to the shore as they could. This was not easy, but they all knew how vital the operation was.

Will, meanwhile, was a great comfort to Emma at this time, and between Philip and himself, they managed to keep her from absolute despair. One of the most consoling aspects of this time was prayer. Will was able to drive them both up to school, where Philip held silent prayer times for any pupil who was fearful. This was especially attended by the children of the Kindertransport. Once again, as in the Great War, Emma sat with the children and comforted them, and in those moments, she was back to her old self. It drew Will very close to Philip and his mother, particularly as he imagined his brother and his friends in France, while he was still working at home.

James, who had once suffered terribly from his experiences in the first Great War, now found himself at the head of a troop of younger conscripted men. He and his troop crossed Northern France at pace, enduring dreadful weather. The men were hungry, wet and weary. They could hear the pounding of explosives in the distance and smell the acrid smoke that drifted across the countryside as they tried to keep away from main roads to avoid discovery by the enemy.

Then, from their cover behind bushes they were keeping close to, James realised, with a sinking heart, that they were, in fact, walking towards a fully armed German troop heading directly for them. *My God, I am leading my troop in the completely wrong direction.*

As his men realised the peril they were in, they ducked in horror, swearing colourfully at James. And yet, to his amazement, instead of fearfully fleeing, they looked to him for his authority.

"*Come on, lads,*" he said as loudly as he dared speak. "*The sooner we board a boat for home, the better, but we've got to reach the beaches first. We can rest when we get there. If you don't want the German army to catch us, we need to move faster than this.*"

He found a courage in himself that he'd hardly known he had as he urged his men a different way. What had happened to the young soldier who could hardly speak without a vicious stammer? He praised God for this transformation into someone who was able to lead others.

But these were black and bleak times for him as he led his men, in complete ignorance of what lay ahead for them, to the beaches. When eventually they struggled across the dunes of the beach at

Dunkirk, his initial relief at reaching their destination turned quickly into horror. How could they possibly survive the constant lethal strafing from the German low-flying aircraft and the German bombers hitting targets on the beach?

Lying out amongst the dunes, trying to keep his men from sinking into hopelessness, the only thing that enlightened James was the thought of Holt House and of Beth.

He felt a guarded relief as he watched a troop ship extend a long pontoon to the shoreline, and his troop were signalled to wade out to it in file. There, soaked through with salt water and attacked unmercifully by tracers from low-flying German aircraft, James clambered shivering on board, last in the file, and shook the extended hand of a naval officer. The boat set off within minutes, but with the constant danger of attack, James did not relax until the White Cliffs of Dover felt close enough to touch.

Later, before being given the short leave awarded to the returning men, he wrote to Holt House describing his adventures at that time. Philip found himself wincing as James described the time they had found themselves walking towards the armed German troop. But he played down the horrors of the rescue from the beach.

The letter arrived just before James himself, for shortly afterwards he got his personal papers for a forty-eight-hour leave and was able to travel home to Shadworth. His knock came on the door just as Emma was serving tea for the children and Philip was amusing them with the story of Dick Whittington.

"*Turn again, Whittington, Lord Mayor of London.*" As he read, he heard Emma answering the door and giving out a scream of delight. The children rushed to the kitchen to see what had happened just as James walked in with his arm round Emma. Tears were in Philip's eyes as he wheeled himself to the newcomer and held out his arms.

"*James, my God, is it really you?*" he exclaimed. But there was no more need for words as James knelt at the foot of Philip's chair and embraced him.

Emma knelt beside James and whispered, "*Time for the kettle.*"

It was a sombre party that ate together that night. Will and Laura joined them to share in the homecoming but talk soon turned to the others who were foremost in their minds.

James wished so much he could bring good news, but he still had no idea of Harry and Ned's whereabouts, nor if they were alive or dead.

"*Tell me any news of Beth,*" he begged, hoping for at least some relief on that front.

"*She is working hard as ever, but I feel keenly that she is too busy to write,*" admitted Philip. "*We've had one letter but nothing more.*"

"*Philip.*"

Philip looked at Emma, and she shook her head.

"*As you said, she is working very hard, and she is allowed to be free of family expectations.*"

Philip paled at the thought. James gave an involuntary shiver.

"*We are not allowing ourselves to worry about Beth,*" Emma said firmly. "*She is getting on with her life and her studies. No news is good news, as I keep reminding her father, but he worries so.*"

Philip knew that, at this time in Oxford, students would be undertaking their summer exams. They were usually set between late May and early June. He could not stop himself from worrying about Beth and hoping that Anatole was not distracting her from her work.

He longed for a letter from her, but Beth was so completely wrapped up in her growing love for Anatole that she had thoughts for little else. She would, of course, have been mortified had she known the anxiety she was causing her beloved father by not contacting him for so long. Meanwhile, Anatole was committed to his efforts to bring back refugees to Britain, but he came to Oxford at every opportunity. He had managed to find accommodation in a pub during these visits, where the owner rented him a room at the back. There, they explored their feelings for each other on the narrow single bed.

James took Emma and Philip to The White Swan, where Milly was still doggedly serving the customers and maintaining the open hospitality of the pub. When she saw the three of them, she burst into tears. Emma hugged her tightly and Philip took her hands in his and assured her of their concern for her, promising her that they were all still praying and hoping that Harry would be safe. The little family was desperate to hear of Harry and Ned's whereabouts, but there had been no shocking letters, so they lived on in the hope that the two men were alive and would get home somehow.

This happy reunion at The White Swan was to be James' last family gathering for a while. He set off the next day to return to his duties in Scotland.

Chapter 41

June 1940

By the fourth of June, the evacuation of the troops from the beaches of Northern France was complete. Once safely returned to Britain, the troops received the paperwork that would rubberstamp their leave to go home for a short respite.

Milly was at the pub some days later pulling the pints when the snug door was pushed open and a grey-haired man on crutches hobbled in. She took one look and abandoned her post with a cry of joy. "*Harry*," she screamed as she flung her arms round him. She felt a huge relief rising in her amid the concern at his use of the crutches.

"It's OK, *my girl*." Harry smiled. "*I've just damaged my ankle on board the motorboat that brought me back. Milly, my darling, how is it with you?*"

"It's *all fine now you're here, my dear. Your family has been looking after me very well. But how I've missed you.*"

"*Let's go down to find my mum. I know she won't rest till she sees me.*"

Milly was only too glad to leave the bar in the capable hands of her deputy and make their way down to Low Shadworth, Harry managing his crutches manfully.

After knocking, Harry and Milly let themselves into Holt House just as Emma was making her way down the hallway to open the door. Her hands met her mouth in shock before she ran the last few steps to reach them. "*My son, my son, thank God you're home,*" she managed to whisper in choked cries of delight as she hugged Harry.

Philip wheeled himself over, a smile split between true happiness and worry on his face. "*Now it's only Ned we need, please God.*"

"*You've seen James? Is there no word of Ned?*" asked Harry, feeling the very familiar ache of anxiety for his brother. But no news had reached any of them.

It was the tenth of June, and Florence was gloomily knitting a jumper for Teddy as she sat on the bench at the front of the Tempests' farmhouse, Daisy beside her.

"*I want to be happy that we know James and Harry are safe, but I can't stop from constantly fretting about Dad,*" Daisy confided.

"*I feel that same worry and it's completely normal that you can't wear the mask of happiness all the time, especially in the face of all we're going through, but we must hope and pray that all will be well in the end.*" Florence didn't share with Daisy that she often panicked while alone that her husband could have perished.

Daisy simply nodded.

Polly, the farm collie, began barking uproariously, and they both looked up through the farm gate and down the line of Long Lane stretching towards Low Shadworth. There, in the distance, was a lone, tall figure coming down the lane towards them.

Florence gasped. "*Daisy, it's your dad,*" she shouted. Mary heard her from the kitchen and appeared at the door, but Florence was already lifting her skirts and running as fast as she could, closely followed by Daisy, straight into the arms of the man in the lane. Ned caught her and swung her round as in the old days while Daisy grabbed hold of his arm and would not let it go.

"My darling girls, you look wonderful. Let me feast my eyes on you."

Mary had hurried out of the house and nearly caught up with them. She was beaming from ear to ear.

"Mother, Mother, come here. It's really me. Harry and James, how are they? Are they still as tough as ever?"

Between the sighs and the glad sobs, Ned related all his adventures, though he left out the part where two of his companion troopers died on the beach beside him from thirst and heat.

Mary ran inside to call Holt House as the others crammed on the bench.

"Emma, your son-in-law is home. Can you pick Teddy up from school and come down, all of you? Bring all the little German chicks too."

And sure enough, holding tight to a skipping Teddy and pushing Philip's chair, Emma and the kinder hastened down to Tempests' Farm.

Such a reunion there was, as Harry and his wife landed too with Will, Laura and Ralphie. Tears were shed as at last, Ned and Harry were able to share all they had been through, each knowing what horrors they had witnessed. As they talked, their wives and children celebrated their presence, ignorant of the traumas they had suffered.

Philip sat quietly beside the two younger men, listening to all they had experienced and thankful that they had managed to return safely. But he was horrified at the terrible losses the army had suffered in that disastrous defeat and saw beyond the joys and high spirits to the task that Churchill was facing.

"*Everest, Emma*," he whispered to his wife. "*It's a mountain to climb, my darling. We are in for a long haul, I do believe.*"

Emma shuddered and clutched his hand very tightly. She knew quite well that, like James before them, their leave would fly by and they would have to report back to their units. But—and Philip had to smile at her courage—she was undaunted in giving them all her unstinting love, with Mary beside her, glowing with their happiness even though she knew it was so very short-lived. And saying not a word to spoil the evening, she and Mary managed to dish up a most delicious supper for them all. It somehow seemed to appear by magic, as the kinder told each other in amazement afterwards.

Yet Philip had a raw, unhealed tear in his spirits that night, a wound that would remain sore until he heard from his beloved Beth. Where was she, and how was she coping? That night, with Emma beside him in their big bed, he held her very close and whispered his desperation. She took the only remedy she could think of to soothe his anxiety and prayed fervently for Beth and Anatole. As the prayer ended, she added: "*And, loving God, please let her write to us so we can know she is happy, for we cannot rest until we hear from her. Amen.*"

"*My darling*," Philip said, "*do you think it is legitimate to ask for a letter? But I hope God has heard that most heartfelt prayer, legitimate or not.*" And he smiled as she settled at last beside him into sleep.

***

It felt unfair waving Harry and Ned off at the station. Florence and Milly turned to Emma and Philip for comfort from their tears as the train disappeared into the distance. Despite the cruelty of the situation, Emma felt a surge of hope as if from nowhere. As she pushed the wheelchair back up to Holt House, she told Philip about it, and he nodded in understanding. But as they made their way up the path to their door, the postman was just parking his bike at the gate.

"A *letter, Mrs Manners*," he shouted out to her.

"*It's not like me to snatch, Sam, but today, I cannot wait to look at it*," she cried, immediately noticing the handwriting on the envelope was Beth's.

Philip watched with Sam as she ripped it open. He knew this was the answer to their most earnest prayer and yet he could hardly believe it. Beth. And how could it be that God had answered it so quickly?

"*Quickly, my love, let's go in and read it. I should have stronger faith, Emma, and we should not doubt Him.*"

And with that, they sat together in the parlour, she at the foot of his chair, and read the precious letter, while postman Sam, grinning all over his face, rode off cheerfully.

Oxford,
8th June, 1940

My dearest mother and daddy,

As I write, I realise how long it has been since I last wrote and I am mortified to think I have been so careless. I hope that you have not fretted about me, for I have been so very preoccupied with all my work and with Anatole.

On top of all that has been the drudgery of the kitchen work assigned to me by the college. Oh, Mother, the number of times I have longed for you to turn up like the good fairy and take over the jobs. I long for home, but I cannot leave my responsibilities. And, truth is, I cannot bear to be away from Anatole, who visits me as often as he can get away.

At least the summer exams are over now and I have survived them. Daddy, if it hadn't been for you sharing your love of Jane Austen and George Eliot with me through the years, I fear I would not have passed. We have had very little in the way of tutoring in our subjects. To tell the truth, it's all topsy-turvy. But I did pass, thank goodness. Now only a year left till I can work with Mr Israel myself.

Philip let out a groan, much to Emma's grief. She knew he would be very unhappy for Beth to end up with Anatole and Wilfrid. She took his hands and made him read on to get over this stumbling block.

Anatole and I have shared our fears for Ned and James and Harry, and Anatole has been terribly anxious about Pieter, though he knows his own position is safe with Wilfrid. Do you think they will intern Pieter, Daddy, after all your hard work to secure his permit? Mother, are the boys safely home from Dunkirk? And on top of all these awful fears, what of George?

You must forgive me for allowing my love for Anatole to take over me so completely. Please, Daddy, be happy for me. When term finally ends, I can't wait to come home and tell you all about it. It's only two more weeks, then I shall see you.

Till then, I send you all my love,
Beth

Philip leaned back in his chair and looked at his wife. "*Dear God, Emma. I love her so much, as life itself, but she stretches us to the limit, doesn't she? What is she planning for herself and Anatole? What does she mean about working at Bloomsbury House? It's all about Anatole, Emma. Is she being really wise, do you think?*"

"*Philip, you have to trust her and be glad we have news of her at last. And, my love, she's coming home soon, so she says. Can't you just be pleased?*"

"*Like you, Emma, I can't wait to see her. You know that. I just don't want her to have her heart broken.*"

"*I know, my darling. But she must be allowed to take her chance, as we did so long ago now. Don't forget the anguish we went through. Now it's her turn to try her wings, and we must support her. Philip, you don't need me to tell you this. And do notice, she hasn't forgotten to think of all the others. It will do her such a lot of good to be home and share it all with us.*"

There were tears in his eyes as he nodded at this reproach. "*Let's go down Long Lane, sweetheart, like the lovers of old we used to be.*"

She stooped and kissed him, and he pulled her down onto his lap and embraced her.

By now, the German army had advanced towards Paris, and there was nothing the French and its allies could do to prevent the inevitable consequence. Paris fell on the fourteenth of June, and by the fifteenth of June, infantry divisions of the German 7th army attacked across the Rhine and took the cities of Colmar and Strasbourg. The French, seeing no hope, asked for an armistice with the Germans. The surrender was signed on the twenty-second of June, and the remnants of the French who had been holding out were ordered to leave their fortifications and were taken to POW camps.

Chapter 42

Elizabeth May – The Family at War, 1940

I stepped off the train at Shadworth Station just two weeks after I wrote home. It was the twenty-second of June, a fateful day in the annals of the war. France had completely surrendered and German divisions were entering Paris—an almost unthinkable prospect a few weeks earlier.

I didn't tell them which train I was coming on because I wanted to surprise them. So, I knocked on the door of my beloved home holding my breath. Would they have forgiven me for my neglect in the past weeks? I had allowed myself to be totally swept up in Anatole's embrace.

Daddy got there first and held out his open arms to me. I knew then he had forgiven any lack on my part. And Mother followed closely behind him, rubbing her pastry-covered hands on her apron and smiling happily.

"*Look who's here, Emma,*" Daddy shouted with a break in his voice. "*Let me look at you, my dearest girl.*"

I knelt beside his chair and hid my head in his lap. He stroked my hair very gently without a word, and Mother simply did what she always did—put the kettle on. There was no need for words, but after a long time of resting there, Mother brought us both a steaming hot cup of tea.

"*My darling child, you've studied and got through a very difficult year. Your letter sounds as if it's been a strange experience in many ways, not what I would have hoped for you.*"

Daddy sighed, and I hastened to comfort him. I knew I had to make them both understand how much Anatole meant to me and I to him. I reassured them that all was well with me and that Anatole took enormous care of me. Daddy was unhappy about all the chores that fell to me, but I promised him they did not affect my work. But though Mother was much relieved to see me, she couldn't forget her worries about George and needed to articulate them. She found it very difficult to think of him flying against German specialist flyers in constant danger of being shot down.

He was attached to a squadron of Spitfires ready to defend our country from the power of the Luftwaffe—a massive force prepared to make Britain agree to peace under Hitler.

"*Philip, I cannot lose another George,*" Mother said with tears in her eyes.

I felt a cold hand choking my heart. "*How has this come about, Daddy? Why must we face such a terrible threat?*"

"*Beth, Hitler's one aim is to force Britain into capitulating entirely to his forces and, to put it bluntly, to put our entire country into Nazi hands.*"

I gasped at the horror of such a prospect.

"*But, my love, Churchill will never allow that to happen. Thank God he has been acknowledged as the prime minister in Chamberlain's place. The country needed to affirm him to face all that's to come. He is demanding a level of endurance and courage from everyone. And the air squadrons must keep the skies as clear of the oncoming danger as is possible. So you see how important the role is the RAF must play, and our own George is a part of that.*"

I looked across at Mother, and we both held our breath in shared fear.

Daddy tried to reassure us though he himself was just as anxious.

"*Come now, my two brave girls. We must not let ourselves be overcome by the fear of it all. We really must trust God to keep our country free of Hitler's evil.*" He looked at Mother with all his love in his eyes and she stood up and squared her shoulders.

"*Philip, we will keep faith and fight our fears, I promise. Beth and I are a very good team and we will indeed do our very best to keep the faith.*"

Daddy smiled at this and somehow, a sense of relief enlightened the room with a spirit of peace. I knew he would use all that prayer can do to keep George safe, and I knew that, if prayer alone was sufficient, my father would hold that in place.

My visit to them should have been an unadulterated time of joy, for I was so glad to be close to them and to the family. But our fears and the issue of my love for Anatole constantly shadowed the visit. Daddy was finding it so difficult to accept that we were together.

We all went down to the farm, where I was welcomed with open arms. Teddy danced around with pleasure to see me. I had time alone with Daisy, who was now very much the mainstay of the farm with Florence. We shared our fears for her father and for George. George meant so very much to us both; he had been our best friend throughout all the different experiences we had shared. It felt horrible to even consider if he were to be in danger.

Laura and Will with dear Ralph, now eleven years old just like Teddy, turned up at Holt House soon after I arrived, and my dear brother Will took me into the garden to ask me all about Anatole. He was very reassuring and supportive, which was a relief. He tried to make me understand that Daddy was so worried because he felt I was too young at eighteen years old, but he promised to look after Father and Mother in the difficult days ahead.

We all got together at Holt House on my last evening before my return to Oxford, Milly too. Mother surpassed herself with a delicious roasted chicken, culled from the hen house especially and smothered in her homegrown carrots and cabbages, with her own immaculate Yorkshire puddings alongside. Teddy and Ralphie simply loved Yorkshire puddings and competed with each other to see who could eat the most.

How I longed to be free to stay there with them with no more fears, but I also knew that Anatole would be looking forward to my return, and I could never deny him that.

I was back in my room at Lady Margaret Hall in Oxford by the twenty-eighth of June after a very painful farewell on the station platform. So many unsaid things were left hanging in the air as my beloved daddy held me very close and Mother just stood by his chair with her head down and tears dropping from the end of her nose.

"*Come back soon, my darling,*" she had whispered, "*and bring Anatole next time.*"

He arrived in the college quad that afternoon, and we almost ran through the back lanes of Oxford to our hideaway in the upstairs pub room. There, we lay together on the narrow bed and kissed uncontrollably. He kissed my eyelids and my nose, he kissed each ear in turn, and I looked into his deep, dark eyes and saw his gaunt cheeks hollowed by the stresses he was bearing for Wilfrid's missions. I felt the thrill of his elongated body stretched out beside me, touching my hips and my thighs that throbbed with longing for him. His hand on my breasts was tender and very sweet.

I wanted to give way to this passion very badly, and somewhere deep inside, I knew we would one day succumb, but he respected me and my parents so very much that he would not break the code he knew they expected of us both.

So we lived and shared everything with each other whenever he could get away. And together, we watched the news of the Luftwaffe's large-scale air attacks with growing horror, knowing George would be trying to stop them somewhere. Somehow, I continued to study hard, but this was only on our separated days. Anatole would often be away for many days with Mr Israel working on different routes for Jewish families to escape the perils of their situations. Sometimes, this involved Anatole travelling into Europe to implement Wilfrid's careful arrangements. This could be dangerous, and for me, it was terrifying. But the daredevil, that was my beloved Anatole, somehow seemed to glory in it.

A special delight during those days was a letter from James that Mother had forwarded to me. He was in Scotland with his battalion, training for their next sortie into the war arena.

Inverary Garrison
8th July, 1940

My dear Beth,

I think of you very often and hope you are happy in Oxford. Your father tells me you have passed the first year and now are starting on year two. Anatole will be visiting you as often as he can, I guess, and I trust you are looking after each other whenever you can. Be happy, my dear girl, that's all I ask.

This town of Inverary is spectacularly lovely, nestled beside a large loch, Loch Fyne. It is encircled by mountains, so I manage to take walks as often as I can when off duty. You would love the place, I know. One of the special things about it is the river that runs down to the loch, and if you're very lucky, you can sometimes spot salmon leaping upstream to spawn. I watched them the other afternoon, then spotted a dipper on one of the rocks. Beth, I wish I could show you it all.

Nevertheless, I often feel homesick for Shadworth and often worry about George in the skies, protecting us from the German air force. I feel so sorry I can't be there for your father and mother and for my mother, to keep them from thinking too hard about it all. We must, as your father never fails to remind me, pray hard for him and for us all.

Well, dear, I shall close now by sending you my love as always,

James

This letter was a great comfort to me. Alongside all the discipline and training James had to undergo, he was still able to see such wondrous things as salmon leaping and dippers in the river. At least he was safe up in Scotland for now. But there was no news of

Harry or Ned, so I hoped and prayed they, like James, were safely training somewhere just as secure.

As the weeks rolled on and July passed into August, the skies grew darker and darker with the constant battle out in the skies. Hitler was determined to bring our planes down so they could no longer interfere with his bombers who were targeting our main ports and all our shipping convoys bringing supplies to Britain. We had begun to feel like a besieged island. So much depended on the RAF Fighter Command destroying the German aircraft, but Anatole reckoned there was a sense of despair amongst the military hierarchy, for we had so few trained pilots against their huge strength.

I thank God Anatole was able to visit me often in those anxious days. He would make me work hard for my course studies, then we would stop work and just lie together on our narrow bed and think back to those golden days when he would meet me out of school, take my hand and walk me home. He was so very grateful for the love he was always shown by Mother and by Father. I think it made him feel he could just about bear the thought of his own parents lost somewhere in the camps.

Then came the decisive moment in the skies. The different RAF squadrons were sent out over and over to fight aerial battles against the German fighters. George was out there somewhere. All we knew was that he was flying a Spitfire—something he had managed to let Daddy know in a very brief note that got through to Shadworth. He purported to be very proud to have shot down two of their

Messerschmitts on one single afternoon. All I could think was of how Mother and Daisy would be shuddering at the very thought, as indeed was I.

Anatole came home with me during that summer period on brief visits, but the one that stands out was our visit to Holt House, where Daddy told us of his battle on behalf of Pieter. Daddy had been shocked and angered by the arrival of a posse of military police at the school, come to take Pieter away to an internment camp on the Isle of Man.

On their arrival, Alan Lorimer immediately sent for my father to prevent such an appalling injustice. Beatrice drove down to Holt House to get him, and as Mother helped him out of the car, he was met in the school courtyard by the men with Pieter between them, under arrest. Pieter was beside himself with shock, but Father wheeled himself in front of them.

"*How dare you. Where is your authorisation for this arrest? This man is a fully accepted teacher in our school and you may not come onto this property without proper permission.*"

As they produced their papers, he took one look at them and told them to follow him into Alan's office. There, he produced from his own old files, files still neatly in rows on the nearest shelves, a folder containing all the details of his various sorties into the immigration department, with clear evidence for Pieter's legitimacy as a serving teacher at the school. Then, as I was told, he accused them of setting out to commit this effrontery without proper checks.

"*How dare you come to our school and expect to deal with a teacher here as an alien? You, gentlemen, are the aliens here, and I suggest you leave forthwith.*"

They left abashed and ashamed.

Pieter told his uncle Frank this story, and it cheered Frank hugely to hear the news of Philip's never-failing care for his Jewish nephews.

But the one thing on all our minds was George, for news of the battles going on in the skies frightened us all terribly. At home at Holt House, in the chapel at the school, down at Tempests' Farm and in mine and Anatole's small pub bedroom, we all held our breath as attack after attack was raged against us and the RAF fought to hold it back.

Chapter 43

1940

They had received a letter from George at the end of August. It was a very brief scribbled note, full of his pride at his squadron's successes in the aerial battles against the fighter pilots who accompanied the big bombers heading for London. He was very vague about his exact whereabouts. Term had started at the school and things seemed on an even keel, though Emma was constantly on edge simply knowing that George was putting himself in danger, with a certain amount of bravado and ineffable courage every day. Or so it seemed from his note.

When she heard the telegraph boy whistling up the path on the morning of the seventh of September, her heart almost stopped in the rush of that earlier memory from long ago when the news of the death of her first son, George, reached her. She screamed, and Philip heard her from the garden, where he was enjoying the sunshine. He wheeled himself in as she answered the door.

"*Thank you*," he said to the boy, aware that Emma was past all niceties and politeness.

Her cheeks paled as she tore the telegram open. Then he grabbed her and pulled her onto his lap as she swooned, reading its contents as she put her head on his chest.

To the next of kin of George Holt: It is with great regret that I have to inform you that George Holt was injured in action on the sixth of September and taken to Southampton Hospital, suffering from acute burns. Please contact Biggin Hill Air Base for further information. Commanding Officer Ryan, 17th Squadron.

Philip waited for the faint to pass and then gently raised her to her feet with utter tenderness.

"*Darling, do not fear. He's alive, love, and now we must get to him as soon as we can. But first, let me contact his squadron leader to get more information. And, Emma, we need to tell Florence and Daisy and contact Beth.*"

Emma put on her coat and ran down Long Lane to the farm with all the speed she could muster as Philip phoned the base. Daisy, gathering up the stubble in the fields, saw her frantic pace and ran to meet her. Emma was exhausted with the emotion and the huge haste with which she had run, yet managed to gasp out the horrible news she was bearing, "*Daisy, it's George. He's crashed and is badly burned.*"

This news was like a poison dart to Daisy's heart, and she grabbed it as if to keep it beating.

Florence had been watching the conversation from the farm window and saw the overwhelmed emotions from both parties. She opened the door to them, dreading what they had to tell her.

"*It's George. He's badly burned and in hospital,*" Emma repeated, the look of sadness on her face immediately worsening, as if she were just hearing the news for the first time rather than being the person relaying it.

Florence was her mother's daughter, and seeing someone needed to take control of the situation, she acted ruthlessly and without hesitation. "*Daisy, you can take Dad's car, as Mother and Philip do need to get to him as soon as possible. And, Daisy, there is no time to grieve over this. I am trusting you to drive to Holt House for Philip and then get them to the station. Then, I assume, you'll want to finish the journey with them. If I know Philip, he will already have found out the trains and the connections through to Southampton.*

"*Mother, just rest for a minute to get your breath back, then let Daisy take you. I shall ring Philip and tell him you are all set to go. I'll get the children out of school and bring them all here. Laura will help, I know. Ralph and Teddy are really splendid with them all and they love coming down here.*"

She was right. Philip had heard how George had bailed out close to his base, as his cockpit was on fire from a direct hit from a Messerschmitt. He had been recovered badly burned from the site and transferred directly by ambulance to Southampton Burns Unit.

Then Philip had checked out the next train through to Sheffield and the connection to London—a route he had covered many times in the past. The final lap of the journey was the fast train from Victoria to Southampton.

Soon enough, though not nearly soon enough for heartbroken Daisy and Emma, they were on the way. At each stop, they had to ask for help with the wheelchair, much to Philip's chagrin, but he managed to haul himself into a seat once his chair was stored.

By taxicab, they reached Southampton Burns Unit and asked to see George Holt. An orderly led the way and they followed hurriedly.

He was lying flat on a low bed, his arms and legs swathed in bandages. A drip was linked into a vein in his hand, which they guessed was giving him the pain relief he needed. The sight of him horrified them, but his eyes were open, and as they approached, a faint voice came from the bed, exclaiming, "*Grandma, Uncle Philip.*"

Daisy threw herself to her knees beside him and Emma knelt by his other side. They could all see the tears springing up in his eyes.

"*My darling boy, we're here,*" Emma said, "*and you are going to recover from this so we can get you home. Just believe it, George. My dear, is it terribly painful?*"

"*I'll be alright, Grandma. I shot down one of theirs before they hit me, so I can be proud of that.*" He turned to Philip, not wanting Emma and Daisy to see any more of his pain and fear. "*Uncle Philip, please stay with me. I need you to make me stronger to get through this.*"

"*Our dear boy,*" said Philip, masking his own emotion, "*we're not going anywhere. We have just got to get you well so we can bring you home.*"

Daisy stood up and leant down to stroke his forehead. "*Think, my dear, dear George, how we will picnic in the farm fields, just like we used to. You have just got to stay patient until you are fit to leave hospital.*"

"*There speaks my very best friend.*" As he spoke, his eyes were closing with weariness, and Philip took charge.

"*Come, Emma, Daisy, we must leave him to sleep because that is the best healer. We will find a doctor who can tell us what to expect, then we must find a place to stay so we can be here when he needs us."*

Many days of sitting beside George followed as the wounds gradually healed, days that reminded Emma of those long hours when she had sat beside Philip after the leg amputation and before they sent him off to convalesce. But the specialist doctors were reassuring. The burns had been limited, not as dangerously extensive as first thought, and were going to heal in time. With care, he would be able to use his arms and legs again.

To Philip, it was a powerful reminder of his own suffering long ago and he felt incredibly close to the young man on the bed. He immediately informed the family of George's situation, including Milly, Harry's wife. Of course, he could not reach Harry, Ned and James, who were away in some distant danger of their own. But when he let his own beloved Beth know, she came straight from Oxford with Anatole.

She arrived on the fifteenth of September, the day that became known as Battle of Britain Day, when the Luftwaffe were finally overcome in their purpose to gain supremacy in the skies and open the way for invasion. This was denied them almost miraculously by the incredible onslaught of seventeen newly equipped squadrons of fighters. Fifty-six enemy aircraft were shot down. The Luftwaffe could no longer make accurate bombing assaults after this defeat and turned to other tactics.

Beth, with Anatole beside her, came like a whirlwind to George's bedside. Daisy was sitting beside a sleeping George, and she put her finger to her lips to warn them not to wake him. She hugged Beth close and shook Anatole's hand as a kind of reassurance.

"*Don't cry, Beth. He's going to be alright. The doctors assure us the wounds are healing under these bandages. They are dressed freshly each morning, and he bears the pain more and more easily.*"

Beth clutched Daisy's hands in hers. "*Oh, Daisy, thank God. I've been in agony since Daddy let me know. And where are Mother and Daddy?*"

"*They went to get a drink and a break. They have watched by his bedside day and night, and I have taken turns with them. Oh God, Beth, I can't bear it.*"

Anatole smiled at Daisy's fervent words. The sleeping George opened his eyes and looked up at the three old comrades gathered round the bed. His eyes widened and then he grinned.

"*Bethy, is that really you? And, Anatole, old friend. What a wonderful sight. Oh God, Anatole. I really copped it, didn't I? But at least I managed to get one of them before I had to ditch my machine.*"

And suddenly, the tears came, and George clutched Beth's hand tightly and lay back on his pillows exhausted. Beth looked across at Anatole, aghast.

"*George, try not to talk. We are all here and we are all very proud of you. The doctors have said your burns are gradually healing, but you have to be patient.*"

There was a cry of delight behind Beth, and she turned to see Philip and Emma returning from their break. Wordlessly, Emma rushed over and hugged Beth close to her before Philip scooped her into his arms.

"*Daddy, Mother, how good it is to see you. I have been desperate to get here to see George. Do you know how long it will be before he can get up and walk again? When can you take him home to Holt House?*"

Philip put his fingers to his lips to hush Beth's questions, far too close to the point of George's anxiety.

Daisy whispered to Anatole, "*We don't know yet how long it's going to take. George is already talking about returning to his squadron, but I don't know if that's ever going to be possible.*"

Anatole understood Daisy's remonstrance and sat beside George to bring the talk back to much more everyday things.

"*Are the Spitfires good to handle, George? I cannot quite imagine you with complete mastery of such a plane. It must be an awesome experience.*"

"*It's just stunning, Anatole. I love flying.*"

"*You mustn't fret, George. That will only delay the healing process. Patience, dear friend. We're all here for you.*"

Watching Anatole, Philip saw the maturity he had now acquired and felt a surge of hope that his beloved Beth was in safer hands than he had feared.

The hospital in Southampton resounded that day with many voices and much laughter as the family gathered round George's bed and cheered him on. For the first time since the accident, Daisy found herself relaxing, allowing herself to enjoy the company. Her cheeks took on a rosier bloom and her spirits lifted. George lay looking round them all and felt a sudden sense of peace that all would be well and that nothing could take away the love they shared.

They all rejoiced despite the horrors the Germans now unleashed on London and other cities, having lost the battle of the skies. The Blitz began in earnest now. But in that ward in Southampton, they felt new hope despite everything.

The visit ended with many reassurances to George of better times ahead together, and Beth and Anatole left for Oxford once more. Philip hugged Emma very close that night and thanked her for the millionth time for being his wife.

As October turned to November, the moment came when Philip and Emma were able to bring George home to Holt House for time to recuperate completely and for his limbs to properly recover from the terrible burns they had withstood. He was able to hobble round the garden holding on to a walking stick and, as his hands and arms began to heal from the awful sores they still bore, he even began to tend the garden, much to Emma's delight.

Milly got to know her stepson very well in those heady autumn days, often visiting when she had no duties at The White Swan. But it was Daisy who claimed his attention the most, often picking him up in her car and driving at top speed to the farm. During that Indian summer, they picnicked often in the fields. Teddy and Ralph, accompanied by Laura, would join them after school, whilst Emma and Florence would make piles of sandwiches to take down to them.

"*I promised you picnics when you got well, George, and here we are at last*," said Daisy, laughing.

Perhaps, best of all, was that Pieter and some of the kinder children would also arrive after school. The German children were closely attached to Pieter now, and they took his lead in all the games they played. On these occasions, while George watched them, sitting close to Philip's chair, they often popped up with questions about his battle with the enemy fighters and how the cockpit fire had happened. Their English was now immaculate, and their settled and comfortable manner gave Philip real pleasure.

One morning, George had a visit from his old squadron leader who had come to check out his fitness and whether he was motivated to return to the field. The squadron leader was a very tall, sombre man, but he gradually unbent as he was welcomed into the family.

Emma led Captain Williams into the garden, where George was idly playing with the chickens. But he stood to attention when he saw his captain.

"*Well, Flight Lieutenant Holt, Rumour has it that you are now ready to take up your position in the squadron again. We are still fighting to prevent the Luftwaffe from achieving their bombing targets and we could do with an experienced airman.*"

"*Sir, I believe I could manage. My scars are more or less healed and the pain has gone now.*"

His captain smiled at his enthusiasm and took the scarred hand gently into his own before shaking it warmly. Philip and Emma, both looking on, were so glad for George to be back to his old self but torn at the thought that he would once more be walking into danger. Emma looked at Philip with a huge sigh, but Philip squeezed her hand in reassurance.

"*Well, Captain Williams, I think you have your answer,*" said Philip. "*Thank you for coming, and you go with our prayers and best wishes for the days ahead. George will be very glad to return, we both know. But please stay a while with us and enjoy my wife's excellent baking.*"

"*Captain Williams,*" Emma interrupted, "*you certainly must not go without a cup of tea. Please sit down for a minute or two and relax. The kettle is on and we shall be glad of your company.*"

She hurried into the kitchen and emerged with cups of tea and a plateful of her delicious cakes. The older man tucked in gladly before regretfully standing up, ready to say his farewells.

"*Mr and Mrs Manners, thank you for your hospitality. It has been my pleasure. George, we look forward to your return.*"

With a smart salute, he left the little family.

This visit was to mark the end of George's long convalescence, and all too soon, the day for his return to his squadron arrived. He would have dearly loved to be able to stay under his grandma's care and the parting with her and Philip felt a very painful one, yet he knew what service he could bring to the fight in the air and something in him loved the daring adventure of it.

Leaving the family at the farm was also extremely difficult, for he had been so lovingly cared for by Daisy. Deep inside himself, he knew she would suffer from being unable, as his cousin, to be a wife to him. He resolved to keep a special place in his heart for her.

Florence observed his parting from Daisy with a saddened heart. She was aware of the feelings Daisy had for her cousin yet believed that Daisy would one day find someone who could give her love untrammelled by external societal expectation.

The day ended and George's departure drew nigh. He was ushered to the station to catch the train back for London and thence to Biggin Hill, where his squadron was to receive him with open arms.

Daisy kept up the brave front till the train pulled away, then Philip took her hand and handed her his handkerchief.

"*Our dear girl, we must once again face up to what this war will bring us next. I happen to know you are as brave as ten lions. We must trust God to keep George and the others safe, wherever they are. Will you help me, Daisy?*"

"*Oh I will, Uncle Philip,*" said the brave Daisy as she pushed his wheelchair up the hill back home.

Chapter 44

1941

Shadworth returned to its quieter, gentler pace after George's departure to his squadron.

Beth was working very hard in Oxford, not only in her books, but also helping with all the domestic duties of her college. Lady Margaret Hall would have seemed like another world entirely to any student who had studied there before the war outbreak. It was buzzing with menial activities accompanying the maintenance of all its housekeeping needs and with very few normal staff. The result of this was that students were exhausted at every day's end, yet there was also the camaraderie that comes from sharing hard work. Beth was always in a state of tension, praying that Anatole would keep safe with Wilfrid.

Anatole came to see her whenever he could in between his many rescue missions with Wilfrid into Europe to seek out and bring terrified Jews to safety. These expeditions were always fraught with danger, but Wilfrid was almost obsessed with the need to rescue everyone he could.

For Philip and Emma, it was very hard to be so very far away from Beth, but they had promised themselves that she must be allowed the space to be with Anatole and to do her studies. They both held their breath and, knowing the passionate love Beth had for Anatole, hoped she would not get pregnant at this time.

Frank Jacques was in constant touch with them, and they knew he fully supported Wilfrid and Bertha Bracey in all their efforts. He alerted Philip to the horrors of the Blitz over London, but the bombings of Sheffield, Doncaster and Leeds were all closer to home. Emma found herself frightened by it all, more than she had ever felt fear before. She and Sheila Thomson often shared their fears, knowing their boys were out there somewhere.

As for news of Harry, Ned or James, there was very little. They only knew that wherever they were and in whatever battalion they had been placed, only their prayers could sustain them.

The Kindertransport children were by now growing up apace and were fully settled into school routine, thriving on the school's curriculum set up for them with Pieter at the helm. Only the smallest of them, now six years old, remained at Holt House and attended the school across the road where all their own children had gone. The kinder at the farm and in school joined in all the Manners family gatherings with zealous joy.

Then, at last, there came a letter from Harry. It came to Milly, who ran down to Low Shadworth as soon as she had read it.

King's Own Yorkshire Light Infantry,
Royal Armoured Corps,
9th June 1941

My dear Milly,

I have managed to access someone willing to take this letter for me to get it posted. I pray it reaches you and that you can take it on to my beloved mother and Philip and all the family.

All I can tell you is that we are being sent out to Burma, but I can say no more, since we are completely constrained to remain silent on the details.

My dear wife, I have no idea how long this posting will last, but you must know I have you in my thoughts and prayers at all times. I have to trust God now for the days ahead—that is undoubtedly what Philip would say. May God keep us all safe.

Your loving Harry

They gathered in Emma's kitchen and hugged each other with a mixture of relief and anxiety for Harry and his regiment. Every day offered fresh anxieties at this critical time in the war, but it struck them all forcibly that time was passing.

On a sunny Saturday at the end of June 1941, in the ancient Oxford Radcliffe Camera, Beth Manners received her English degree, watched by her beloved father and mother, Anatole and Daisy, who were the ones honoured to receive the much sought-after tickets. She had been awarded an Upper Second in English Literature—the subject that her father had excelled in many years before.

Philip could not contain his pride in his child's success. "*Emma, she is following in my footsteps, something I never dared hope. But, Emma, she's done it.*"

His wife leant over and gently kissed his forehead. "*My love, of course she has. You began to teach her a love of books when she was just a tiny thing, and now it has all come to its proper conclusion. I'm so glad for you, dearest. You know how you inspired this gardener's wife all those many years before. Oh, Philip, many blessings have been poured on us in spite of the most tragic circumstances."*

The tears fell, and Philip handed her his big white handkerchief, smiling.

"*Emma Manners, none of this could have come about but for you and your indomitable spirit.*"

They all ate together that evening at Browns' Restaurant—a place where Philip himself had occasionally eaten as a young student. He knew it served the very best roast meats and pies and wanted them to savour the pleasure for themselves.

"*Mr and Mrs Manners,*" said Anatole as he cut into a slice of succulent roast beef, "*I can never thank you enough for allowing me to share in your family and to be able to call Beth my own. How I wish my own dear mother and father could have been here too. Who knows where they are now, but I pray God they may still be alive.*"

"*Oh, Anatole, don't be sad tonight,*" cried Daisy.

"*Yes, my dear boy,*" said Philip, "*we must be patient and not lose hope. Meanwhile, we are trusting you to look after our Beth. She has whispered to me that she is hoping to work in Bloomsbury with Wilfrid and Bertha Bracey. Is this part of a grand plan?*"

"*Philip, I have asked Beth to be my wife,*" said Anatole. "*I have the ring for her already. All we need is for you and Emma to give us your blessing so that we can be married and she can come to London as my wife.*" He set down his knife and fork, then looked round them all hopefully.

Emma gave a short cry and covered her mouth in shock as Beth blushed crimson. Philip had prepared himself for something like this after Beth had told him what she wanted to do. He took Emma's hand and squeezed it reassuringly.

"*Mother, Daddy, be pleased for me,*" Beth said. "*It's what I dearly want. And whatever happens in all the dangers Anatole faces in his work with Wilfrid, I shall be his wife.*"

And so the day ended, Beth having received her degree and now full of excited anticipation of a marriage with the man she had loved from girlhood.

Beth and Anatole were married very quietly on her birthday in the chapel of Philip's school with only a few guests in early September 1941. It was quiet of necessity, for indeed, as George later laughed, everyone had gone to war. But George himself made it and Will came with Laura. Will had been reprieved from a call up, thanks to his age and his status as an important craftsman. Frank Jacques and Wilfrid Israel came from London, and Alan and Beatrice, Milly, Edna and Sheila Thomson and all the kinder children with Teddy and Ralph joined together to make it a sparkling ceremony despite its modest status.

Pieter, of course, was Anatole's best man and spoke movingly in his speech of those other absent ones. Daisy, looking on, was not unaware of the wisdom he demonstrated in his words, nor of the figure he cut as he stood tall and very handsome in his new suit, which Emma had insisted she was going to buy whether he liked it or not. But the absence of James in particular, unable to get away from Scotland, left Beth with a small corner of her heart sad with regret.

Philip made a speech celebrating the love that had begun when they were still a schoolboy and a girl. When he went on to say how they must always remember those who could not be with them, those they all longed to see again, Ned and Harry and James, there was not a dry eye in the house.

As Anatole took Beth in his arms that wedding night, it was the zenith of all her hopes. And when Philip took Emma in his arms that same night, it was a much gentler embrace, but nonetheless wonderful in the expression of their love grown through their many years together.

Chapter 45

Elizabeth May – Life Under the Shadow of War, 1941 - 1942

On my nineteenth birthday, the eighth of September, I found myself a married woman living in a flat that Wilfrid had generously found for us. I was so very happy despite the many people I missed terribly, of whose whereabouts we knew nothing. Harry's only letter to Milly had informed us his troop was heading for Burma, but Florence had heard nothing of Ned's battalion and my treasured letter sent from James more than a year ago had only told us he was training in Scotland.

Nevertheless, Anatole and I were idyllically happy. Being together without constraint and working in Bloomsbury beside Bertha Bracey was very rewarding. We often visited homes where she had managed to place refugee orphans. She was tireless in serving the needs of those children, and I know Anatole had a great respect for her. I liked her very much.

The one shadow over all our pleasures was the fear I felt for Anatole, who remained absolutely faithful to Wilfrid and always committed himself to whatever enterprise Wilfrid embarked on no matter where or whatever the risks. I dreaded those calls from Wilfrid asking to speak to Anatole, and I could never persuade Anatole to refuse him because he always reminded me that, in that way, he was somehow closer to his mother although she was physically lost to him.

When I told Daddy of my fears, he always steadfastly reminded me that I must trust that God would have it all in His hands and to let my fretting be. I found that difficult to believe, and I know I shocked him when I argued the point with him. But Mother, always anxious for Harry and Ned, understood. She would remind Daddy of all the weary times they had shared, when God had seemed very far away. Daddy would nod at those reminders and beg our pardon, yet he would insist that, though no safety could be guaranteed, God would help them through. Somehow, his faith helped me to draw courage.

As the days and weeks slipped by, we anxiously devoured the newspapers every day for any news. Mother fretted about Harry, out in Burma, and about Ned, whose troop was stationed in Morocco, serving with the Mediterranean force. Meanwhile, Mary Tempest, despite her age, was tireless in sustaining the life of the farm, and Daisy had pronounced herself farm manager in organising all the farm's yields and driving supplies across to the troops wherever they were called for. The farm became a kind of pantry of riches, sustaining the brigades nearby.

She told me she felt herself to be an actual soldier in the KOYLI brigades she assisted. KOYLI stood for King's Own Yorkshire Light Infantry, but we all grew used to using the acronym. The soldiers who came to the farm to help load up their orders of supplies used to flirt with Daisy and one or two asked her out, but she would have none of them.

George sometimes flew over the farm, and he would dip his wings three times to tell us that was his plane. Daisy and he had arranged that, and with all of us, she gloried in it. Indeed, we were all very proud of George.

I sometimes felt homesick for Shadworth, and I was very thankful that Daddy and Mother were steadily holding the fort there. I was desperate for them to stay fit despite the fact they were now in their seventies. Sure enough, they remained a source of great strength to the life of the school. As the months of 1942 rolled by, I was confident that all would be well at home.

Chapter 46

1942

Moulmein,
Southern Burma
July, 1942

My dear Milly,

I write to you with no idea whether this note will reach you, but I write with the forlorn hope that it might.

My brigade is in disarray, as we are being pursued relentlessly by the Japs, with the express purpose of driving our entire army out of Burma. Life is tough, my dear Milly, and the heat extraordinary.

The Japs have begun building a railway from this vicinity, which, I guess, will be to improve their links with troops in Siam. We are meanwhile trying to hold them back, but it's tough terrain and morale is low.

All I really ask, Milly, is for you to keep well and keep the home fires burning! That is for all my family down in Shadworth.

Your Harry

Milly ran all the way down to Holt House and found Philip enjoying the sunshine out in the garden. She practically ran into his arms.

"*Steady, my dear. What is it?*"

"*Read this,*" she exclaimed, and he took the note from her, rapidly gathering the implications of it.

"Milly, don't despair, love. All will be well." He kept hold of the note tenderly, smiling positively. *"We must be patient till we get more news. Harry can look after himself and has done for many years. You'll see."*

Emma came hurrying out to them, rubbing her hands dry on her apron. *"Milly, are you OK, my dear? Is Harry alright?"*

"Don't panic, my darling," Philip quickly reassured her. *"He is fine, but the news is not great. Milly is feeling shocked by it, but she need not be. Harry will be fine."*

Emma hastily took the letter from Philip and read it. She soon realised the anxiety it had produced for Milly, and she herself felt a tingle of ice down her spine. What if Harry were to be killed in the fighting, or, if captured, what would happen to him? Rumours of the excoriating behaviour of the Japanese commanders were rife. But she swallowed her fears and became her usual practical self.

"Milly, come on inside. I'm going to make tea and we'll just have a quiet time together and digest this. Philip, can we do anything to find out what's going on?"

He shook his head sadly. He knew news from the Far Eastern Front came terribly slowly, and all they could really do was to wait for more information, perhaps from news bulletins from out there.

Emma hugged Milly, and she dried her tears. The two women had become the best of friends since the men had gone away, both sharing the same anxiety over Harry. Of course, Emma had major anxiety over the others too, but Florence and Laura seemed to find comfort in each other more than with her.

"Come on." Emma took Milly's hand and led her indoors. There, she made two cups of tea, placing

one in front of Milly, who was already sitting at the kitchen table, and one in front of herself.

Milly placed both hands around her cup, as if she could warm the cold emptiness she was feeling inside. "*How I long for this awful war to be over, Emma. I don't feel I have had any real time with Harry.*"

"*I understand that, Milly. But take courage. Harry has come through the first war and I am confident in him.*"

Milly silently took a sip of her tea and stared off out of the window. Emma wished she felt as confident inside as she was portraying to Milly, but the truth was, she thought often of her beloved son who hadn't made it out of the previous war and it set off extra fear in her. She'd seen firsthand the reality of war, the reality of grief, and she wasn't sure she could cope with losing a second child.

They sat together quietly, perfectly comfortable in each other's company. Perhaps it was the fact that they weren't alone that was healing.

Milly sipped the last of her tea and stood up, pushing the chair under the table. "*Thank you for your company; I think it was exactly what I needed. But I must get back, for I'm on duty at The White Swan later today.*"

"*If we have any further news, we'll reach you straight away, Milly,*" said Emma as she gathered up the cups and put them into the sink.

Milly smiled thankfully and waved her goodbye.

Emma went back outside, pushed Philip's chair into the shade of the oak tree and took a deep breath. She thanked God for her husband and for her beautiful garden. The roses were in full bloom and the bees were busy working their way amongst them. The dark purple lavender bush nearby gave off a delicate perfume into the air.

There was a click of the latch on the gate, and Emma and Philip smiled as young Ralph appeared. Laura and Will closely followed.

"*Philip*," said Will, rushing into the garden with a grin. "*I am so pleased to have had a letter from James. It's good news. He is planning on visiting his mother and calling in here en route from somewhere deadly hush-hush. He seems to be thriving in his Scottish posting but as busy as ever. I know Beth will be thrilled to hear news of him. Perhaps we should get her over here for a couple of nights.*"

"*Is Will more at peace in the Home Guard now, my dear?*" Emma asked Laura very quietly when she had her to herself. "*I do get anxious moments when I worry about him feeling left behind by his peers, but I'm sure he is doing just as much good working here. If only he could see that.*"

"*Emma, I really think he has found a role with the other men now. And did you know he's turned into the school gardener? Following in James' footsteps.*"

"*Why, that's amazing. James, for one, will be absolutely delighted to hear about that.*"

And with that, Emma hastened into her kitchen to make tea for the little party and to load the table with sandwiches and cake. Despite flour being rationed, she always seemed to manage somehow.

Chapter 47

1942

James had planned to visit home to arrive just in time for Beth's twentieth birthday. He wrote Philip a brief note announcing his intention:

I don't want to miss Beth and Daisy's birthdays this year, my friend. Will it be fine with you and Emma for me to stay a night or two? Much to tell!

Yours,

James.

Emma just laughed when she read this and immediately rang Beth at Bloomsbury House. She reached Bertha Bracey first, who hastened to find Beth to come to the phone.

"Mother, *what is it?* Is *Daddy alright?*" were Beth's first, somewhat anxious words. She could not help the thought that an unexpected phone call from her mother might mean bad news about her father.

"*Of course he is and can't wait to see you. James is coming home for a very short holiday and is going to stay with us at Holt House. He wants to be there for your birthday. Can you get away, my darling?*"

"Oh *joy*, Mother, *I wouldn't miss him for the world, but I shall have to leave Anatole; he's off on another scary mission with Wilfrid. At least it'll take my mind off it. And, Mother, it'll be Daisy's twentieth too, so she will want to be there as well."*

"We'll make it a celebration birthday tea, shall we? Please beg Anatole's pardon that I am doing it when he can't be there. Love you. Bye, my darling."

Meanwhile, Philip wrote a short but enthusiastic note to reply to James:

We can't wait to see you. Come at once!

It was September the eighth, the day of Beth's birthday, Daisy's having been the day before, that James drew his car up by the gate to Holt House after driving down from Inveraray. He sat for a moment and took a deep breath, knowing Emma would have got his mother to come to meet him there and all the Tempest family would be gathered to greet him too. He had to admit to himself that of all his beloved family, it was Beth whom he especially wanted to see. But he did not allow himself to dwell on such a thought, which he felt to be just a little illegitimate. No. Instead, he pictured them all, one by one.

He had no longer than a couple of seconds to himself before Beth, closely followed by his mother, was struggling to open the heavy Jaguar door. She was shrieking with frustration at being unable to budge it, so, smiling, he opened it, and she nearly fell over on the dusty road.

"Well, hello, my little one. That's a fine way to greet a long-lost traveller."

"James, don't tease. And here's your mum as desperate as I am to be the first to greet you."

James succumbed to the embrace from his mother, squeezing her hand as he did so. And before he knew it, all Emma's invited guests congregated around him with cries of pleasure.

Beth took his hand and led him up the path to the door of Holt House, where her father was waiting in his wheelchair with Emma beside him.

"*Philip, Emma, how very glad I am to see you. Daisy, happy birthday, my dear, and, Beth, can you both really be twenty years old? It makes me feel very old.*"

"*Come on in, James, and sit down,*" invited Emma. "*These excited young ones can come and help me make tea.*"

She bustled off to check that there was nothing missing from the wonderful spread she had laid out.

James relaxed all the tense muscles that he carried every day as he gradually felt himself perfectly at home. Despite all the restrictions of wartime, Emma had prepared, with Beth's help, a substantial tea. There were bread rolls laden with cheese, hard-boiled eggs and baby tomatoes, sausage rolls and quarters of pork pie. Emma had even managed to make a glorious trifle topped with a thick layer of whipped cream, which James was particularly fond of. How long it had been since he had eaten so well.

As they seated themselves at the table, Philip looked around, feeling that this loving gathering was somehow a taste of heaven.

Later, after the party had split up homewards, James was left with the three Manners. James and Emma sat on the big old settee next to Philip, while Beth sat at her daddy's foot.

"*I am now working on a very special and urgent task, training troops for the moment when the Allies will return to the fields of France to retrieve the land the Germans have occupied,*" James shared with them. "*This will be no easy matter and it has to wait until the moment is right, possibly more than a year away.*"

He could say very little else, but it was enough to convey the magnitude of his undertaking.

"*But*," James said, laughing, "*at least we do it all with the glorious backcloth of the lochs and mountains.*"

Beth took a great deal of comfort from the thought, but she also found it, in general, a real comfort to have James with them, even if only briefly.

Her mind sped to Anatole and Wilfrid as she relaxed at her father's foot. If only they could have shared this evening with them, but instead, she had tearfully packed them off on another mission to reach refugees in hiding. Wilfrid had not allowed Anatole to tell her his destination; he was meticulous at keeping everything absolutely confidential, particularly when the mission involved occupied territory. And indeed, Beth had accustomed herself to swallowing down her tears to wave them off whenever it was necessary. And then her thoughts took flight to those very distant places where Harry and Ned might be at that very time.

Oh, if only this fearful war could be over and everyone safely home, she thought.

Chapter 48

1943

That thought would be repeated many times as 1942 turned into 1943. Florence's usual stoicism was stretched hugely as she heard nothing from Ned except brief notes assuring her he was alive and well. She had heard that his battalion was somewhere in the Mediterranean, preparing to invade Sicily—news that had come indirectly from a source close to Bertha Bracey. Bertha knew of Florence's desperate longing for news and had reported this information to Emma and Philip as soon as she heard it.

But then, in early February, a telegram arrived at The White Swan. Milly opened it, her heart in her mouth. She was horrified at what she read. Harry's regiment had come under severe attack and Harry, along with many of his compatriots, had been captured. She felt herself shaking but knew it was important to get down to Holt House. She landed at the door out of breath and trembling uncontrollably. She handed the telegram to Emma, who quickly took in the news and rushed to tell Philip. As she told him, Emma felt a cold hand on her heart as she realised what this meant. Yet she knew she had to keep a brave face on for Milly's sake.

"*Emma, Philip, what will it mean for Harry? I've heard terrible things about the Japs and their treatment of prisoners.*"

Philip knew full well the implications of this capture. Harry would be a prisoner of war under the Japanese, whose reputation was notorious. Prisoners of war would be sent to work on the railway being built by the Japanese to link Southern Burma with Bangkok. He sighed deeply, much to Emma's chagrin, for she knew that Milly was hanging on every nuance of response from Philip. She squeezed his hand to remind him to be gentle, and he smiled at Milly in an attempt to reassure her.

"*Philip, what do you think? Will he be alright?*" Milly demanded to know again, the silence making her feel even worse.

Philip took both her hands in his and squeezed them. "*My dear Milly, we must pray that God will keep him strong and that the rumours of mistreatment are overexaggerated. And we ourselves must stay strong for Harry's sake.*"

Milly gasped, and Emma, herself feeling the old sense of dread she had so many times had to conquer, sat down with her on the old settee. There, the tears of both women flowed, and Philip felt suddenly hopelessly inadequate.

He was saved from this feeling by the arrival of two friends coming straight home from school in Cranston, both having passed for grammar school there three years earlier. Ralph, with Teddy close on his heels, bounced into the room.

"*Grandad, we have both been picked to play for the school football team. Isn't it wonderful?*" yelled Teddy. Then they both stopped dead, seeing their grandma and Aunt Milly looking so sad.

Emma nodded at Milly, and they both made for the kitchen as the boys continued to tell Philip all their news. Emma gave Milly a hug, and they both had to smile at the excited boys.

"*I'll be alright now, Emma*," said Milly. "*I don't know what I would do without you and Philip. But we do have to put on a braver face for the young ones.*" She then set to work helping Emma cut cake and put out biscuits for the lads.

Thus, the news of Harry became part of the tensions that always now stayed with them all. Not knowing what was happening to their menfolk was very hard to bear. They knew little of Ned, of Harry and indeed of George still flying with his squadron, though James at least did not feel so far away.

Beth came home often as the year swung round. Whenever Anatole was away with Wilfrid, she retreated to her place beside her father's chair, where he loved to relax in the parlour. Meanwhile, Emma had been secretly watching Beth's girth gradually growing rounder. Emma was desperate to share her suspicions with Philip, but she wanted to wait till she could be absolutely sure. In the end, she had no need to wait, as Beth stood up, the fireplace a backdrop behind her, and shared the news she could no longer contain.

"*Mother, Daddy, I have to tell you some very exciting news. I can hardly believe it, but I am pregnant. Are you pleased? You are going to be grandparents all over again.*"

Philip took a moment to take in the information, then shook his head, letting out a sigh, the excitement not yet outweighing the shock. "*I am dumbfounded, my darling,*" he said. "*This is astonishing news. How long have you suspected?*"

"*I knew it already.*" Emma smiled. "*It was when you couldn't get into your blue dress. I have watched with interest your waist grow larger.*"

"*Emma Manners,*" broke in Philip as Beth shrieked at her mother, "*you have known this remarkable truth and kept it from me? How could you?*"

Emma ran to his chair and embraced him. "*My darling, I felt I should let Beth tell you.*" She turned to Beth. "*When do we expect this wonderful arrival, and is Anatole pleased?*"

"*Mother, he can hardly believe it and is so, so thrilled. And the doctor says it should be due in August. A summer baby, Mother. Oh, what fun we shall have with him... or her.*"

Philip watched them dancing together with such energy, and he felt a pang of envy that he could not join in. There were times when he still felt his disability keenly, but he managed this sadness with prayer, resting his grief in God. Now, at this very special time, he prayed silently for his beloved daughter and for Anatole, and Emma observed tears pricking at his eyes. She let go of Beth's hands and ran to him, and only then did his tears flow. He gave in completely to the emotion as Beth too came to comfort him.

"*Daddy, my daddy, it's alright, this baby will come safely and be your best friend. Just wait and see.*"

He put his head in his hands. He was so unutterably grateful for this blessing endowed on him through so many trials, so many painful tribulations. But, with that thought, he drew himself up.

"*My darlings, please forgive me. Beth, it's only that I am so proud of you and very glad about this glorious news. I feel grateful that we've come through so much.*"

Beth went back to her favourite seat by his chair. Emma, ever practical but full of the same passion she had always felt for them both, muttered a quiet, "*I'll make tea.*" She scurried into the kitchen to blow her nose very loudly. Beth and her beloved daddy looked at each other and collapsed into laughter.

Beth was right about Anatole's joy at the news of baby, though, like Philip, he was anxious that she keep herself and baby well. Philip watched her very closely at every visit, so afraid something would spoil her delight. But she remained absolutely well and strong as the weeks went by. Her only complaint was to Emma when she admitted, "*Was it like this for you, Mother? Baby kicks a lot now and I find the weight of him sometimes hard to bear, though I wouldn't dream of telling Anatole.*"

Her mother laughed at this. "I *remember being much the same with Daddy when you were on the way. It must run in the family, my love.*"

Daisy and Florence were delighted at the news of Beth's pregnancy though Daisy kicked herself at the pang of envy she felt at the news and Florence was desperately sad for her daughter.

"*I am so pleased for Beth, but I really wish Daisy will find the same happiness one day,*" Florence admitted to Emma. Emma gave Florence a hug. She understood well the pain it was causing.

"*Oh, Florence, how I wish I had a magic wand to wave for all things to be free and joyful. I pray for Daisy every night. She needs to find a young man for her own self.*"

Indeed, Emma did pray for Daisy each night, as she did for all the members of the family, but above all, she prayed for the end of the war. She dearly longed for a time when all her family could be out from under its shadow and free to live in the light. In particular, she yearned for the safe return of all her sons and shared this thought with Florence.

"*Pray God, Mother, it will bring my dear Ned safely home.*" This was Florence's deepest concern.

Now the days wore on. It was a hot summer and Beth found it unbearable at times. On these occasions, she went home to Holt House, and Emma would lead her upstairs to her own shady room, where she would lie down to rest. Philip loved to hoist himself up the stairs to sit beside her bed, often wiping her hot forehead with a damp cold cloth. They spoke little, but each of them simply relaxed in each other's company.

Wilfrid Israel, who was very fond of Beth, would occasionally visit Anatole and her to check all was well. She had grown close to him as she worked with him, though he was always taciturn and serious. Wilfrid knew well what Hitler had in store for the Jews of Europe. He wrote about his belief on more than one occasion, claiming that Hitler had in mind to send the Jews to faraway annihilation centres in Eastern Europe, but no one seemed to accept this as credible. Whenever he visited Holt House, he shared his views with Philip, knowing that Philip understood. As for Anatole, he trusted his mentor and willingly accompanied him on his missions to rescue Jews in danger.

Beth and Anatole made the most of their little flat in the days before the birth, the August date outlined as the due date. They made their spare room into a nursery for the little one and Beth decorated it with pictures of animals and toys.

"*Doesn't it look perfect?*" Beth enquired of Daisy, who was visiting them that day in May.

Daisy teared up taking in all the little details Beth had added to the room. "*Oh, my dear Beth, I really envy you terribly. Forgive me. Please let me share this baby with you. That will help.*"

Beth put her arm around Daisy. "*Of course you can. But keep steady, my dear friend. There will be a time for you, I feel sure. I know Daddy holds you in his prayers all the time.*"

"*You're right.*" Daisy smiled. "*And this baby will help us to endure these awful times.*"

Beth nodded. "*I hope so, Daisy, and I trust that the baby will be a talisman of hope for us all, but I cannot help being afraid every time Wilfrid asks Anatole to help him on a mission. I know he takes terrible risks.*" She shuddered suddenly though the sun was warm and bright.

"*You know what Uncle Philip always says: 'Trust God',*" said Daisy. "*We must try.*"

The two girls gave each other a reassuring hug, and the moment was gone.

Chapter 49

March 1943

Beth and Anatole grew increasingly attached to Wilfrid despite his shy and reclusive nature. He kept all his concerns close to his chest, but Anatole had somehow broken through the carefully maintained shell he had built around himself. Philip admitted his surprise to Emma of Wilfrid's very real affection for Anatole. And indeed, it seemed that Anatole had grown to love him as a replacement father. Wilfrid often went for supper in their small flat and relaxed as he sat musing over all the work he and Anatole had in hand.

On the night of the twenty-fifth of March, Wilfrid came over for what Beth hoped was just another supper, especially with the baby's arrival not far away now. But it wasn't to be.

Wilfrid gave out a huge sigh and glanced across at Anatole. "*It's time we admitted to your dear wife that we have plans to leave tomorrow.*"

Beth let out a gasp of dismay. As the time for the baby's arrival neared, she wanted Anatole close to her more than ever.

"*Beth, the Jewish Agency has requested that I go to Lisbon to coordinate the rescue of a large group of Jewish refugees, and I have asked Anatole to come with me. Can you forgive me, Beth, for taking him away again?"*

Anatole, however, gave an exclamation of frustration. "*Wilfrid, you know Beth always supports our work. There is nothing to forgive.*"

"*And, Wilfrid,*" Beth reiterated, swallowing down her fears, "*you know that's true, of course he is going with you. I wouldn't want it any other way. But you must promise me again that you will both take great care.*" Although she wouldn't admit it in the moment, she was disappointed that Anatole was putting his work first again, then she felt immediately guilty for thinking it.

Wilfrid took her hand and, in a courtly gesture, kissed it. His gratitude was palpable, and Anatole, watching her, thanked God for his understanding wife.

Supper ended, Wilfrid said his farewells and Anatole took her in his arms, but she pulled back and put a finger to his lips.

"*Come, darling, we must be practical now. What should we pack for the journey? You know I'll cope. Just remember to hurry back, won't you?*"

That night, they slept in a tight embrace until morning dawned. Beth took a firm hold of her courage so as not to give way to all that she felt. She waved them off in the cab to the airport, then she abandoned her brave face and wept into her pillow. It was not long before she phoned her mother and father to unburden herself of the news.

In Shadworth, Emma looked at Philip with deep concern.

"*Philip, how much more do we have to endure? Let's tell her to come home and await his return here with us.*"

"My *darling, she's brave as ten lions, but we'll certainly get her here if she'll agree."*

Beth's favourite place whenever Anatole had to work with Wilfrid was always home and at the foot of Philip's wheelchair, so she took no persuading to catch a train home to Shadworth on the thirtieth of March. There, Emma and Philip cosseted her as in the old childhood days.

Chapter 50

June 1943

As the first of June dawned, Beth awoke early knowing the return flight was due to leave and head for Bristol. She had the details from Anatole: BOAC Flight 777.

It was Philip, already up and downstairs, who got the shocking news of a plane shot down, listening as he always did to the early radio news broadcast. His heart sank with a terrible sense of dread. He held his breath, his whole body in an icy grip as he prayed and waited for further news. He had a horrible feeling that what he feared most would in fact be the truth.

And it was. A plane carrying a group of passengers en route to Bristol from Lisbon, BOAC Flight 777, had crashed into the sea. Anatole's plane. There were no survivors.

He sat silently in his chair, unutterably stunned, with thoughts of that daring youth with whom he had remonstrated countless times. And now that boy was dead. And his own treasured daughter would receive this deathly blow. He wanted to fall to his knees in prayer, but he worried he wouldn't have the strength to pull himself up again. He remained in his seat and closed his eyes.

"*Lord God, you have accompanied me throughout all my dark days, but now, once more, I turn to you. God, help me to endure this blow. It's difficult to believe I can. Yet, 'I believe, oh Lord. Help thou my unbelief.'"*

As Philip groaned, Emma tiptoed downstairs to find him. She took one look at his face and instantly knew something was awfully wrong. "*What's happened, darling? Tell me quickly.*"

He simply looked at her in grief. "*The whole crew and passengers on the flight from Lisbon are dead in the sea, after attack by a German fighter plane. Emma, I know it's Anatole's flight. How can we tell Beth this?*"

They heard a step creak and turned to the stairs, where Beth ran down the last few steps and fell at her father's foot.

"*What has happened, Daddy? Oh my God, Mother, it can't be. No. Oh no, no, no!*" Beth let out a scream that resounded through the house. The shock overtook her and she fell into a dead faint.

Emma knelt down and held Beth tight, rocking her. "*I'm so sorry, my Bethy. So, so sorry.*" Her grief mixed with her daughter's took over, and she couldn't stop her tears from dripping onto Beth's arm.

Within minutes, there was the sound of a car door slamming and the front door being opened, and Pieter appeared, having driven himself down from the school in reckless haste. He too had heard the news. Anatole had told him his return flight, as he always did when he was on an overseas mission with Wilfrid.

Emma's face was set and grim; his dear friend Philip was sat in stunned silence in his wheelchair. Pieter knelt down next to Emma and oh so gently lifted Beth from Emma's arms into his own. Then he laid her on the old settee and held her close until she opened her eyes and looked round, at first puzzled. Seconds later, it came back in all its awfulness.

"*Pieter, it's Anatole and Wilfrid, both dead. I don't think I can bear it,*" Beth almost screamed. "*How can I, Pieter? And for you too, after all that's happened to your family. Pieter, it's too much to stand.*"

Pieter, still holding Beth close, felt himself succumbing to the horror of it all. He turned to Philip, holding out his hand. Philip, sensing he must now play his part in bringing them all to a calmer place, took his hand. Beth sat up and Philip wheeled his chair round to be next to her.

"*Beth, be steady. Think how Anatole would want you to be brave. You are carrying his baby, and you must now dig deep to the resources I know you have.*"

"*I will try, Daddy, but I have to live with this terrible sadness now, and I'm not sure it will ever be any easier.*"

And with those few words and a last kiss on her father's forehead, she fled upstairs to her room.

Emma had a sudden memory of Philip lying on his hospital bed realising that the doctors had taken his leg and her comforting him with every ounce of love she had for him. She knew that, throughout the trials they had to face, their love was always sufficient. And she knew with complete certainty that the love they all shared here and now, in this very tragic circumstance, would also be sufficient.

Slowly but determinedly, she rose to her feet. "*Let's have a cup of tea, my dears, and let's ring the farm and tell Florence what has happened. Pieter, did you see Laura before you left school? We must let Will know if not.*"

"*Yes, Laura was just arriving as I left, but she promised to get home as fast as she could.*"

"Then we may find ourselves besieged by all our loved ones soon. Philip, can you ring Milly? I could do with a bit of help."

Philip smiled momentarily at his indefatigable wife, but his main concern was for Beth. He hauled himself upstairs to sit by her. She was staring into space where she lay, and he bent and kissed her.

"Take comfort, my treasure. We are all here, and we will get through this, believe me."

Even to Philip, his words sounded trite and hollow, but Beth stretched out her arms to him, and he leant and embraced her. Her face was wet with tears.

There was the sound of footsteps mounting the stairs, first the two boys, Teddy and Ralph, followed closely by Daisy and her mother. Finally, Will appeared at the door. He knelt beside her bed.

"Beth, oh, Beth, I am so sorry. I don't have words to tell you how much. This is awful. But, my lovely sister, we will come through even this, I promise you, and we're all here to help you."

Chapter 51

Elizabeth May – Coping with Grief, 1943

I truly believe it was their love that pulled me through. The agony of losing Anatole was almost too much to bear, and for months after the disaster, all my energy had been sapped away. If it weren't for my baby quietly growing inside me, I might never have bothered to go downstairs and face everyone. It was really quite overwhelming to see everyone, and they all came, even Bertha Bracey, quite heartbroken at Wilfrid's passing and very sad for me, Anatole's widow. Ugh, how ugly a word that is.

I remember Beatrice arriving with the biggest bunch of flowers I had ever seen, and she hugged me enough to take my breath away while Alan looked on, somewhat embarrassed. Dear Edna had begged a lift with them.

"*Thus a whole life is swerved out of its trajectory*" was exactly how she put it. And I couldn't have put it better myself, for indeed I felt slightly unhinged, purposeless even.

The best visits were yet to come, and by this time, Daddy had persuaded me to go into the garden. I remember it was a most beautiful July day, like the summer days I had spent so deliriously happy in our garden as a child, with the chickens clucking around my feet. I heard his engine roaring and stopping before I saw him. Daddy sat quietly beside me in his wheelchair, his love for me palpable, staunch and soothing. He smiled at the arrival of James and the pleasure on my face.

As he came through the gate, my heart leapt. My dear old friend who had coaxed and cajoled me all my life. He ran over to me and threw his arms round me. He had come at full tilt, driving all the way from Inverary, barely stopping to fill up the petrol or to eat. I knew how impatient he would have been to get to me. And there he was. I looked up at him and saw the tears coming down his face, matching my own.

"James, is this how it feels when your heart bleeds? For I think mine is bleeding."

"Bethy, my dear Bethy, I got here as quick as I could. So sorry, darling."

"My dear James, how glad I am to see you. It's a treat to have you back. Please don't go away again."

Daddy shook his head in frustration at me for making such a silly comment, for I, and everyone else, knew full well he would have to go back. Indeed, he already had to drive off to pick up Sheila, his mum, but he wasted no time over that and ushered his mum in to see my mother in the kitchen.

Mother appeared and, as you might expect, after many more hugs, she retreated into the kitchen to make yet more tea. Before long, the whole Tempest family arrived from the farm to welcome James, and Mother ushered everyone inside. I followed and silently sat down on the old settee.

Daisy wordlessly crept onto the settee beside me, knowing that the silence between close friends was all that was needed. But she also had some good news to impart.

"I've heard from George, and he tells me he is coming home on the weekend. He can't stand being apart from us when we are coping with this awful loss. Oh, Bethy, will that help you to feel just a little bit better?"

"That will be a great comfort. I love him dearly. But, Daisy, he can't replace my own Anatole. No one can."

As I spoke, the tears started to flow yet again. I felt rather awful that this good news wasn't somehow enough to soothe my pain for even a moment.

James, watching, perched on the arm of the settee and leaned over me. "*Are you OK, little one? Is this too much for you? Say one word and I'll whisk you back into the garden.*"

A great sob rose up inside me as he asked, but I managed to speak. "No, *James, I am enjoying the sight of everyone. And Daisy brings excellent news: George is coming at the weekend. If only I could stop crying.*"

His eyebrows rose slightly with surprise, but he held back his happiness, as if it felt unfair for him to be happy when I was in such emotional distress. "*Why, Daisy, George will do all of us good. And maybe Beth will cheer up a little.*" He looked anxiously at me.

"*Teatime,*" Mother called from the kitchen.

The discussion ended and we all made our way to the kitchen. As I looked at all the smiling faces surrounding me, I felt a terrible pang for my beloved Anatole. It swept over me in waves of untold sadness. I couldn't quite believe it. Perhaps it was all a mistake and he would walk in in just a minute. Then, like a hammer blow, it hit me like a punch in the stomach. Oh God. No. I suddenly wanted to scream out for him, for the friendship and joy we had shared. The pain in my aching heart wasn't going away. I wasn't sure it ever would.

Daddy, watching my face, announced it was time for Grace. Everything stopped. All the kindly visitors stood still at Daddy's word.

"*Oh, Lord, be present at our table now. Bless each one gathered here, but bless also, we beseech you, those who cannot be with us. We pray for all our loved ones and especially for those who are already at your heavenly table. May the food now before us refresh us in our faith in you as we commend them into your loving mercies. Amen.*"

Chapter 52

Elizabeth May – Time Heals, 1943

Two months after his father's death, Andreas Philip Otto Czernik arrived smoothly, named after two grandfathers and with a first name to recall his German/Austrian heritage. Everything telescoped down to caring for him: nappies, sleep routine, feeding. My nipples became raw and very sore, but my darling mother rubbed lanoline into them after each feed. Oh, how he grew. He was a very beautiful baby, and I yearned for his father to be able to see him. If only...

As the autumn advanced, the old saying "*Time heals*" came into play. There were good distractions, and I very slowly began to recover. In a sense, I didn't want to feel better. The loss of my darling Anatole was profound and so I needed to hold that loss ever before me. It almost felt like a betrayal of him if I found myself laughing or enjoying those dear ones who were always ready to cheer me up. And of course, they all loved Andreas.

Our minds travelled often to the Japanese camp where our own Harry was imprisoned and to the soldiers in Europe planning for the invasion of France, Ned included. My father held them all in his prayers every day whenever we gathered together around my dear mother's feasts that she unstintingly prepared for us all, including the kinder. We were all looking forward to the fifteenth of December, as it was to be Mother's seventy-sixth birthday and Daddy had arranged for everyone to come to Holt House to celebrate. I think it was his way of helping everyone to let go of the pain and terrible sadness that had overtaken us all in that anxious time, not least me, for he desperately wanted me to emerge from my grief and live again, for Andreas' sake.

I remember watching the birthday guests as they assembled. It was a joy as James drew up at the gate and hastened over to me. Will was clutching Laura's hand very hard, glad not to be far away, but at the same time regretful that he was only on the home front. I watched as Laura lifted her face to him and gave him a most loving smile. Pieter smiled across at me as I stood with Mother and held Andreas. I believe he was thinking, as I was, of his homeland and of his cousin, Anatole, and the dear families still lost to us.

Daddy had invited Beatrice and Alan with Edna to Mother's party, and they were engrossed in conversation with James. Mary and Florence were responsible for the delicious meal into which we all tucked hungrily and then, at last, Daisy stepped into the big kitchen holding a large box. Once opened, its contents revealed a most beautiful cake all decorated in pink and white with rosebuds iced around the edge.

"*Dear Grandma*," announced Daisy, wreathed with smiles, "*look what Philip has ordered from Hagenbach's for your and our delectation. Happy, happy birthday, Grandma Emma*."

At this, my beloved father wheeled himself up to Mother and took her in his arms. "*Nobody deserves this more than my dearest wife. Thank you for all the years, my Emma.*"

Everyone cheered and Ralphie and Teddy gave a loud whoop of delight. Much hilarity followed as the younger ones played hide-and-seek all around the garden.

I crept away to settle Andreas for bedtime, and Daddy followed me. He loved to help me with snuggles and prayers, and tonight it was difficult because the little chap had enjoyed an exciting day. Andreas moaned and whined as I rocked him, shushing softly.

There was a knock on the bedroom door and it opened slowly, James peeping his face round. "*Could I help with bedtime?*"

"*Of course,*" Daddy said before I could respond.

I handed Andreas to James and sat on my bed to watch the two of them share in dressing him in his nightgown and saying prayers with him. I still felt a deep sadness looking round my own room, realising the only item from the nursery there was the cot, all pictures, toys and teddies still boxed away.

Daddy laughed at James' clumsy attempts to get Andreas' hands through the sleeves. But, sure enough, dressing complete, thumb in mouth, he closed his eyes and slept. James looked on with some astonishment, seeing how easily sleep had overtaken him.

I put my hand gently on James' arm and whispered, "*He's just really tired.*"

By the time we got downstairs, the guests were all drifting away and Mother was doling out hot drinks to see them on their way. James was staying overnight before heading back to Inveraray, so at last we could put our feet up and relax. But first he had to see his own mum home, and he left with her, promising to return.

I used this moment to thank my beloved daddy for his clever plan to cheer me up and once again celebrate my darling mother. Mother's face shone with pleasure as she thanked Daddy and gently kissed him.

"*And, my darling, how has it been for you?*" asked Daddy.

"*I am alright, Daddy. I miss Anatole so badly, but I am surrounded by love, so how can I not begin to feel better? And, Mother, isn't Andreas a joy for us all?*"

"*He is, darling. That is truly a gift of grace.*"

Daddy smiled at this comment. Mother was taking over his role as comforter, and it came as natural to her as breathing.

I found, to my surprise, that the days no longer crawled interminably in the shadow of my grief. I am sure it was all because of my beloved Andreas. The joy of being a mother somehow relieved the desert within that I had inhabited for so long.

When Christmas arrived, despite all the rationing, we were able to celebrate it in the old way. The whole family gathered at Tempests' Farm, where Mary and Florence, with Milly's help, conjured a turkey feast out of anything that could be eaten. The turkey was one of Ned's choice flock, now down to the very last bird. Florence assured me that Ned would approve. The apple sauce came straight from our apple trees at Holt House, the vegetables were all dug out of Tempests' fields, and Mother had stored dried sage for the sage and onion stuffing. Last, but not least, Mary had made a very large Christmas pudding for our delectation. Every contribution was well appreciated and, as we came to the end of the meal, Will stood up to speak.

"*Let's not allow this moment to pass,*" he said, "*without acknowledging the debt we owe to Mother and Father for the support they have given. So many families have known loss and grief during these war years and perhaps we have been more fortunate than some. But our share has been hard and we have felt the shadow of death around us. But at all times, their guiding hands have brought us through.*" Choked with tears, Will stopped and Emma put her hand to her throat as she felt his pain. It took a short while before Will could continue. "*I can't finish this tribute without a special mention of my own beloved wife, Laura. She has been my constant companion through my own dark days. She left her life behind to be with me and has given me a son, of whom I am very proud.*"

Ralph beamed with pleasure and I do believe his face actually glowed that night. Laura blushed and smiled back at Will. I'm sure it helped to encourage him on.

"*But now, Florence, it's your turn, dear sister. You have been a rock on whom we all trusted and you have never given up your belief that Ned will soon come home. And, Milly, you know that we will not be complete until Harry is back with us too.*"

Florence put her hand up to stop him saying any more. She took hold of Mary Tempest's hands. "*Oh God, may they really come home soon,*" she whispered. At the same time, Milly turned to Emma and Emma put her arms around her.

This brought back to me my own terrible loss, a loss that would never be redeemed. I clutched my heart as she spoke and felt a terrible ache that would never leave me. My darling daddy wheeled his chair round to Andreas' highchair, lifted him out and held him out to me.

"*This little chap is here to remind us that his daddy is still with us in our hearts though he has sacrificed his life for the sake of others, so no more tears now. We have to live and work towards the day when this ugly war will be over.*"

"*Amen to that*," resounded around the table. As I cuddled my sweet Andreas, the weight of sorrow left me once again.

And so Christmas 1943 passed as war raged around us, and we all hoped and prayed for an end to the conflict and for a new and lasting peace.

Chapter 53

1944

Shadworth awoke to the new year with a fresh sense of purpose. The school maintained its high standards under Alan and Beatrice's care and down in Low Shadworth, Emma and Philip cared for many from the quiet of their home in Holt House.

The day came when James' own mother was found lying on the kitchen floor while a kettle was boiling itself dry on the nearby hob. Her neighbour, Margaret Trimble, was alerted by the sight of steam pouring out of an open window and went into the house to find Sheila lying prostrate. Sheila Townsend, the good doctor's widow, had at last succumbed to her failing heart. James was sent for, and he drove at speed from Inveraray to deal with all the duties that death brings. When he left the empty house, bereft of his mother, he knew he would find comfort at Holt House, to be greeted by Philip and Emma with unbridled affection. Though they were unaware of it at the time, his work was now intense, as he had been appointed to a team immersed in the planning for the D-Day Allied invasion of France.

But this did not prevent him from seeing Andreas and Beth whenever he was able to visit. On these occasions, he and Beth would walk the little boy in his Tansad pram down to the fields to watch the trains, a particular treat, bringing back James' own trainspotting days. Andreas gurgled with delight whenever James appeared.

But Inveraray always called him back, as he had an important role in the careful planning of operations. Beth would not allow herself to feel sad at his departure, though sometimes she admitted to herself that she wished he could be nearer. Her yearning for Anatole remained the same.

Of course, Milly knew that she must wait until the war ended to find out what had happened to Harry, and Florence kept her patience as she waited for news of Ned. She might have been less equable had she known that Ned was preparing for the D-Day landings, wherever that might be. None of them knew that the day they all awaited with bated breath had been set for the sixth of June.

Ned was to be in a landing craft with a group of soldiers landing on French soil close to Caen. Indeed, Florence found that Ned would hardly speak at all afterwards about his experience landing on the beach in Normandy with a hail of gunfire aimed at the crafts that were landing almost right in front of the German guns. Being soaked to the skin with seawater and with the blood of several of his dead friends was a hellish memory for Ned. He remembered clearly pulling the craft to shore and then heading off towards the French hamlets scattered in the fields around them. Then he followed his battalion leader to reach the road that led to Paris, still very much in ignorance of all the detailed planning that his captain was following.

By some miracle unscathed, Ned became a part of the Allies' liberation of Paris, and as soon as he could, he sent Florence a brief but cogent note reassuring her that he was alive. It was enough to encourage Florence and bring back her smile and her tranquillity. Emma was relieved to find her daughter so much more relaxed, while she and Philip were truly relishing having Beth with them. Philip found intense pleasure simply sitting in his wheelchair nursing little Andreas, who found the place on Philip's lap was perfect for the chance to suck his thumb and watch the world go by.

As harvest time was underway in all the fields around Shadworth, a renewed hope was born. There was a sense that Hitler was in retreat and, just perhaps, there would come a day when this brutal war would be over.

It was a misty autumn morning in Shadworth when James pulled up outside Holt House and beeped his horn. Philip was already out, sitting in the garden in his chair, and he wheeled himself forward before outstretching his hands to greet him warmly.

James offloaded what he believed to be good news. "*Philip, allied troops are advancing towards the east and Berlin. Can you believe it? It seems we are pushing back harder.*"

Philip frowned, not quite seeing the situation in such a positive light. "*James, I am horrified at the news of our policy of firebombing the German cities,*" he confided anxiously. "*Oh God, James, how many will die because of such policies? I must speak to Frank Jacques and get him to persuade the government against it. James, I know it's probably hopeless, but I feel I need to do something.*"

James shook his head, understanding his dear friend's anxiety and indeed feeling it himself, but he knew, as the saying goes, desperate times call for desperate measures. "*Philip, I wish I could reassure you on the point, but I know that they will definitely go ahead, and nothing you or I can do can stop it. Hopefully, it might bring an end to this war more quickly.*"

Beth appeared holding her little boy, who immediately stretched out his arms to James. Philip, watching James' face, suddenly recognised the depth of feeling in James' response.

Lord, bless this man we have loved all his life, and may all things good fall to him when the time is right. Amen.

Philip squeezed Beth's hand as she stood beside him. She knew Philip's anxiety about the horrific excesses of the war.

As the days passed, they all listened with bated breath as news came in of the horrors the troops had come across once they crossed the Rhine and moved towards Berlin.

Emma could hardly bear to hear of the sufferings of so many trapped in the death camps. The Holocaust, in all its virulence and, as Philip called it, its wickedness, was revealed in Belsen and in Dachau as our soldiers discovered the camps. And of course, there was the question of whether they could locate Pieter and Anatole's lost relatives. This brought Pieter down to Holt House many times, where Philip, with Frank Jacques, was trying everything he could to discover what had happened to them. But nothing surfaced of Otto Czernik or Franz Staab and they had to give up their fruitless research.

"Daddy, I'm almost glad Anatole is not alive to hear this," Beth confided in her father, who simply shook his head in sorrow.

Pieter could not avoid knowing the full ghastly details of what emerged, and he had terrible nightmares nearly every night. His only comfort came from walking in the fields round the farm, often pushing Beth's Andreas in his pram. Daisy usually accompanied him, which turned into a great comfort.

"Perhaps it is my Andreas' innocence that somehow helps him," Beth confided in her mother. And Emma gave her a hug, her only response, for she was deeply disturbed at the effect the uncertainty was having on Pieter.

In school, many of the boys were deeply troubled and anxious for their own families. Alan drove over to Holt House to ask Philip to renew his prayer times in the college chapel, a request that Philip was very pleased to answer. Alan would pick him up in his car and then, with Emma, the two of them set up the chapel as it had been all those years earlier in the time of the First World War. Pieter found himself very thankful for these special quiet times in chapel and admitted to Beth that he was beginning to feel just a little bit calmer.

Gradually, the autumn leaves started to fall and the mornings brought a misty haze over the landscape. Beth was enjoying the wonders of Andreas' progress from baby to toddler. He walked early, aged only thirteen months, and she loved showing him the leaves all in heaps on the path to the farm and how to shuffle through them as a game. Little though he was, he toddled energetically through them in glee.

On one of James' visits, she took him down Long Lane to show off her little one's progress. James watched him with deepest pleasure but also with a very serious face.

"*What is it, James, suddenly so serious?*"

"*I wish I were just a little bit younger, Beth. I sometimes feel like a very old man as I watch the little one. Why, Beth, you are still a youngster. You are only twenty-three and I have reached the grand old age of forty-five.*"

"*James, how could you? You are only as old as you feel. Never say such a thing.*"

As she spoke, little Andreas held out his arms to James to be picked up. James had to square his shoulders and stop himself from brooding as he picked him up and threw him in the air to shouts of joy.

"*You do know that you have made me able to live again, my dear friend, don't you? I'm not sure what I would do without you, James.*"

"Beth," he replied, "*I have loved you for a very long time, ever since your mother presented me with a very small baby to hold in my arms. But, Beth, I must confess, I no longer love you like an old uncle, and I'm far too old for you, yet I would like to take you in my arms now and kiss you as if I too were twenty-three.*" The words came tumbling out, but he broke off and simply looked at Beth, who was standing there with tears streaming down her face.

"*Oh God, Beth. I wasn't going to say that to you.*"

"*James, do you remember George Herbert's poem, 'Love'? Do you remember that line, 'Who made the eyes but I?'"* And then Beth, standing on her tiptoes, reached up to him and kissed him long and sweetly.

Andreas got hold of a tuft of James' hair and pulled it hard, then he lunged out to his mother to catch him, and Beth, by now laughing and crying all at once, caught him and sat down on the leaves with a bump. James joined her, there on the autumn bed, with the little boy between them.

James gasped in wonder at what had seemed to him an impossible moment, with a surge of joy. "*Can we do this, Beth? Would Anatole be hurt by such a thing?*"

"*I don't for a minute think so. He would like his son to have such a father as you.*"

This astonishing and most delightful encounter now became subsumed in a long and very passionate embrace, in which one little boy was somehow entangled.

At last, they got up, and each taking Andreas' hands, they set off back to Holt House with news to share.

Philip was at the door into the garden, sitting in his wheelchair, enjoying the late autumn sunshine when he saw the three of them coming up the path towards him. He clapped his hands as he saw Beth and James smiling tenderly at each other.

"*Emma,*" he called over his shoulder, into the house, "*you need to come out and see this.*"

Perhaps my prayer is being answered here and now, he thought as they approached.

"*Daddy, my daddy, can you believe us if we tell you of the morning's wonders?*"

Philip smiled at this, and Emma, taking it all in in a flash of comprehension, ran to the two of them with a cry of delight.

Philip's voice broke with emotion as he addressed them. "*So you have got there at last, you two sleepyheads? It's taken a while for you to see the truth, hasn't it? But Mother and I could not be happier for you, my darling Beth. And, James, my dear old friend, congratulations.*"

James took Philip's hands in his and spoke very quietly. "*Philip, how is this with you and Emma? Your beloved daughter, and I, old enough to be her father.*"

"*James, you can be assured that her mother and I could not wish for a happier resolution to the tragedy of Anatole's untimely death. My old friend, we only know how much she means to you and give you our blessing.*"

Beth flew at her father and landed at her favourite place next to his chair. Emma smiled at her impetuous daughter, knowing the depth of all she had suffered, but now knowing she had found sweet relief. James, still unable to take in the momentous thing that had happened to him, stood numb and silent. Then he simply held out his hand to this woman he loved, and she took it and rose to stand beside him.

"*Why, I've been loving this man all my life, but now, I will be his absolutely, and I'll thank God every day for it.*"

"*Is there something I should know?*" came from the gate, and there stood Will. "*Laura's been telling me I'm blind, you two. And now I see for myself. Sister, dear, are you happy? Can this man make you so?*" And, to Andreas' surprise, he lifted Beth off her feet and swung her round as if she were still little.

He already knew the answer for himself and threw his head back and laughed. His mother looked at him and smiled. This big son of hers made her incredibly proud. She knew he and Laura and Ralphie made a very good team, and she could wish for no better. If only Harry could be home and safe for Milly. She knew Florence was confident that Ned would be home, for the short missives Florrie had received from Ned had been full of optimism. That left her darling grandson, who was flying raids over Europe and had been promoted to squadron leader.

"*My darling*," she said to Philip, interrupting the cries of pleasure they were all sharing, "*can you say a prayer for us all and for a safe homecoming for everyone?*"

Philip looked up at his wife and nodded. He felt that words could not quite say all that he was feeling at this moment. But he could try.

"*Lord God, we want to thank you today for this new understanding between Beth and James. And we want to ask you especially to keep safe those who are far away, fighting for the freedom of everyone: Ned, Harry, George, our own beloved children. This is the prayer of all our hearts. Amen.*"

He covered his face with his hands as he finished the prayer and the tears fell.

Beth rushed to him and kissed the top of his head. "*My darling daddy, all will be well. How many times have you reminded me of those words?*"

He smiled, and James leaned down to him and shook his hand. James knew his old friend had lived through many of life's ups and downs. But one little boy had had enough solemnity for one day and now made his presence felt by grabbing James' coattails and pulling him away. The atmosphere of solemnity at last turned to laughter.

Chapter 54

Elizabeth May – A Hopeful Future, 1944 - 1945

That day in autumn, my eyes were opened to a truth I had resisted for some time. The love James had for me was able to flourish after such a very long wait, but I kept Anatole always sacred in my heart, of course. James understood that and never resented the part that was reserved for him.

They were very different lovers. Anatole—young, exuberant, passionate—made love to match his impetuous nature. He would catch me in an embrace wherever we might be and strip me of my clothes, with a million kisses. His lovemaking was strong, fervent, searching me for a response to match him. And so delicious.

But James was oh so tender and took me so gently. It was an ecstasy of pleasure, and I would lie back afterwards and relax with deep satisfaction.

And on one such night, he held me in his arms, his head next to mine, sharing my pillow, and spoke quietly to me. "*Marry me, Bethy. Let's do the job properly.*"

I looked at my bare ring finger, my rings from Anatole now stored away in a jewellery box, and smiled. "*Dear James, I am already married to you in my heart. I didn't think we needed to be 'proper', as you put it.*"

In my ignorance, I had simply assumed we would be together for ever, so in truth, I already felt married. James laughed at me then and I turned to face him. Indeed, words cannot describe the look of deepest joy that shone on his face at the mere thought that I was his now and always.

"Let's set a date, my darling, when all our boys are safely back," I suggested.

James nodded in approval. *"Then I want to take you with me to show you Inveraray as my wife. What do you think? And, my darling, I want to buy you a ring."*

We shared this idea with my father and mother. Although she was not getting any younger, my beloved mother was always thrilled to make a feast and Daddy would always support her.

All that remained was to await the return—please, God—of our absent ones.

As the Soviet Red Army moved steadily westwards towards Berlin and our troops moved closer and closer eastwards, Hitler must have known the end was coming. We were holding our breath in Shadworth for the outcome, and at last, the news came flooding in: Hitler had committed suicide in his hideaway bunker below the Reich building.

The thirtieth of April—a date to go down in history recording the death of one of the world's most evil protagonists. My little man, Andreas, understood nothing of all this, but he danced with me in the garden of Holt House as Daddy watched us from his chair. Mother came out of the kitchen bearing cakes, for she knew there would be an onslaught from our extended family down from school to celebrate with us.

A plane flew over us as we danced, and Andreas shouted, "*Look, Gandad, is it Nunkie George?*"

Daddy laughed and laughed at this, but when the plane circled round and flipped its wings, we knew the little one was right.

As Stalin insisted on his own signature on the surrender documents, it was May before the unconditional surrender was finally complete. My dear sister, Florence, spent many quiet times with us at Holt House during her anxious wait.

Then one day, the gate rattled and footsteps were heard along the garden path. Daddy was in the garden enjoying the summer sunshine, but we heard him give a loud shout of joy and dashed out to see. There stood a tired, greying man, weary yet full of hope. Florence flew out of the kitchen and flung herself into his arms.

"*Ned, Ned, can it really be you?*"

"*Why, my Florrie, of course it is. I'm home. Now, let me feast my eyes on my wife.*"

Florence simply looked at him as if she were soaking up every part of him. And Ned—the serious, earnest farmer that he was—took her face in his hands and kissed her gently at first and then very passionately as we all looked on. Unabashed, Ned just grinned at us all in his utmost relief.

We had one of our own back safely, and you may imagine the pleasure Mother took as she brought out the goodies she had been baking. Afterwards, my father took charge.

"*Florrie, take him home and have some quiet time together before Teddy gets home from school. And rest, dearest Florence, this is your space now.*"

"Thank you, Philip, that's just what my heart is telling me," said Florence. *"Come on, Ned, you have a farm awaiting its farmer."*

Ned hugged my mother and shook Daddy's outstretched hand. Then he lifted his huge rucksack, put an arm round Florrie's shoulder and headed for the gate.

Daddy leaned back in his chair and lifted Andreas onto his lap. Andreas had watched all the proceedings amazed, but now he snuggled up to his grandad and put his thumb in his mouth.

"Who will be next, Emma, my darling? We can only hope the Japanese will surrender soon and that Harry will be released."

"Oh, Philip, if only he has survived the ordeal. I am tired of all this torment I feel still."

"Emma, courage. Hope is still very much alive, you know."

Daddy kissed the top of Andreas' head.

Chapter 55

Elizabeth May – The End in Sight, 1945

Although there was peace at last between the Allies and the German army, still the battle raged on in the Pacific. As a matter of pride, the Japanese would not surrender, so they fought on. Milly would often come to Holt House in distress, as she knew that nothing could release Harry until the war was truly over.

Andreas always brought her back to her cheerful self. He loved Milly, and she brought him little playthings—a toy boat to sail in the bath; a wobbly man; some plasticine, which he managed to get all over the place. It must have been a comfort to watch him enjoying her gifts as she survived those very hard days.

A milestone at this time was to be his second birthday on the first of August, and James was driving down to be with us. I had begun to miss him terribly whenever he had to return to his office in Inveraray. I increasingly longed for the right day to come when we could be married, but we had sworn to each other that all our dear ones were to be home with us on that day. This visit was therefore much anticipated, and I had whispered to Andreas that James would be coming for his big day.

Sure enough, as he played in the garden, he must have heard James' car heading down the hill to Low

Shadworth. He broke out into a toddle to stand at the gate and watch. I hastened after him, and there indeed was James, tossing the little one up in the air to cries of delight.

"*He has some kind of special sense that you are near, my dear,*" I said as I reached up to kiss him. He embraced me but then became more serious.

"*Beth, it means so much to me that this little boy knows me and, perhaps, already loves me, as his mother does. I am very privileged, Beth, my love.*"

Father wheeled up to him and shook his hand, with a delighted smile on his face. Next came Mother, wiping her floury hands on her apron. We were all joyful at seeing him, and I, most of all. Everyone was coming the next day to share in Andreas' birthday.

As I enjoyed the sheer warmth of James' love for me, I thanked God for His grace in dealing with me.

The next day, oh how we celebrated. Will and Laura with Ralphie came early to get all the goodies out for the party, and Ned and Florrie with Daisy and Teddy joined in, playing silly garden games with the little one. Then came Pieter with Milly, whom he had picked up in his car. All this for a little one, but of course, it was really to celebrate Ned's safe homecoming and to join together in praying for an end to the war.

As the conversation continued around the garden, I noticed that Daisy was sitting wistfully on her own on the grass. Pieter went over and put a gentle arm around her shoulder. Daisy smiled gratefully and leant back against him. I saw her visibly relaxing and that there was a new, unanticipated hope awakening.

Andreas scurried up to Daisy and landed a kiss on her forehead. James, watching the little chap, put his arms around me and held me. It was my turn to lean back against one who loved me, and I thanked God for him.

Five days later, we were thrown back on the anxiety that was never far away. Truman, newly taking the office of President after Roosevelt's death, gave the word for the successfully tested atomic bomb to be dropped on the Japanese city of Hiroshima. Many thousands died that day and in the ensuing days. Yet Japan did not surrender and, to our horror, a second bomb was released over Nagasaki.

Nevertheless, it took the Soviet invasion of Manchuria to bring Emperor Hirohito to surrender on the fifteenth of August. Then at last, the agreement was signed by General MacArthur on the second of September.

The broadcast that announced the finality of all the suffering simply started with: "*Today the guns are silent. A great tragedy has ended. A great victory has been won.*"

I will never forget my darling father's face when this news broke. He frowned grimly and then wheeled himself to my mother's side.

"*Emma, I can hardly contemplate the suffering that has been brought on the innocent people of those cities. Emma, I don't know what words I can use in prayer now. Help me, my darling. The inhumanity of man to man. Oh God, Emma.*" He put his head in his hands. He knew the devastation in Japan would not be over for a long time, detracting from any satisfaction that the war was over.

"Steady, Philip. You will get the words, you always do. We'll just be quiet and hold the people in our thoughts, and when you feel able, please pray."

Daddy sat for another few moments, then put his hands together in the age-old way. Andreas was watching him, thumb in his mouth, but he copied him solemnly. It was a tender moment.

"Dear Father God, we are few and far away from the agonies that are destroying lives and yet this prayer reaches out to them. We ask you to be very close to those in whatever circumstance they are facing. In your mercy, give them the courage they need and your grace to enable them to go on living. May it be a comfort to know that many people will be holding them in prayer, just as we are.

"And we pray that there can now be an end to this horrific warfare and that peace will indeed prevail. Amen."

And my little son repeated, "*Amen.*"

If anything could have made Daddy smile, that was it, and we all smiled then. If Harry had survived, we all knew now would be the time for him to be released.

In the following days, Milly left her colleagues to manage The White Swan, in which they willingly cooperated, and she came down to Holt House and stayed with us. Andreas was thrilled, for he loved the treats she brought and her unstinting patience with him.

Life went on quietly now. Announcements on the radio that soldiers from the Japanese camps were beginning to come home simply made us even more anxious. Then, on a late October day, Will had a phone call.

"*Hello, who's speaking?*"

"*Will. Will, it's me. Let them all know.*"

"*Harry?*" He gasped with pleasure and relief.

"*As soon as I get my discharge papers, I'll be heading home. Oh, my brother, how I long to see you and Mother and my dear Milly. Is everyone well? Is Philip still managing his wheelchair, and what about my little sister?*"

Will raced round to Holt House to tell us about his call the second it was over. Once Harry received his discharge papers, he would head for Kings Cross at the first opportunity. He would have to change onto the Shadworth train in Sheffield and would let us know when he was due to arrive.

The relief was enormous, though all had different reactions to this news. Milly was alight with the anticipation of seeing him. Mother went very quiet, as if she was afraid something might stop him at the last minute, and who could blame her? The long, long wait was nearly over, and now perhaps there could be a rest from all our anxieties. He also knew, of course, that now, at last, James and I could be married, for we had sworn to ourselves that we would wait till everyone was safely back.

When we finally heard the news that Harry was on the final stretch to Shadworth, Mother and I rushed around getting ready, but Daddy stopped us.

"No, *my dears. Let Will drive Milly down so she can have the moment she has earned, and we can be patient for just a little while longer.*"

Mother kissed him then, and the loving look he gave her at that moment made me want to cry.

We had a job to do while we waited, one that wouldn't have been done there and then had we gone to Shadworth Station. There were others who must be told of this special arrival. Up at school, down at the farm. And I had to get my dear James home from Inveraray as soon as possible. I rang his office and waited for him to answer.

"*James, Will's had a phone call—Harry's coming home. Milly's gone to meet him at the station. And, my darling, you need to get on the road. Do you think you can get away?*"

I couldn't see the excitement on James' face, but I could hear it in his voice. "*I'll be on my way as soon as is possible, my darling. Oh my. What wonderful news.*"

I must confess I sometimes forgot how important he was up there in Scotland. He used to laugh at my ignorance and then always indulge me.

When the moment came, Will drew his car up to the gate of Holt House and helped Milly into it. She had put on her favourite dress and red lippy, as she called it. She looked like a young bride all over again. Andreas tugged at her skirt to be picked up, and she lifted him high and laughed at him. Then they were off.

Will told me afterwards that the sight of Harry as he carefully got off the train came as a shock. He had expected his younger brother to leap down and rush to them, but Harry had aged at that cruel Japanese camp. He had been beaten and punished over and over as the railway track was being laid, sleeper by sleeper. His shoulders were stooped, his back was bent and he was leaning heavily on a walking stick, yet Milly swallowed the unpleasant surprise and readjusted her picture of the man she loved. Harry stood looking at her, and she looked back with a loving and reassuring smile, then took his free hand and kissed it with intense love. At this, Harry seemed to straighten his back and smiled with a huge and obvious relief.

"*Milly, you've got yourself an old soldier.*" The tears were coming as he spoke. "*Can you still stand being married to me?*"

Will felt the fear and dread in Harry at this question, but Milly met Harry's fear and banished it for ever.

"*Let's go home to your mother and Philip. They are longing to see you, as I was. And now I am the happiest of wives.*"

No more words were necessary now. Will helped him into the car and drove to Holt House, where they were met at the gate by Mother, Daddy, me and Andreas.

He emerged from the car and was immediately overwhelmed with hugs, everyone trying hard not to unbalance him.

"*Harry, my darling son, welcome home,*" cried Mother, and Philip held his arms out to him and led him into the Holt House kitchen, which was warm with the hot oven. Mother was cooking a feast.

"*So much to tell you all. And who is this?*" said Harry as Andreas ran up to him.

"*Harry, meet my son, your very own nephew.*"

"*I'm Andreas and Mummy says you are my nunkie. Are you a proper nunkie like Nunkie Will?*" Andreas grinned up at him.

"*I sure am.*" He reached down and stroked his hair, then he looked back up at me with his eyebrow raised. "*And who's the lucky man, then?*"

"*Anatole is his father, but... he's not with us anymore.*" No matter how many times I said that out loud, it didn't get easier, always feeling as if fresh pain were shooting through me.

Harry's eyes widened. "*Are you trying to say...? Oh, Beth, I am so truly sorry.*" He pulled me into a hug.

"It's OK." I forced a weak smile. "*In truth, life has to go on, and not to be 'OK' is one of the hurdles that life throws at us.*"

"So, *is there another, then?*"

"*Yes, and it's James. We are engaged to be married.*"

He silently seemed to mull it over, picturing it in his head, then nodded his approval. "*My God, Beth, you never fail to amaze me. What a glory. And, for me, out of the blue.*"

Harry stood still for a moment at this extraordinary and unexpected news, then he lifted Andreas onto his shoulders and did a funny little jig while Andreas giggled and giggled. Then he stopped beside Milly and gently dropped Andreas down onto her lap.

Oh, we all gloried in Harry. And gradually, as the evening wore on, more and more very glad people arrived on the doorstep and acclaimed him. Ned was speechless as he embraced him. Pieter came from school, while Teddy and Ralphie played silly games with Andreas, to huge chortles of laughter. Milly simply sat next to him on the old settee and held his hand in mute pleasure.

Mother's feast was a huge bowl of stew that warmed the cockles of everybody's heart. Even Andreas, tired little boy as he was, tucked in heartily. We all hid our shock at how the experience had aged our dear Harry, indeed terribly. He was no longer the stalwart youth who had gone out to fight so bravely in 1918.

"Tomorrow is another day, my dear friends, and this chap must get some rest, not to mention time with his wife in peace. So I am calling a stop to the celebrations until tomorrow," Daddy finally said after a couple of hours of celebrating. He nodded understandingly in Harry's direction, for he knew Harry would be absolutely exhausted after the long journey homewards.

"And who knows, tomorrow might bring our last two wayfarers home. George tells me he is due in tomorrow and James is setting off early in the morning."

I gave a cry of surprise at this news, and Daisy came over to me and screamed with pleasure as she hugged me, her oldest and dearest friend.

Daddy wheeled himself over to me and took both my hands in his. *"All will be well, my darling. Let us enjoy this moment now."*

Chapter 56

1945

At last, peace had come and lives could return to a gentler, quieter pace. At Holt House, Emma had all her sons home safely, though the word "all" belied the fact that her youngest son, George, namesake of the younger George, was never able to return. Yet in this year of grace, 1945, she had many grandchildren, all of whom adored her and, in particular, her beloved husband, Philip. Philip himself rejoiced in all Emma's progeny but in particular, the child he himself had fathered, his own Elizabeth May—Beth, as everyone knew her. She and Andreas, a tot of two years old, were the apples of his eye, and now at last, there was to be a marriage of her to his old and very dear friend, James.

James' father was the good doctor who had nurtured him through his worst days after losing his leg and the one who had brought all Emma's babies into the world, though—and here he smiled to himself—Molly Townsend had had quite a lot to do with Beth's arrival.

Beth and Daisy enjoyed a glorious time in Leeds choosing the dress for this long-awaited event. Beth was to marry James on her mother's birthday, the twenty-second of December. She was to be married in the school chapel, dedicated to services in the Quaker tradition. This, for Philip, would be a crowning moment in his life. He had served as head of the school and led many services in the chapel. Indeed, the chapel was a kind of home to him. Many boys had prayed with him there in their hours of greatest need throughout the two world wars. Emma had often stayed by his side during these precious, sacred times, and boys, he believed, had emerged from the chapel better able to bear whatever cross they had to carry.

Now to give away the only child born of his marriage, Beth, to James, son of the doctor who had brought him through his sufferings, was a kind of benediction for Philip. And the grounds of his beloved school had been maintained and loved by James in his younger years before the war denied them all the normal pleasures of life. Of all men, Philip trusted James to treasure his Beth just as much as he did. He was well aware of the sadness Beth would always carry for her first husband, Anatole. Little Andreas was there to remind them all of the passionate, sometimes arrogant, young German whom Beth had loved in the first flush of youth. And Beth had promised her beloved father that Anatole would never be forgotten by James or herself.

Emma, meanwhile, was enjoying having her grandson George home. Since his mother's death early in his life, he had been another son to her. She had brought him through all the traumas of youth and seen him off to Oxford with huge pride. Now he was a squadron leader in the RAF, having proved his worth in the long, hard-fought war.

She and Philip had walked down to the farm to share these tranquil moments with Mary Tempest. In Mary and Florence's warm farm kitchen, Emma basked in the quietness, knowing there was no more need to await bad news. Mary smiled to herself, knowing all the many trials that had been overcome to reach this joyful point in their lives. Florence gave her mum a hug, and Philip simply sat and enjoyed the sense of peace and blessing in their company. Florence had been Emma's only daughter in an abundance of sons until Beth arrived, and Emma knew how much Mary missed Ron. The two women had been friends for many years, and it was a luxury to be able to spend time with Mary without any pressures, for she was content that Milly was preparing the wedding breakfast at The White Swan for James and Beth. For once, she could simply enjoy being the mother of the bride.

As she later pushed Philip's chair back up Long Lane home, he reminded her of all the good things to look forward to.

"Can you believe it, my dear? After all we've gone through, we can truly celebrate your birthday this year on our own Beth's wedding day. This will be a crowning joy, my dearest wife."

Meanwhile, James had driven Beth all the way up to Inveraray, leaving Andreas in the tender, loving hands of Laura and Will. In Inveraray, she was greeted by his many colleagues, all very keen to see James' young bride-to-be. They were to live in a cottage there for their first married home until James relocated to London, which would take only a few months. Beth was thrilled to meet his friends and to see the most beautiful Loch Fyne. James was teased unmercifully by his friends about having himself such a lovely young bride, and Beth took them to task for it.

"*Why, he is younger than the young in me, you'd better believe it,*" she told them all.

Something in James relaxed and breathed easy at her words that day. She had, almost unknowingly, taken away his anxiety about his age with that remonstrance.

As he set out on the long drive home, he stopped the car for a moment as they looked back at Inveraray nestled in the hills behind them.

"*Do you know how much I love you and have always loved you, Beth, my life and my love?*" he whispered.

Beth leaned over and kissed him there and then in the narrow passing place on the mountain road. "*I do know, my dearest, and next week we will seal the promise.*"

Chapter 57

December 1945

It was the twenty-second of December 1945 and Emma's birthday when James and Elizabeth May "plighted their troth" to each other in the school chapel, surrounded by their beloved family and very dear friends. The air was redolent with the scent of the beautiful white lilies decorating the chapel. Philip, in his wheelchair, sat at the front to welcome everyone. It was, for him, one of the most precious moments in his whole life. A little boy, all wreathed in smiles, carried the ring on a bright red cushion to his grandad. Even so, through his son, Anatole was present with them. Then Will lifted Andreas up for the congregation to see his sweet and happy face before taking him back to sit with Laura.

"*I, James Thomson, take you, Elizabeth May Czernik, to be my lawfully wedded wife, to have and to hold from this day forward . . .*"

Beth could see the tears in her father's eyes as James spoke these words, and she, in her turn, took James' hand and gave her whole heart into his keeping.

As they sang the hymn that had strengthened each one of them through the many hard trials and tragedies they had all faced, Beth looked across at her darling mother, who smiled back, her face transformed with the love she felt for her daughter.

"Not *for ever by still waters, would we idly rest and stay,*

"But would smite the living fountains from the rocks along the way."

Yes *indeed,* thought Philip. *There have been many rocks and painful, tragic moments, but there are many "living fountains".*

As he looked around the chapel, he rejoiced at each member present in that special wedding service. And he was so very proud of the beautiful, elegant bride, in the straight white satin dress with the wreath of flowers around her beautiful chestnut curls. *My Beth. My daughter.* She caught his eye at that moment and smiled her sweet smile reserved for him as he contemplated the joy of the scene surrounding him.

Here is Milly holding tight to Harry's hand; and here is George, Emma's beloved grandson; Mary Tempest, next to her own dear son, Ned, who is holding Florence's hand tightly. Here is Will, holding my own grandson in his arms, with Ralphie and Teddy beside Laura, both very smart in their bow ties and wedding suits. And what a debt I owe to Alan and Beatrice for keeping my school alive through these years of war. And alongside them is Pieter Staab, standing close to Emma's granddaughter, Daisy. Dear Pieter, the only one remaining alive from his own family. And Frank Jacques has made it all the way up to Yorkshire despite his age, with tears in his eyes.

Philip's hand shook a little as these thoughts crowded in on him. Yet he watched Beth and James join their hands together as James placed the ring on Beth's finger.

"*With this ring, I thee wed; with my body, I thee worship.*" And then, holding her to him, James reached down and kissed her.

There was a resounding clap that echoed round the chapel.

Andreas leapt out of Will's arms, shouting, "*Hurrah.*"

Emma hurried to stand by her beloved husband as they shook hands with all the guests, rejoicing at this special loving moment. And Harry, so world-weary after the horrors the Japanese had laid upon him, grinned round his united family. Will thanked God for the day he had travelled to find Laura, to share with her the sadness of the loss of his dear friend and comrade. Now she was the mother of his own dear son, who carried his old friend's name, Ralph. Emma could almost read her children's minds as she stood with Philip and rejoiced at last.

After all the trials of recent years, it seemed as if, at last, there was a resolution of all the past agonies and past joys in this moment of special grace for Beth and James and for everyone gathered there. A new era had begun and life seemed possible again.

Beth looked up at James, and her eyes shone with tears for her family, for her first love, and now, for their future together.